PRAISE FOR JOHN BURNSIDE'S

THE GLISTER

"Burnside builds mood and atmosphere with fearsome skill."
—*Chicago Sun-Times*

"A scary, fascinating exploration of innocence and evil, and the thin margin that often separates the two."
—Scott Smith, author of *The Ruins*

"By turns beguiling, sinister, playful and never less than mesmerizing. . . . [*The Glister*] will haunt you."   —Irvine Welsh, *Guardian*

"Proves John Burnside is also a master at the creation of dread, tension and mystery. What a dazzling book this is."   —Peter Straub

"A hauntingly mysterious . . . story about disappearances and environmental decay."   —*Toronto Star*

"Like a latter-day Jekyll and Hyde, Burnside can turn from luminous verse to prose that keeps you up at night. *The Glister* is such a novel."   —*The Financial Times*

"*The Glister* is wickedly good. Burnside writes with a dark and beautiful splendor."   —Keith Donohue, author of *The Stolen Child*

JOHN BURNSIDE

THE GLISTER

John Burnside is the author of the novel *The Devil's Footprints*, the memoir *A Lie About My Father*, as well as five additional works of fiction and eleven collections of poetry published in the United Kingdom. *The Asylum Dance* won the Whitbread Poetry Award, *The Light Trap* was shortlisted for the T. S. Eliot Prize, and *A Lie About My Father* won the two biggest Scottish literary prizes: the Scottish Arts Council Non-Fiction Book of the Year Award and the Saltire Society Scottish Book of the Year Award.

THE GLISTER

THE GLISTER

| A NOVEL |

John Burnside

ANCHOR BOOKS
A DIVISION OF PENGUIN RANDOM HOUSE LLC
NEW YORK

FIRST ANCHOR BOOKS EDITION, FEBRUARY 2010

The Library of Congress has cataloged the Nan A. Talese/Doubleday edition
as follows:
Burnside, John
The glister : a novel / John Burnside.—1st ed.
p. cm.
1. Missing children—Fiction.   I. Title.
PR6052.U6683G55 2008
823'.914—dc22   2008012141

Anchor Books ISBN: 978-0-307-45533-8
eBook ISBN: 978-0-385-52949-5

Book design by Maria Carella

www.anchorbooks.com

Hist, then. How dost thou know that some entire, living, thinking thing may not be invisibly and uninterpenetratingly standing precisely where thou now standest; aye, and standing there in thy spite? In thy most solitary hours, then, dost thou not fear eavesdroppers?

HERMAN MELVILLE
Moby-Dick, or, The Whale

Buoyed up by that coffin, for almost one whole day and night, I floated on a soft and dirge-like main. The unharming sharks, they glided by as if with padlocks on their mouths; the savage sea-hawks sailed with sheathed beaks. On the second day, a sail drew near, nearer, and picked me up at last. It was the devious-cruising *Rachel*, that in her retracing search after her missing children, only found another orphan.

HERMAN MELVILLE
Moby-Dick, or, The Whale

THE
BOOK
OF
JOB

HOMELAND

In the beginning, John Morrison is working in his garden. Not the garden at the police house, which he has long neglected, and not the allotment he rented when he was first married, but the real garden, the only *garden*, the one he likes to think of as a shrine. A sacred place, like the garden in a medieval Resurrection. To anyone else, it would look like nothing more than a patch of flowers and baubles, set out in a clearing amid the poison wood, just above the old freight line; but then nobody else could ever see its significance. Morrison created this garden himself and he has maintained it for seven years: a neat square of poppies and carnations, dotted here and there with the knuckles of polished glass and stone that he collects on his long walks around the Innertown and the wasteland beyond, filling the pockets of his police uniform with worthless treasure as he pretends to go about his duties. Of course, these days, he *has* no real duties, or none he could ever believe in. Brian Smith saw to that, years ago, when Morrison made the one big mistake of his career—the one big mistake of his *life,* other than marriage.

That was the day when Smith talked him into concealing the first of the Innertown disappearances. Now, with five boys missing, Morrison is almost ashamed to show his face on the street. Not that anybody knows about the lie, the confidence trick, that he has perpetrated upon them all. People want to know where the Innertown children have gone, but aside from the families of the missing boys, nobody expects anything much from *him*. They know he doesn't have the training or the resources to track the boys down, and they also know that nobody beyond their poisoned tract of industrial ruin and coastal scrub cares a whit about what happens to the Innertown's children. Even the families give up after a while, sinking into mute bewilderment, or some sad regime of apathy and British sherry. After more than a decade of dwindling hopes for their town and for their children, people have become fatalistic, trying to find, in indifference, the refuge they once sought in the modest and mostly rather vague expectation of ordinary happiness that they were brought up to expect. Some choose to believe, or to say they believe, the official line—the line Morrison himself puts out, with more than a little help from Brian Smith. In this version of events, a story full of convenient and improbable coincidences, each of the boys left the Innertown of his own accord, independently and without speaking a word to anyone, to try his luck in the big wide world. Some say this story is credible, boys being boys. Others say it is far-fetched, that it seems most unlikely that all five of these bright children, boys in their mid-teens with families and friends, would wander off suddenly, and without warning. Among this group, there are those who say that the boys have, in fact, been murdered, and that they are probably buried somewhere in the ruins of the old chemical plant between the Innertown and the sea, where their mutilated bodies will decay quickly, leaving no trace that could be distinguished from the dead animals and anonymous offal that people find out there all the time. This latter group gets restless on occasion, usually just after a new disappearance. They demand a full investigation, they want independent outsiders to come in and conduct an official inquiry. They write letters; they make phone calls. Nothing happens.

Mostly, however, the town goes about its business; though, these days, it would seem that its sole business is slow decay. Of course, Morrison's business is to walk his beat, make himself visible, try to suggest that law and order means something in the Innertown. This is his function, *to be seen*—but Morrison hates to be seen, he wants to be invisible, he wants, more than anything, to disappear, and on this warm Saturday afternoon in late July, he is out at his secret garden, weeding and clearing so the few flowers he planted in the spring might not be smothered by grass and nettles. To begin with, this makeshift shrine had been dedicated to Mark Wilkinson, the first boy to disappear—the one that Morrison had, in fact, found. Later, though, it became more generic, a memorial to all the lost boys, wherever they might be. Nobody else knows about this garden, and Morrison always feels nervous coming out here, afraid of being caught out, afraid someone will guess what all this means. The shrine is fairly well concealed, because the event it commemorates happened, as such things must, in this hidden place, or somewhere nearby at least. Once, he found the little garden kicked apart and trampled, the flowers uprooted, the glass and stones scattered far and wide, but he guessed right away that this was nothing more than the usual vandalism. Some kids from the Innertown had come across his handiwork and smashed it without even thinking, in the routine way that kids from the Innertown have in everything they do, but Morrison is fairly sure that they hadn't realized what the shrine meant, and he simply built it up again, plant by plant, pebble by pebble, till it was, if anything, better than before. Whenever he can, he comes out here to maintain it. When yet another boy vanishes into the night, he extends it a little, adding new plants, new heaps of sand-polished glass and stone.

He finds the best stones on Stargell's Point, his favorite place nowadays, because nobody else ever goes there. Even the kids avoid it. Everybody understands, by now, that the entire land under their feet is irredeemably soured, poisoned by years of runoff and soakaway from the plant, but in most areas nobody quite knows the extent of that souring—whereas Stargell's Point was always recognized as a black spot, even back in the good old days, when the people believed, through sheer force of will, that the chemical plant was essentially safe. They believed, of course, because they *had* to believe: the Innertown's economy depended almost entirely upon the chemical industry. More to the point, there were people in the Outertown, up in the big houses, who had an interest in ensuring that things ticked over without too much fuss. The Innertown folk, the ones who actually worked at the plant, had from the outset been made aware of the appropriate precautions to be taken while going about their duties, but they had always been told—by the Consortium, by the safety people, by all the powers that be—that the danger was minimal. They had wanted to believe they were safe because there was nowhere else for them to go, and they had wanted to trust the managers and politicians because there was nobody else for them to trust. Naturally, they worked hard on being convinced. In the early days, some of them even smuggled home bags of the stuff they were making out at the plant so they could spread it on their gardens. It was an act of faith, utterly perverse and so, they hoped, all the more powerful.

Later, when it was too late, they began to see what was really going on. They heard the rumors about bribery in high places and anonymous death threats against potential whistle-blowers, they heard how the Consortium had influential contacts within the supposedly independent firms charged with the care and safety of the plant's workforce, but they hadn't known what to do about it. A few years after Morrison left school, the plant had finally been shut down, but its ruins were still standing out on the headland, all around the east side of the Innertown, acres and acres of dead real estate, running from the gutted administration buildings at the junction of East Road and Charity Street, through a series of vast, echoey kilns, warehouses, waste-processing units, and derelict production blocks, all the way to the loading docks on the shore, where great tankers rusted beside the slick, greasy waters of the firth. You could see evidence wherever you looked of the plant's effects on the land: avenues of dead trees, black and skeletal along the old rail tracks and access roads; great piles of sulfurous rocks where pools of effluent had been left to evaporate in the sun. A few keen fishermen found mutant sea creatures washed up on the shore, where those great boats had once been loaded with thousands and thousands of drums of who knew what, and some people claimed that they had seen bizarre animals out in the remaining tracts of woodland, not sick, or dying, but not right either, with their enlarged faces and swollen, twisted bodies.

The most convincing evidence that some evil was being perpetrated on the headland, however, was the fact that, for as long as the plant had existed, the people themselves had not been right. Suddenly, there were unexplained clusters of rare cancers. Children contracted terrible diseases, or they developed mysterious behavioral problems. There was more than the usual share of exotic or untreatable illnesses, a sudden and huge increase in depression, a blossoming of what, in the old days, would have been called madness. Morrison's own wife had got sick in the head and, even now, nobody was able to say what was wrong with her. She drank, was the cruelest explanation, but she had been a drinker in her younger days and she had been fit as a fiddle back then.

Now, everybody blames these problems on the plant, but they don't have the energy to do anything about it. The plant had been their livelihood; it had been their best hope. Everyone knew its history, in the official version at least. People could tell you how, thirty years ago, a consortium—it had a fancy name, but it was always referred to, simply, as the Consortium—a local and international consortium of agricultural and other companies, started making various products there, but nobody remembers, now, and it seems that nobody really knew back then exactly what chemicals were manufactured, or what they were used for. Morrison's father, James, had worked at the plant, and he would insist that it was all harmless agricultural material: fertilizers and pesticides, fungicides, growth accelerants or growth retardants, complicated chains of molecules that got into the root or the stem of a plant and changed how it grew, or when it flowered, or whether it set seed. Other people said it was more sinister than that: maybe the bulk of what they processed out on the headland was innocent enough, but there were special facilities, hidden deep inside the plant, where they made, or stored, chemical weapons. After all, they would argue, it doesn't take much to change one substance into another; break a chain of molecules here, add an extra chain there, and what had been a mildly dangerous herbicide became a weapon of war; alter the temperature, or the structure, or the pressure, and stuff that you had once bought over the counter in the local hardware shop was transformed into a battlefield poison. To this day, they would claim, there are sealed buildings that nobody, not even the safety inspectors, was ever allowed to enter.

After a while, when the children started to vanish, new theories were put forward. The boys had stumbled into one of those secret facilities and been consumed by a cloud of lethal gas; or they had been taken away for tests, either by top-secret government scientists, or by aliens, who had been observing the plant for decades. Morrison has always known that this is all pointless speculation, of course, because he knows the truth about the disappearances. Or rather, he knows the truth in *one* case because, on a cold autumn night seven years ago, it was his bad luck to find Mark Wilkinson suspended from a tree, a few yards from the spot where he now stands. A few yards, no more, from this raggedy patch of garden flowers and colored glass where he lingers beside a phantom grave, trying to think of something to say. It isn't prayer he intends, on these visits, so much as some form of communion: he wants, not to send Mark's soul into some happy otherness, but to hold it back long enough for the boy to understand and, so, forgive.

Morrison was never very much convinced by the idea, taught to him in Sunday school, that forgiveness comes from God; he could never see why God needed to forgive us our trespasses, when He was the one who made us how we are. Even as a boy, however, he had believed in the forgiveness of the dead. When he was little, his mother would take him on Sunday walks to the cemetery on the West Side of the Innertown, not far from where the better-off people lived. James Morrison wouldn't come, he'd always be too busy, but his wife would lead young John and his little sister out to the Innertown cemetery, and all three would sit down on one of the benches dressed in their Sunday best to enjoy a picnic lunch by their grandmother's headstone. It would be a quiet meal, solemn, though not at all morbid. Afterward, out of respect for the dead, Morrison would pick up every spilled eggshell, every curl of orange peel. The dead fascinated him by the way they lived on, alone in their names, each one separate from the others, and he wanted to erase any trace that he, or his family, might leave in their solitary domain. Once, when he was fifteen, he had gone for a walk in the cemetery with his first girlfriend, a slightly plain but funny, generous-hearted girl called Gwen. He'd intended it to be nothing more than a walk, but almost as soon as they passed through the cemetery gates she had grabbed hold of his arm and kissed him, right there, among the gravestones and the rhododendrons. That kiss hadn't quite worked because they hadn't tried this before, both of them shy and Morrison not sure if he liked Gwen as much for her looks as he did for her personality. That was why he had hesitated, probably; but the truth was that, at first, he hadn't wanted to go on, with the dead all around him, watching from their separate resting places across the cemetery. He'd tried again, though, for the girl's sake, and this time they did it right, Gwen tilting her head like they did in the movies, so their noses didn't get in the way. After that, they kissed for a long time, maybe a minute, not quite knowing how to stop once they had got started.

As soon as he and Gwen parted, however, that kiss began to worry him. He didn't want to upset or insult the dead, because they were alone in some silent otherness—and that, he had realized, was why they could forgive us. He'd never had any doubt that the dead were better for being dead: they were beyond all the petty concerns and trivial disputes and anxieties that trouble the living. They breathed with God. That was how Morrison had imagined them as a child: breathing God's air, but never seeing Him, always alone. It was up to them to watch us, dispassionately, from a distance, and they forgave us the more easily for that. It wasn't God's job to forgive, it was theirs. They saw, and they understood, but God couldn't understand because God's standards were so high, and because He always got so bloody wrathful, smiting and striking down here, there, and everywhere. So, being perfect, He gave the job of forgiveness to the dead. It was logical, when you thought about it. Morrison liked to think of it as a form of delegation.

He'd found the Wilkinson boy by accident, at the end of a chain of ordinary incidents and events that, in themselves, should have added up to nothing. It was Halloween, around ten in the evening; Morrison had been at the old vicarage, dealing with a minor vandalism incident, going out on foot because he felt he needed a stretch, and because, at that time, he thought people found it reassuring to see a policeman on the beat. The weather had been pretty harsh, clear but bitterly cold for the time of year, and Morrison had been on his way back to the police house to brew up some tea when he came upon a man and two boys at the near end of the West Side Road, which led out to the old rail yards and the little wood that everybody in the Innertown called the poison wood, because the trees, though still alive, were strangely black, a black that didn't look like charring or the result of drought, but rather suggested that the trees were veined with a dark, poisoned sap, black, but with a trace of livid green in the essence of it, a green that was bitter and primordial, like wormwood, or gall. The boys looked scared and unhappy, but they also had an embarrassed air, and Morrison had been suspicious to begin with. He thought something had happened to frighten them, but he wondered if they were as innocent as they wanted to appear. He hadn't been in the job long, and his first line of defense in most situations was skepticism. That was what he thought being a local policeman was all about in the end, a contagious sense of calm and a readiness to take things with a pinch of salt. Still, these boys had been scared, no doubt about that; though, to begin with, he couldn't make much sense of their story, other than that it had to do with a boy called Mark, some old den out by the poison wood, and a spool of cotton thread.

Meanwhile, the man with them, a middle-aged widower called Tom Brook, whom Morrison knew somewhat through family connections, wasn't helping matters any. In a gray cardigan and blue corduroy trousers, though without a coat in spite of the cold, Brook had the look of someone who has just left his cozy living room, pulled on a pair of boots, and gone out into the night without thinking. It was a look Morrison had come to know well, the look of someone singled out, in the middle of ordinary matters, by chance, or perhaps by fate. Trouble was, Brook had got one garbled version of the story already, and he kept asking questions that, for Morrison, had no context and so only confused matters.

"All right," Morrison said, finally. "Let's start this again, at the beginning." He spoke slowly, quietly, as he had trained himself to do, to inspire calm in others. He had practiced his calm look in the mirror, as he ran through lines in his head that he thought would be reassuring. He wished he looked older. Or not so much older as more experienced. People knew it wasn't that long since he'd worked as a lowly security guard—a night watchman, in effect—at one of Brian Smith's properties in the Innertown. To date, he'd not learned much in the job, but he *had* learned one thing, which was that people didn't quite trust young policemen. "Who, exactly, went where and how long ago?" As soon as he finished speaking, he was annoyed with himself. He'd just broken one of his principal rules. One question at a time. Take it slowly. Keep everybody calm, get one person to talk.

Tom Brook looked at the boys, then shook his head. "Well," he said, "I know it sounds odd. He's only been out there a short while, really." He turned to one of the boys, who had started to cry openly now. "It's all right, Kieran," he said. "The policeman's here. We'll find him—"

"Find who, Tom?" Morrison's mind was already drifting back to tea and digestives at the police house. Maybe to sit awhile with Alice, quietly together at the kitchen table, in those days before sitting with Alice had not been a chore. This was going to be nothing, he could feel it. Maybe he was new to the job, but he had an instinct for police work. This would be nothing more than a silly prank, or some misunderstanding. He didn't want to spend the rest of the night wandering around the poison wood, looking for some runaway who'd only been gone for an hour and a half.

"It's Mark Wilkinson," Tom Brook said. He already seemed less sure of what had transpired. Morrison's native skepticism was obviously catching. "They say he went into the woods and he hasn't come back."

Morrison looked at the boys. It was odd: they really had got a scare, that was obvious, but the taller lad seemed as much embarrassed as frightened. The boy Brook had addressed as Kieran was smaller, a little stocky, but with a sweet, almost girlish face; he was close to desperate, a step away from hysterical even, looking from Morrison to Tom Brook as if he suspected that they were the ones who had made his friend vanish into thin air. "So," Morrison said, "tell us exactly what happened. From the beginning."

In spite of their different emotional states, the boys were utterly consistent. It seemed they had been playing a game out in the woods, and because the game was an old Halloween ritual, probably dating to pagan times, Morrison quickly returned to his suspicion that this was all a storm in a teacup, that the disappearance was some kind of schoolboy's hoax, a piece of silly theater that had simply gone too far. Possibly the taller boy, whose name was William, had been party to the hoax all along, but then something had happened that wasn't in the script, which left him torn between worry and skepticism—and also embarrassed, because the game they had been playing was a girl's game, one that Morrison only knew about from one of those "Did You Know" type articles he'd seen in the paper the previous week. Maybe Mark, or one of the others, had read the same article about how, once upon a time, a girl would take a bobbin and tie it to one end of a length of cotton thread. She would go out into the woods and, after repeating the necessary spell, she would toss the bobbin out into the dark as far as it would go, keeping a tight grip on the other end of the line. The bobbin would fly out into the darkness and land some distance away, hopefully still attached to the line, while the girl stood waiting for some sign—a movement, a tremor, something tugging urgently, or gently, at the line, calling her out into the dark. The article had said that, when they followed the line out to where the bobbin had landed, those pagan girls believed they would meet their future lovers in spirit form, and so perhaps learn who it was they were to marry when the appointed time came. Mark had suggested to the others that they should play this game out in the poison wood, to make it more real; he had even seemed to think the trick would produce some result, that there really would be someone waiting in the dark at the end of the line.

"So what did you think you would find?" Morrison asked William. "You're a bit young to be thinking about a wife."

William looked even more embarrassed than before. "We weren't looking for *wives*," he said, with obvious distaste.

Morrison gave him an encouraging smile. "So what were you looking for?" he asked. William stared at his feet then, not wanting to look any more foolish than he already felt. Morrison turned to Kieran, who had begun to calm down. "How about you?" he said. "What were you looking for out there in the woods, son?"

Kieran shot a glance at William, who shook his head but kept his eyes fixed on the ground. "We were looking for the Devil," he said, after a moment. "It was Mark's idea. He said this thing about girls and husbands and stuff was all rubbish, it was really a trick to find the Devil." Now that he had stopped crying, he seemed angry. Or indignant, rather—and Morrison sensed that Kieran was one of those boys who would grow up angry at the world for occasionally including *him* in its problems.

"The Devil?" he said, in his best skeptical-policeman's voice.

Kieran stared at him. "Yeah," he said angrily.

Morrison turned to Tom Brook. He wanted to say something

reassuring, to tell them all that this was either a hoax gone wrong, or one of those minor mysteries that everybody laughs about afterward, but Brook spoke before he could say anything. The man looked both sad and relieved.

"You don't go looking for the Devil, son," he said. Both boys looked up at him then. He was the older man, so he had their attention. "Didn't anybody ever tell you that?" he said. He turned to Morrison and gave a sad, but conniving, smile. "You don't need to go out to the woods searching for the Devil," he said again. "The Devil finds *you*, doesn't he, Constable?"

That had been the story. Daring himself to look the Devil in the eye, Mark Wilkinson had thrown his bobbin into the dark reaches of the poison wood and, when nothing happened, he had walked out alone, tracing the line to where it had fallen. The last thing he'd said to the others before he vanished into the shadows was that, if he didn't come back right away, they shouldn't wait for him. Then, with a laugh, he had walked out of the ring of flashlight and vanished among the trees. William and Kieran had waited a long time for him to come back, but they were too scared to go out into the Devil's night to look for him. Instead they had panicked and run, leaving their one flashlight behind. Morrison heard their story patiently and decided that the best thing—the only thing—to do was to pack these boys off to their beds, and go out into the poison wood to investigate. First, though, he would go by the Wilkinson house, to see if young Mark was tucked up in bed, laughing at the trick he had played on his friends, while congratulating himself on his lucky escape from the Devil. It was nothing, this story, just a kids' game, and Morrison was surprised the boys had got into such a state about it. Still, the poison wood was a pretty scary place at night, even with company and a flashlight.

"All right. Here's what we'll do," he said, "I'll go out there and take a look. If nothing else, then maybe I'll find your torch, at least. Mark is probably back at his house now, watching TV. You boys get off home, too. There's nothing to worry about." He turned to Tom. "Maybe Mr. Brook could see you back?"

Brook nodded. "It's not far," he said. "I've got nothing better to do," he added.

That was when Morrison remembered what a very special anniversary for Tom Brook this night was. It was a story everybody knew, a story Tom would trail silently around with him for the rest of his days, defined by this one event, this one painful fact. For it had been around this time last Halloween that Tom's wife, Anna, had died from a huge, inexplicable growth in her brain that had eventually driven her insane. She had been reduced, at the end, to an abject, desperate creature who, lying in her own bed, believed she had been buried alive. For several days before she finally gave up the ghost, she'd clawed desperately at the imaginary box in which she thought herself enclosed; when he had gone round to the house briefly to see if he could do anything to help, Morrison had been reminded of the story of Thomas à Kempis, the saint who really *had* been buried alive, a fate that was only discovered years later, when Thomas was disinterred for a more distinguished burial site after his canonization. Contemporary descriptions said that the body was wizened and twisted, the arms curled up under the coffin lid as if the author of the *Imitatio Christi* had died while trying to push his way out, the fingertips a robin's pincushion of splinters and dried blood, where he had scratched and clawed at the wood in his desperation to be free. Morrison had heard that story in school, while his mother was on her sickbed; after she died, he would go to the churchyard and lie on the grave with his ear pressed to the ground, listening. He had been terrified that his mother was still alive down there, with six feet of earth holding her down, scratching and crying to be free. When he'd heard about Anna Brook, Morrison tried to imagine how he would have felt if he'd been obliged to listen to his mother calling his name, in some bloodied darkness deep under the ground, and been unable to do a thing to help her. That had been Tom Brook's fate: to see his wife buried alive, to watch her clawing at her coffin lid, to hear her screaming for help, and be forced to sit helplessly by. Tom knew, as Morrison knew, that his wife wasn't actually buried alive, that her predicament was imaginary, but her agony was no less real for that. It had been a terrible time and Morrison was disgusted with himself for forgetting this anniversary so easily. "Thanks, Tom," he said. He wanted to say something else, something commemorative perhaps, but he didn't know what. He turned back to the boys. "There's nothing to worry about," he said. "Everything's going to be fine."

———

Over the next few hours, Morrison went about his business with a feeling more of irritation than concern. He stopped off at Mark Wilkinson's house before he did anything else because, as he'd told the others, finding the boy there was the most likely scenario. When he got to the house, however, at just after eleven o'clock, the Wilkinsons were watching television and they seemed more upset at being interrupted at the crucial point in the film than anything else. They certainly didn't seem concerned for their son. After showing Morrison into the front room, they hadn't even switched off the television, though the mother did turn the sound down a little. Still, all the way through the interview, they kept sneaking glances at the screen, to see what was happening. This annoyed Morrison, who also found it difficult to sit in a room where a TV was turned on and not be distracted. Though he hardly ever watched it at home, it struck him as a fairly innocent distraction and it was company for Alice when he was out and about. That night, however, there was something dully obscene about those images flickering on the screen and the sound of the actors talking, dialogue spoken just quietly enough that, even though he didn't care a whit about what they were saying, Morrison found himself straining to follow. Perhaps because of this, or maybe because the parents seemed so unconcerned, the interview did not last long. It seemed the boy hadn't come home yet, but the Wilkinsons made no show of being worried. "Mark often stays out late," the husband said, darting a quick glance at the screen. Clint Eastwood was pointing a gun at somebody.

"He's stayed out all night a couple of times," the wife added. She seemed oddly blasé about it, as if she didn't much care what the boy did, or what might happen to him. Morrison thought, talking to them, that it was no surprise Mark was out there in the dark, wandering around in the poison wood, playing stupid games to scare his pals. In fact, the longer the conversation went on, the more he disapproved of these people. At the same time, however, he knew he didn't have any right to judge them. He didn't know what their lives were like. You only had to take one look at them to know that marriage to either one couldn't be much fun. "He just goes off, without a by-your-leave." She glanced at the TV. "I think it's his way of teaching us a lesson."

"I see," Morrison said. He sounded like a policeman from a TV program himself at times. "So, can you think of any reason why he might have wanted to teach you a lesson tonight?"

The woman gave him a sharp glance. She had sensed his disapproval and she was none too pleased. She turned to her husband, whose face was as blank as a TO LET sign; then, with nothing doing there, she swung back to Morrison and gave him a bitter smile. "Probably," she said. "Nothing would surprise me with him."

Morrison was working hard not to show his exasperation. "Well," he said, "do you know of *anywhere* he might have gone?"

The woman didn't look at him, but kept her eyes defiantly on the screen. "He might have gone to my sister's," she said.

"Your sister's?"

"Yes," she said. "Sall's."

"And where is that?"

"Oh, she's not there *now*," the woman said, with an oddly triumphant expression. "Sall's dead. Somebody else lives there now." The woman seemed as indifferent to her sister's death as she did to her son's apparent disappearance.

"He just goes over there, sometimes," the man put in. "He loved Sall," he added, a little wistfully, Morrison thought.

"She spoiled him," the woman said. "She didn't have kids of her own."

Mr. Wilkinson had started to get interested now. "Well," he said, "she couldn't, could she?"

His wife shot him a warning look and he slipped back into semi-torpor. "Anyway," she said, "he goes over there and hangs about. God knows why." She gave Morrison another of her tight smiles. "I mean, he *knows* she's dead."

It was around then that Morrison decided he didn't see any point in continuing any further, so, after noting down the aunt's address and a few more-or-less token questions, he stood up. The Wilkinsons stayed where they were, on the sofa. "Well, I wouldn't worry," Morrison said. "It's probably just a bit of Halloween high spirits."

The woman looked at him. "Probably," she said.

Morrison stood a long moment, then the man finally got up. "I'll get the door for you," he said.

"Don't worry," Morrison said. "I'll see myself out." The man looked surprised at this, then relieved. He sat down again and turned to the television. By the time he got to the front door, the TV was back at normal volume.

———

As he closed the Wilkinsons' gate, Morrison had debated whether to let the matter go for the night and follow up the next morning—and without a doubt, he would have been better off if he had. If someone else had found the boy, there was a good chance that things would have turned out differently, not just in this one case, but in all the cases that followed. On another night, perhaps, he would have gone back to the police house, to check in with Alice and have a cup of tea, but that night, something nagged at him, something he couldn't put his finger on. So he'd fetched the car and gone over to the poison wood to take a look. Even then, he'd been in two minds and he'd considered just going home and waiting till morning, thinking himself a fool for bothering. If the parents didn't think the boy was in any real trouble, he asked himself, why should he? About half an hour into the search, however, he found what looked like a little den among the trees, a natural shelter of scrubby bushes and rubble, the kind of place where some lonely child might go to hide out. Not a place for a gang, but a secret, enclosed space where a boy with more imagination than friends might sit out late, playing at wilderness. Or that was what it looked like at first; it was only on closer inspection that Morrison saw that it was really the first in a series of such closed spaces, the first tiny room in a series of rooms, one leading to another, until, in the fourth, he found a strange little bower where someone had made an elaborate display, all glinting, colored fragments of glass and china, the bushes decked with swatches of stripy fabric, the floor splashed here and there with what looked like tinsel and glitter. It was all new, a special place that someone had just built—a *bower*, like those elaborate structures that some exotic birds make, when they want to attract a mate. At the same time, it also had the feel of a chapel, a special place set aside for prayer, or contemplation, or possibly sacrifice— and it was as if that thought, that wisp of an impression, drew Morrison's torch beam away, dancing over the cold, glittering floor of the den across a wall of twigs and tattered scraps of nylon and old curtain fabric to the body. A boy's body, Mark Wilkinson's body, suspended from the bough of the largest tree; suspended, perfectly bright and neat and—this was what disturbed Morrison most, this was what his mind kept going back to afterward—absurdly gift wrapped, at the throat and around the chest and ankles, in tinsel and bright lengths of fabric, like a decoration or a small gift hung on a Christmas tree.

Morrison knew it was Mark Wilkinson right away, though there was no reason to be so sure: the face was covered with blood and grime and there were faint creases in the dirt on his cheeks, where he might have been crying—though Morrison wasn't sure of this, because the boy's face looked oddly calm, even though his eyes were open and he was suspended in the tree like a figure from some makeshift crucifixion. Morrison didn't know why, but he was convinced that whatever had happened here had only just finished, maybe only a few minutes since. Still, he didn't have to check the boy's pulse to know he was dead. Yet it wasn't the fact of death that horrified Morrison so much as his own reaction to the crime scene.

It was nothing like the climactic moment in a film, where someone discovers a body and screams: he didn't reel away in disgust, he didn't cry out or run to fetch help. Worse still, he didn't remember who he was and start doing his job. Instead, he came to a halt at every level of his being. He came to a total standstill in his mind and in his nerves and in his blood, suddenly drained of energy and will, captivated by the horror and, at the same time—and this was what transfixed him—by the sense that there was some kind of meaning in all this. Had he got there soon enough to intervene, or a few hours later—the next morning, say—it might have been different. There would have been something to do, set actions to perform; or everything would have been frozen and drained of color, a crime scene, a collection of evidence that someone, though probably not John Morrison, could have read like a book.

At first sight, it appeared that the boy had been brutally treated, deliberately and systematically wounded, in a process that easily could have been mistaken for torture. Yet later, when the image of this place had sunk into every fiber of his bones and nerves, Morrison would not have called it that. Mark Wilkinson's hands had been bound—bound, yes, yet loosely, almost symbolically—with a length of very white, almost silky rope, and most of his clothes had been removed, leaving him so thin and stark and creaturely that he looked more like some new kind of animal than a boy in his early teens. His skin was very white, in the unmarked areas between the mud stains and grazes, but what struck Morrison most forcibly was the look in his eyes, a look that suggested, not fear, or not just fear, but recognition. That was what shocked him most: the boy had a look in his eyes that suggested that he had seen, at the moment of death, something he knew, something he recognized— and it took Morrison a moment to realize what he was now witnessing, a moment to work it all out, not thinking, just feeling, just ticking like a machine for remembering and connecting, and then he understood that what he was seeing wasn't the result of a torture scene, but of something that, to him, seemed much worse.

What he remembered then was a passage in a book he had read, a passage that described how, when the Aztecs performed a human sacrifice, they would cut the heart from the still-living body, and he recalled how he had shuddered at the notion that a whole people, an entire culture, could believe that this was the only way to protect their crops, or to ensure victory in battle. It had revolted him, that these things had actually happened, that this was how people had once spoken to their gods. To believe in human sacrifice, not as some secret, ugly, perverted thing, but as a glorious act; to accord the highest honor to the priest who scooped out that living heart and raised it to the sun, not once but time after time, in ceremonies that might claim tens, perhaps hundreds, of victims, had seemed to him obscene beyond imagining. Yet it had also seemed mercifully remote, the ugly, absurd practice of a primitive, warlike race. Now, however, as he stared into Mark Wilkinson's pale, muddied face, he understood that his death had meant something to his killer, something religious, even mystical. He didn't know *how* he knew this, he simply did. It wasn't the scene of the crime that told Morrison what the killer felt; it was nothing rational and it was certainly nothing he could have put into words had someone come, at that moment, to question him, or prod him into doing his job. No: it was something about the arrangement of the body that struck him, an arrangement in which he sensed the reverence of a last moment. No matter how incredible or disgusting the idea would have seemed to him at any other time, Morrison sensed, for one fleeting and terrifying moment, that there had been reverence here, a terrible, impossible tenderness—in both the killer and his victim—for whatever it is that disappears at the moment of death, an almost religious regard for what the body gives up, something sublime and precise and exactly equal in substance to the presence of a living creature: the measured weight of a small bird or a rodent, a field mouse, say, or perhaps some kind of finch.

Morrison had to fight the temptation, then, to cut the boy down, to undo the ceremony of what had been done to him, to cover him up and not let him be seen like this by anyone else. He wanted to deny this sacrifice, he wanted to invalidate it—but then the realization came that what he really wanted was to bring the boy back to life, to reverse the process through which he had suffered and died, and that was something nobody could do. And it was then that John Morrison understood, with a sudden and brutal clarity, that he wasn't a real policeman after all, because he did not have what it took to deal with this. He could already feel some brittle structure crumbling in his mind and, as he stood staring at this sacrificed child, everything he had hoped for when Brian Smith unexpectedly wangled him the job of town policeman collapsed like a bad wedding cake. When he'd joined the police force, he had never expected to find a body. Or not like this, at least. People died in the Innertown all the time, as they die elsewhere. They died of strokes, old age, lung disease. Occasionally, they killed themselves, or were made strange by some random accident. Morrison had already had his fair share of those, and he'd been obliged to deal with the aftermath, or make notes, or stand at the edge of some family's bewilderment and grief and pretend he had a reason to be there. Mostly, though, his neighbors died privately, with no need for an official presence, and Morrison was as removed from those deaths as he was from their other secrets. Some of them died from causes that were, and would forever remain, unknown, because no authority on earth wanted to determine what those causes were. The Innertown wasn't a healthy place to live; the trouble was that, for most people, there was nowhere else to go. This was why so many also died of things that no doctor could have diagnosed—disappointment, anger, fear, loneliness. Not being touched. Not being loved. Silence. In the old days, even hardnosed GPs would talk about dying from a broken heart: now cause of death had to be something more official. Still, nobody had been murdered in the Innertown, not in Morrison's lifetime, and he was glad of that, at least. He might have wanted to be a policeman all his life, but he had never wanted to be one of *those* policeman, like the ones he saw on television, finding bodies, stalking the killer, refusing tea from a friendly, but now slightly anxious woman, because he was about to tell her that her child had been tortured to death. That was all very well for the cinema, or crime magazines, but Morrison had never thought of it as real police work. What Morrison had wanted was to be a small-town bobby, walking the beat, a face familiar to everyone, a person people could trust. He wanted to work with the familiar and the tender; he wanted to be able to know what he was dealing with, learning all the time as he went along till he had a body of knowledge and understanding that he could pass on to whoever replaced him. He wanted, in other words, to be part of the community, a man as well known and reliable as the town-hall clock. He wanted to tap the barometer as he left home in the morning and know the chances of rain that day; he wanted to buy a paper on a Monday and read about the town gala, or some minor local sporting victory. Not this. Not some child, hung out on a tree like a sacred offering.

It was this chain of thought, this sense he had of something collapsing in his mind, that wrong-footed him. It came as a shock, afterward, that he could have done such a thing, but it only shocked him later, when he had become capable of feeling anything more than he had at the scene. At that moment, in his confusion and terror and the horrible emptiness of it all, what he had done seemed not so much the best as the *only* thing to do, his one possible escape. He had just realized that he was too tender a soul, too soft a man to see through the work he had chosen. He had just seen himself as wholly lacking in all the virtues he had thought would come with time and experience, but which, he now knew, were intrinsic, at least in some basic form. A man either *has* courage, good sense, and a certain impenetrability of spirit, or he does not. Morrison did not. He was weak, lacking, frightened. Because he could not do the one thing he most wanted to do—because he could not reach out and bring this boy back to life—he wanted to close his eyes and run away to some safe place where nobody would ever call on him to do anything again. When he thought about it later, he would see that he knew he was making a terrible mistake even as he made it, and he also saw that he had been guilty of nothing more than a moment's fear, a mere hesitation. He hadn't known what to do: it was that straightforward. He wasn't a real policeman, he'd been pushed into the job when Constable Fox had died suddenly, after a fall from his bicycle. It was his employer, Brian Smith, who'd suggested he take the job if it was offered and he'd leapt at the unexpected opportunity, but he'd never been confident of his abilities as a policeman and now, facing his first real test, he was paralyzed with the fear of making some unforgivable error. Of course, he told himself that he was only looking for advice. He told himself that what he was doing was simply a courtesy, a show of respect to the man who had made him a policeman in the first place. He wanted to send out a warning, in case this tragic event had repercussions that had to be dealt with. This was what he told himself; yet he knew in his heart that he was lying. The truth was, he wasn't big enough to deal with a murdered child and he was afraid of what would happen if he called this in all by himself—and so it was that, in his terror of making a mistake, he walked up to the old red telephone box on the outer road and made the worst mistake he could have made. He called Brian Smith.

CONNECTIONS

A FEW DAYS BEFORE HIS ELEVENTH BIRTHDAY, BRIAN SMITH developed a passion for puzzles of every kind, and jigsaw puzzles in particular. He liked the way they made connections, how a great pile of a thousand or more random pieces could be transformed, simply by matching shapes and colors, into a perfect likeness of the Venetian canal scene or the lush tropical garden depicted on the box. His parents, who didn't think of him as particularly intelligent—or, indeed, as especially interesting or likable—soon took to buying him all the puzzles they could find, delighted to provide a distraction that would occupy their charmless and more or less superfluous only child for hours at a time, allowing *them* to get on with the more pleasant aspects of adult life, like drinking, or playing bridge with the Johnstons—a childless, and so wildly fortunate, couple who lived two doors along the street, in one of the quieter districts of the Innertown. It didn't concern them that, on the surface at least, their sturdy, unsmiling son had nothing at all in common with those bright, bookish children who normally delight in logic problems. Nor had they ever been unduly troubled by the fact that, as young Brian progressed dutifully through primary school, his teachers not only described him as below average, lazy, and almost entirely lacking in flair or imagination, but also implied that he was universally disliked by both staff and pupils. The truth was that this did not surprise them in the least.

What those school reports failed to mention explicitly was that their son was suspected of playing a wide range of cruel and humiliating practical jokes on the other children in his year group. Apparently, he was particularly vicious toward female pupils. He would find a way of placing fake blood or real excrement in a girl's satchel, or he would lace another child's black-currant drink with a special dye that turned her urine bright red. He left dead frogs and birds in desks, he sent Valentine's and Christmas cards with cruel messages or captions—never handwritten, always clipped from newspapers and magazines—or he would send photographs of stick-thin children in stripy Belsen pajamas to the fattest person in his class, a pasty, desperate-looking girl called Carol Black. He put drawing pins on chairs and slipped tiny shards of glass or copper wire into apples and toffees. For several months running, he paid special attention to Catherine Bennett, the class beauty, who regularly discovered pools of sour milk, or sticky masses of Cow Gum and horsehair among her belongings. On one occasion—the morning of her tenth birthday, to be precise—she found a sheep's eye and a packet of Love Hearts on her desk when she came back from milk break. Everybody knew who had put them there but, as with all Brian's other little acts of pointless malice, nobody could prove anything and the boy's parents were never informed. Most of the teachers could see that it wouldn't have mattered anyway. As was so often the case, the child's behavior was an all-too-obvious symptom of parental indifference.

Brian's nasty streak had disappeared, however, when he discovered the world of puzzles. Logic games, join the dots, jigsaws, anagrams, crosswords, number sequences—these things provided him not so much with distraction as with a means of salvation. Solving a puzzle, he could see how *everything* was connected and he was privy to the secret order that underpinned the day-to-day world that had so bewildered him till then. Solving a really *difficult* puzzle would give him a deep, almost physical satisfaction that lingered for hours, or even days afterward; at an age when other boys locked themselves away with a fistful of tissues and a dog-eared copy of *Fiesta*, Brian would go to his room and take out a thousand-piece jigsaw, or some elaborate wooden puzzle that his mother had picked up in a junk shop. There were even times, during his teens, when he seemed to disappear: on rare days out with his parents, or all through the long hours of a school day, it was as if something had been switched off in his head, so it wasn't like being with other people at all, it wasn't even like being present, it was just *nothing*— and Brian was grateful for that, because Brian didn't *like* people. In the puzzles, everything depended on the connections, the logical sequences, the intrinsic order that was always waiting to be discovered; but with people there were no connections, and no logic—or at least, nothing very elegant or interesting. Compared to a number puzzle, or a complicated jigsaw, people were like those dodgem cars at the fair, going round in circles and bumping into one another noisily to no real purpose.

———

So it was that, during the years when he was lonely and despised, puzzles had saved Brian Smith from the world and kept him true to himself, in spite of everything. Yet now that he is a man, he has no time for puzzles. He still sees the connections between one thing and another, but the links he discovers are larger and more tangibly rewarding than those he once made by constructing a coral reef or the Trooping of the Colour from awkward little pieces of dusty cardboard. Now the connections have everything to do with people and the ordinary, day-to-day world, because people and events are the pieces that make up his puzzles now—and *now* everything is different, because the problems are abstract. There's nothing to hold in your hand, there's no starting point of a number sequence or an anagrammatized word to work with. What he works with now is people, and when you ignore what people feel and want, when you see them as objects in the *fullest* sense of the word, they become the most interesting pieces in the most compelling and elegant puzzle of all.

And the rules of the game are much the same as before. There is only one acceptable solution to any puzzle and Brian Smith's job, pure and simple, is to discover what it is. Join all the dots. Fit all the pieces together. Everything is connected to everything else, so anything is possible. If what you are looking for is pain, you find the patterns that make pain possible; if all you need is love, then love is what you are bound to find, even in the most unlikely or dangerous places. What Brian Smith looks for, what he can see where others see nothing, are the patterns that lead to money. In fact, it is Brian Smith's gift to see, where others do not, that *everything* leads to money. Another man's disaster, another man's hell—in any situation, no matter how terrible, a man can make money, if he will only discover the connections between one thing and another. The proof is there for all to see in the newspapers and on the television every day. War. Terrorist atrocities. Natural disasters. Thousands of people die, or lose their homes, cities are washed away or reduced to ashes, and the cameras fix on that human-interest story, that tragedy, these people stumbling out of the smoke and ashes and into the cameras, that woman sitting alone on her roof in the midst of the flood. Devastated, the newsman says. They always say *devastated*, because *devastated* makes good television. Behind the scenes, though, away from the cameras and the lights, somebody is making money. Somebody who sees the connections while everyone else is distracted by the devastation. Brian Smith finds it fascinating how the rest of the world seems to miss this obvious fact. Sometimes, in his lighter moments, he talks to his man Jenner about it.

"What do you see?" he'll say, looking up from his paper or his computer screen. "What comes into your mind when you hear the word 'Africa'?"

Jenner ponders a moment, then shakes his head. He doesn't see much, which is his greatest virtue. Big, quiet, totally serious, he is a man of action, a type that is easier to use than almost any other.

"In your mind's eye," Smith says. "What pictures do you see?"

Jenner tries. He looks into his tidy, rather spartan memory and scrapes some old news footage together. "Kids," he says. "Kids and flies. Barren desert. Refugee camps."

Smith nods. "Exactly," he says. This is what everybody sees when they think of Africa. This, or some jolly, smiling, infinitely malleable native in a brightly colored print dress. But what Smith sees is money. Every disaster, every civil war, every famine makes somebody rich. You can be one of those smiling, malleable natives, or a stick-thin AIDS-infected refugee lying on a bed of flies in a transit camp. Or you can be rich. As long as one exists, the other is possible for whoever can see the logic. Which is obvious to everyone, of course, even to a man like Jenner. This isn't some special knowledge or insight that Smith alone possesses. The only difference is that he alone, or he alone among his immediate circle of acquaintance, is prepared to place his trust in that logic, because for him, money is an entirely abstract entity. For Brian Smith, only the logic of money exists; everything else is invisible.

Yet it had taken him a while to see that logic, and a while longer to understand that a man could apply it in a place like the headland—and there were times when he regretted the first few years of his adult life, a dull, almost somnambulist period when he had failed to realize his true potential. With the benefit of hindsight, of course, he can see that this error is forgivable. All the time he was growing up, all those wet Saturday afternoons and winter evenings by the dusty lamp in the dining room, he had been rehearsing his gift, making connections, searching out the logic in apparent chaos, but everyone he knew, his parents, his teachers, his classmates, they had all been utterly blind to his peculiar abilities— and that had rubbed off on him. Those others had seen him as just another working stiff, doomed for a dead-end office job or some middle-management position at the plant, and for a while he'd been taken in by that sad little scenario. This is how a place like the Innertown works: it holds on to its own, it holds on and draws them under and, mostly, they just let themselves slide, doing all they can to pretend that nothing bad is happening to them, because nothing—*nothing in the world*—is as contagious as the expectation of failure. That's how Brian Smith sees it now, looking back. He had been infected with some local disease. He had been *contaminated*— and his parents were more culpable in this than anyone else. So it is a matter of quiet satisfaction, looking back, to know that it was his parents who got him started on the road to money. It wasn't what they had intended, of course, and if young Brian could have foreseen the fatal accident that killed them both, on the short walk back from the Johnstons' house after a night of sherry and bridge, he would not have wished such a death upon them. Not because he loved or even needed them very much, but because it was too messy, too random. A drunk driver, a couple of tipsy pedestrians, broken glass, blood, a girl screaming. Right outside his house, on the night of his eighteenth birthday. Nobody would wish for chaos on that scale—and yet this event, as random and inelegant as it seemed, had been the making of him. Everything he possessed, everything he had achieved, he owed to that drunk driver, and the Johnstons' insistence, after a last rubber of bridge, that his parents should not put their coats on just yet, but stay awhile and have one for the road.

The life insurance money had surprised him, but that sum, along with what he raised on the house, had given Brian Smith the start he needed. Three months after his parents were buried, he had given up on any idea of working for someone else and started his own business, the Homeland Peninsula Company. To this day, nobody really knows what this Homeland Peninsula Company does but, from almost the first week of trading, Smith prospered. He played the markets to begin with, he made his little pot of money into a bigger pot so that, when he received the second gift of his career—the closure of the plant—he was ready to take advantage. Nobody wanted to take on the job of cleaning up after the

Consortium, but Brian Smith saw that money would have to be thrown at this particular problem. It was politics, pure and simple. Nobody out in the wider world cared about the people in the Innertown, or the environment, or the employment opportunities that might be created by attracting new investment to the eastern peninsula, but it was in all their interests to have somebody local— somebody like Brian Smith—make a good show of developing and regenerating the area with the subsidies and grants they made available. That way, they threw a little money at the problem and somebody else took on the responsibility. A fair amount of money did flow into Homeland Peninsula's accounts, not because the Consortium felt guilty or generous, but because the politicians needed to be seen to be doing something. What made Brian Smith rich wasn't Consortium money, it was public money, and the great thing about public money is that it doesn't stay public for long. Nobody checked to see if Homeland Peninsula could deliver a safer, cleaner Innertown; what mattered was that Brian Smith created the illusion of preparedness, the illusion of competence. Most important of all, he was a familiar face. He knew the problem on the ground, he had his finger on the pulse. What the people here needed was somebody they knew, somebody they could trust.

Before long, Smith was involved, sometimes openly, sometimes discreetly, in everything that happened at the eastern end of the peninsula. Suddenly, it seemed, he had unheard-of connections to the outside world, to politicians and large commercial concerns, and he conducted business with all kinds of powerful and dubious people—yet he never left the peninsula and, mostly, he stayed in his newly acquired house in the Outertown, looking after his garden, or sitting up all night in his office, with its wide bay windows looking out over the former golf course toward the sea, making calls, reading the newspapers, surfing the Internet. He loved the Internet. It was like a great jigsaw puzzle in the ether, an abstract realm where, no matter what happened in *this* world, a new logic ruled, a new order was possible, and money and information flowed everywhere, to anyone who had the sense to find it. Yet in spite of his love for this abstract space, where nothing was fixed, so everything was possible, Smith also knew the value of local, real-world connections. As soon as he'd started up in business for himself, he'd started reaching out into his own community and making a mental list of the people who might prove useful. In this he was totally democratic. Nobody, however mean or low, was irrelevant to his purposes. The poor, the criminal, the rejected—nobody was without potential. It had been a drunk driver who'd got him started in business, after all. A small favor that cost him very little might be a waste of time, but it might as easily provide unexpected returns. This was the logic that had led him to adopt Jenner, a man who had proven both unquestioning in his loyalty and totally without scruple or hesitation when a tricky situation needed to be managed—and that same logic had governed his decision to take on Morrison and his sad little wife, Alice, when they had nobody else to see them through the difficult times. Alice Morrison—Alice Taylor as was—had been a pretty, slightly crazy party girl in her teens, though to look at her now, you'd never know it. It had come as a surprise to everyone when she'd married John Morrison, that dim, self-pitying doormat of a man who'd stumbled from job to job before ending up working as a security guard at one of Smith's Innertown properties, but she'd soon gone back to her former ways, drinking and running around with her old crowd while Morrison was at work, doing the usual crazy stuff that small-town girls do everywhere, when there's no future to speak of, and nobody is paying much attention. Finally, though, she'd got herself into a drunk-driving jam that would have attracted everyone's attention—and that was when Smith had stepped in. The previous town policeman, Constable Fox, had presented a temporary problem, but then he'd had that unfortunate accident with the bicycle and his people had taken him home to Strabane in a box. Meanwhile, a little bewildered by her lucky escape, Alice had gone home and stayed there, sad and alone but more or less respectable, while the party went on without her. With the town policeman's job vacant, Smith had arranged for Morrison to be appointed as Fox's successor and it had been gratifying to think that he had reached the point where he had the local policeman in his pocket, even if the potential benefits weren't immediately obvious. That was the thing about potential, it was beyond prediction. It stayed hidden until it showed itself, sometimes in the most surprising ways, according to its own logic.

So that night, when the phone rang, and his modest outlay had borne unexpected fruit, Smith wasn't altogether surprised. Things had been going well for quite some time, but the ugly little scene that Morrison had uncovered could easily have been the spanner in the works. The last thing Smith wanted was publicity, a more professional police inquiry, the press, some kind of public investigation. There had been times, over the last year or so, when he'd considered using Morrison in some minor way, but he had always held back and kept the policeman in reserve. Now, thanks to his patience, that small investment of time and effort had come good big-time, and Smith couldn't help feeling a little surge of satisfaction as he put the phone down and turned to Jenner. "I've got something for you," he said, sitting back in his chair.

Jenner nodded. "All right," he said. He was trying not to look pleased, but not quite succeeding. He did this often, because he thought business was a serious matter, and he felt it would be unseemly to let Smith know how much he enjoyed the more unsavory tasks he was given to perform. It was endearing, this slight scruple, the true mark of a man of action. Even more endearing, though, was Jenner's gravity, the way his manner made it clear that he was capable of doing *anything* in Smith's service. Sometimes, Smith sensed his disappointment that he hadn't been called upon to kill anyone yet—to really *kill* someone, with his own hands—but that disappointment, merely hinted at, was always tempered by an unspoken agreement that it was only a matter of time before they came to that point in their work together. This was a possibility that Smith not only did not discount but found just as gratifying, for reasons of his own. For now, though, however exaggerated Jenner's gravity might seem, Smith knew it had to be respected and he adopted a suitably serious look. "This is something that has to be handled *discreetly*," he said. God, it was a privilege, being Brian Smith. The sheer pleasure of giving a man like Jenner work he could enjoy, the absurdly cinematic quality to this talk about handling things discreetly. For one dangerous moment, he almost allowed himself a pleased, yet ironic, smile—but that would have spoiled the moment for Jenner, who did, after all, so look forward to the dirty work, in whatever form it presented itself.

MORRISON

LATER, MORRISON TOLD HIMSELF THAT HE'D MADE A simple, once-in-a-lifetime error of judgment when he'd called Smith. But that wasn't quite true. Mistakes don't happen in a single, decisive moment, they unfold slowly through a lifetime. They grow invisibly beneath the surface, running for years in the dark like the roots of some patient fungus till something erupts at the surface, some slick, wet fruiting body full of dark spores that stream out into the wind and travel for miles, tainting everything they touch. That was how it was with Morrison: his big mistake had been in ever having anything to do with Brian Smith in the first place, but there was no way he could have avoided that. The fact was that he was bound to Smith in ways that he hadn't even begun to understand and, on what he would come to think of as *that fateful night,* he was only doing what Smith had expected him to do all along. He was following his nature.

It was a man who picked up, but it wasn't Smith. Morrison knew Smith's voice, and this man was someone else altogether, someone who spoke in a quiet, very formal way, quite unlike Smith's hearty, almost jovial manner. Morrison did not know this person but, whoever it was, he obviously existed as a buffer between Smith and the outside world, and the policeman had had to insist a little to get put through. As he stood waiting, hearing an exchange of voices somewhere in the background but unable to make out quite what they were saying, he remembered the visit Smith had made to him, the very first night he had moved into the police house. The local boy made good had been his usual, friendly self, though Morrison knew that the bottle of whiskey he'd brought, and all the work he'd done behind the scenes, first to make Alice's problems go away and then to set Morrison up as the only possible candidate for the police job, were favors that would eventually be called in. That was how it worked and Morrison knew as much, but he also knew that beggars couldn't be choosers. If you wanted to get on in the Innertown, you had to take whatever help you could get, from whoever was ready to give it—and that was usually Brian Smith. Besides, he'd had no choice but to smile graciously, accept the whiskey—though surely Smith knew that he didn't drink, that he never touched a drop because of Alice—and in so doing, accept the invitation that went with it. Not that anything was stated in so many words. Smith didn't ask for favors, he offered them. Nevertheless, it took nothing more than a smile and friendly handshake for Morrison to know that his soul was being claimed, and there was no turning back, once he'd accepted that bottle of whiskey and returned that insinuating smile. It was, of course, no accident that Smith's gift was something Morrison could not use.

"Call on me anytime," Smith had said, standing in Morrison's new hallway in the police house. He had only stopped by for a moment, on his way home from a meeting. Or so he had said.

"Thank you," Morrison had answered, feeling dwarfed by this big man in his fancy black coat and expensive shoes. He had only been in the house two days. "Though I'm not really supposed to accept gifts—"

"Nonsense," Smith had said. "We're all in this together and we're going to work together to make this a better place to live. Businesses, schools, the police. We should think of each other as friends and colleagues. What better way to show friendship than to offer a small gift, of congratulations and"—he had smiled then, because he had found his former night watchman's weak spot— "respect."

Now, facing a crisis he could never have been expected to handle by himself, Morrison was having to beg to get through to his supposed friend and colleague. "It's an emergency," he said. "A police matter. I can't emphasize how urgent or how important it is."

The man wavered a moment, then consulted with his boss. Morrison heard the voices in that warm, faraway room, and stood waiting, wondering how much more change he had. Finally Smith came on the line.

It hadn't taken the big man long to grasp the situation. "All right," he said. "It's good that you called me. That shows clear thinking. You just wait there, and I'll send someone."

"Send someone?"

"We need to sort this out quietly," Smith said. "God knows what will happen if it gets out. We can't let this get in the way of our larger goal. We certainly don't want the whole world coming down on us. And think of the boy's parents. They're better off thinking their son has run off to join the circus than having to hear this awful—" He thought for a moment, like a PR man finding the right copy. "This awful, awful tragedy. Wouldn't you say so, Constable?"

Morrison didn't know what to say. There had been a trace of irony, he thought, in the way Smith had put the question. *Constable.* "I think," he began. He wanted to say that "this" *had* to get out, that there was no other way, that there would have to be an investigation before another child was murdered. He wanted to protest, to take back the call. He wanted to scream. Instead, he stood silent, unable to say anything. He wasn't a policeman, he was an employee of Homeland Peninsula. The police uniform might just as well have been livery.

Smith broke in quickly. "We really don't want some big investigation over this," he said. "The people of the Innertown have had enough to deal with, and we don't want to dash their hopes for the Homeland project. That's the last thing they need." He listened for a second, trying to judge the quality of Morrison's faraway silence. He seemed satisfied. "I think we're agreed on the best way to handle this," he said. "You just stay there. My people will be right with you."

Twenty minutes later, a man whom Morrison recognized vaguely as Jenner arrived in a black van. He was dressed in a suit and tie, but he looked like a ditchdigger, with his huge hands and his flat nose. He parked the car by the telephone box and got out.

"You must be Morrison," he said. He had that air of calculated affability that let you know he didn't give a fuck about you or anybody else.

Morrison nodded. "I really think Mr. Smith—"

Jenner laughed. "Mr. Smith doesn't do this line of work," he said. "That's why he's got people like us." He looked Morrison up and down in the half-light. "Well," he said, "people like me, anyway."

Morrison wasn't offended. He felt sick to his stomach by now, and he was beginning to understand what he had done. Being insulted by a navvy in a suit was the least of his problems. "Listen," he said, "maybe we should take a step back—"

Jenner took hold of his arm. "It's all right," he said. "Just show me where the kid is, and I'll sort it out."

"But what do we tell his family?" Morrison said, trying to slip his arm free.

Jenner tightened his grip. "We don't tell anybody anything," he said. "Mr. Smith asked me to make it very, very clear to you that this is strictly *entre nous*." He leaned closer. Morrison could smell his aftershave now, and he felt sicker than ever. "*Is* that very, very clear?" he asked.

Morrison nodded. He was trying to remember what *entre nous* meant. "Clear," he said finally, pulling his arm free just as the man let go.

"Good," Jenner said, cheerfully. "Now. Where's this body?"

———

After he had been shown to the den among the trees, Jenner told Morrison that he wasn't needed anymore, and the only full-time policeman on the east peninsula walked back up to the road in a haze of exhaustion and misgivings. He didn't look back. Two days later, he had called Smith, to find out what he was supposed to do next, but Smith's secretary said he was away on business.

"When will he be back?" Morrison asked. He knew she was lying, and he knew that she knew he knew.

There was a moment's hesitation at the other end of the line, before the woman answered. He recognized her voice, she was a woman he had known in school, but he had to think for a few seconds before he could place her. Elaine Harris. That was it. A plain girl, with very pronounced grayish freckles on her arms and face. "He'll call you on his return," Elaine said, her voice flat and slightly hard. By her tone, Morrison could tell she was looking to someone—probably not Smith, maybe Jenner—waiting for instructions.

"It's quite important," Morrison said. "It's police business." He felt stupid as soon as he said it, as if he were making an idle threat and, at the same time, playing a role for which he wasn't quite right.

"He will certainly call you on his return," Elaine Harris said and, before Morrison could think of what to say next, she hung up.

For a long time after that, Morrison had wanted to quit. His small world had fallen to pieces, and he didn't know how to put it back together again. He felt as though someone had broken into his body in the night and switched everything to its lowest setting: his blood, his heart, his nervous system—they were all just barely working, just ticking over. Every now and then, when he was alone, sitting at his desk or lying awake in the middle of the night, alone even when Alice was lying right next to him, it came to him that he would probably live like this for another thirty or forty years, then die without anyone even noticing. He lost interest in work, in his garden, in Alice. She seemed to want to help but, as she kept telling him, she couldn't help if she didn't know what the problem was, and he didn't dare tell her. After a while, quietly, and with only a little bitterness, they had reached a kind of stalemate that had lasted a surprisingly long time before Alice started drinking again. Not long after that, she had the first of her little *incidents*, as she liked to call them.

Meanwhile, the other boys began to disappear, one by one, at intervals of around eighteen months. The first to go was William Ash, the boy who had been with Mark that Halloween night. After that, two years passed, then Alex Slocombe vanished, quickly followed by a little Scots-Italian kid called Stewart Riva. Finally, just a few months ago, Liam Nugent had gone out for a walk and never come back, though he'd been seen with a sports bag over his shoulder, and his troubled relationship with his drunken father was a matter of record, so it was easy for Smith's people to suggest that he'd just given up and run away. With each new case, Morrison resolved to go back, to start again. He told himself he would accept his punishment for his part in the cover-up, if it would help stop this nightmare. But he hadn't made his move, and he was always aware of Smith—and Jenner—watching him from the genteel shadows of the Outertown. Gradually, by degrees that weren't quite apparent as they happened, Morrison had settled into a small, clouded, unshakable limbo. All he had left was this shrine, and even that was unofficial, a guilty man's secret. Meanwhile, he had to sit with the parents while they filled out missing persons reports, he had to lie to people about what he thought had happened to their children. William Ash. Alex Slocombe. Stewart Riva. Liam

Nugent. No trace of those boys was ever found, so it was easy to say that they had simply run away, leaving a life without prospects for the bright lights and the big city. The reward for Morrison's continuing silence, if it could be called a reward, was a more or less honorary inclusion in Smith's lowest circle, not as an equal, but as a hireling, doing little jobs that Jenner brought him: smiling, ironic Jenner, who knew that all this was just a sop, a way of keeping Morrison busy and, at the same time, testing his loyalty. He knew that if he refused just one of these little jobs Smith would let Jenner loose on him, and there was no doubting where that would lead.

Now, eight years later, he is in limbo, and he's thoroughly used to it. All he has is this little garden, three square feet of flowers and broken china and glass. It's something at least, so better than nothing and, late in the day, far, far too late, it's almost honorable. Morrison has always believed that, in spite of its troubles, in spite of its history, the Innertown is really just an old-fashioned town with a police house and a library, soft autumn days of leaf drifts along the high street and girls playing hockey in the fog, summer fetes and white Christmases, children growing up and having children of their own. It's a town that remembers its dead, a town where everyone remembers together, guarding the ancestors in their ancient solitude, long after they might have imagined themselves forgotten. It is, in other words, a good town, a town where people have detailed and carefully nurtured memories. Here, an elderly woman will cut flowers from her garden some weekday morning and carry them in a shopping bag to the cemetery, where she will leave them on the grave of a long-dead school friend. It is a simple act of remembrance she intends, nothing more: she will not stay long, perhaps pausing a while to pick up a few stray sweets wrappers or tidy the gravel before going home to her radio and her baking. Or a man in his middle years, a husband and father, will find himself, some damp October evening, reading the banal inscription on the grave of a girl he knew in school. He is not at all sure why he is there; somebody else would cite nostalgia, sentiment, a midlife crisis, but that's far too simple an explanation. The girl he remembers now never existed; for most of the years she spent being alive, he hardly noticed her, or perhaps it would be truer to say that she hardly noticed him—but once, on a warm summer's night at the town dance, or on some hazy winter's afternoon at the end of term, she had smiled at him, and they had gone for a walk together, or stood talking awhile in the school foyer, and he'd realized how miraculous she was. Two days later, she was dead: a tumor, a rare infection, a hole in the heart. It wasn't uncommon, in the Innertown, that such a girl might die young, but this girl had stayed alive long enough to make her mark, to take up residence in his imagination. To haunt him. Now, through her, he mourns and celebrates everything that life has denied him, all the beauty, all the magic. This is how it happens: the dead go away into their solitude, but the young dead stay with us, they color our dreams, they make us wonder about ourselves, that we should be so unlucky, or clumsy, or so downright ordinary as to carry on without them.

Yet more than any of those kind citizens, Morrison is an expert in mourning—though what he mourns has never been altogether clear to him. The boys, yes; but he doesn't mourn them enough to seek justice on their behalf. He mourns his marriage, especially now that he and Alice have turned from each other and, almost noiselessly, carried on with their separate, quietly desperate lives. He doesn't understand that. It might seem a cliché, now, but when they'd first met, he had known that Alice was the only woman he would ever love. She'd had that quality some people have, if not for everyone then at least for one magical other, of making existence itself feel like a promise. And she had seemed so close to begin with, as much a friend as a wife, even if they had never talked that much. Back then, they hadn't felt the need. She was there, he was there. Later, though, when he needed to be touched, coming to her in a fog of inarticulate longing—a wordless longing to be touched and, in that healing touch, forgiven for a sin he wasn't able to confess—she had just collapsed inward, like one of those sensitive plants they used to grow in school, so there was nothing there, no point of contact. She didn't even like it if he looked at her for too long, as if even that was an impossible demand he was making on her. At such times, she became clinical, almost brutally analytical. "I can't help you," she would say, "if you won't tell me what's wrong." As if what he wanted was *help*.

Whenever she did that, whenever she crumbled in on herself like that, it made him think of that plant. *Mimosa pudica*, that was it. Pale green, slightly downy plants, with their sensitive, fingerlike leaves and perfectly engineered stems that simply folded at any contact till they were all but absent. A fingertip, the nib of a pen, even a single water drop. That was all it took to make the whole plant collapse. A single touch, and everything fell away, till all you were left with was an indifferent, infinitely patient absence. Sometimes, Morrison feels that this is what he mourns more than anything: that this is the true source of his grief. He had expected to be touched, he had thought that was what married folk did for each other: they touched. They healed each other with this simple instrument. He has never understood why Alice doesn't feel the same way. Now, he hasn't touched anyone, and nobody has touched him, for years. When Alice started having her episodes, he'd hoped this would make a difference, he'd hoped that they were finally equal, in their need if nothing else, and could start again. It was almost laughable, now, to think that he had ever been so foolish.

ALICE

IN THE POLICE HOUSE, ALICE KEEPS HAVING THE SAME dream: pink, nerveless fish with lacy, desirous mouths are all around her face, butting and probing at her lips and eyes, eating her away, cell by cell, as she lies half naked and alone on what ought to have been her marital bed. Only it's not a dream, because she's not asleep, and she isn't altogether sure she's alone either; for the last several minutes, she's had the sense that someone is there, in the room, someone or something that feels like a child saying its prayers in some corner that she cannot find. There was a storm in the night, but she'd only been half aware of it, lying on the bed in a tight sleeve of pills and vodka. She had kept those well hidden, and for once Morrison hadn't found them—she always calls him by his surname now, even when he isn't there, even in her private, silent thoughts, because she never wants to allow her contempt to slip or dwindle. She has no intention of letting him get away with anything: not the years of indifference, or the compromises he has made with the good people of the Outertown, and not the part he has played in what she has begun to consider, in herself, an incurable illness. This is the main symptom, this slow realization, as she comes to herself and the pink fish slip back into her mind's haze, that her waking dream, and the quiet, childish voice that she can barely make out in some far angle of the house are the first signals of what she and Morrison choose to call "the shakes." This is the word they have always used for her delirium attacks; it's Morrison's word, in fact: she remembers him using it first, and she is annoyed, still, that it stuck. Now, whenever she drinks, even a little, she is struck down by the shakes; it happens every time and she still can't get herself to stop. Normally, she has to hide the bottles of pills or booze when Morrison is at home and she takes every possible step to conceal them, even though, half the time, she is desperate to give them up, to lock herself away and, with a little help from someone or something, make some kind of honest attempt to cure the incurable.

As often as he can, Morrison stays home and watches her, probably waiting for her to say something that would allow him to help. This last night, though, he has been out till late, presumably doing something related to the storm, some minor work for which Smith and his cronies find him useful, and which he is only too happy to do. He knows it is hardest for her at night and he does what he can, even though his attention is unwelcome. These days, however, with the disappearances still unsolved—five boys gone, now, and no explanation for their sudden absence—and with so much happening in the background, he is out a fair deal on what he chooses to call police business, which means that he comes home to find her, from time to time, listening to voices in her head or staring at something that *he* knows isn't even there, and the odd thing is, she despises him for his normality, she despises the fact that he knows, without a doubt, that everything she sees and hears at such times is a hallucination. She doesn't care if he comes home and finds her unconscious, or finishing off the last of the drink on the porch at the back, where at least it's cool. She has learned to live for the passing opportunity, the lucky moment. What she does mind is how easily he dismisses those phantoms that populate her world, phantoms that, if anything, should be just as real for him. After all, they are his children too, the only children their marriage has bred.

Morrison would say the shakes are caused by the drinking and the pills, and that's that, but Alice isn't so sure. Who's to say that the shakes don't come first, in some quiet, or hidden, form, driving her to do those things to herself, just to be at peace? She doesn't like passing out from drink, it's not what she ever wanted to do with her life. She remembers the time when she and Morrison first met, how sweet and thoughtful he was, and how he had his own ways about him, before he fell in with Brian Smith. At one time, he had wanted to do his job according to his own standards, he'd been determined to make a fresh start. When he wasn't working, he would do stuff in the garden, making things grow, taking a childish pleasure that he didn't even try to disguise in bringing in fresh vegetables and setting them out on the kitchen table, firm orange carrots with dark crumbs of soil still clinging to them and those bright curly leaves, radishes, turnips, lettuce, all of it a minor celebration, the man happy with his work, the produce looking good and clean and tasting fine, in spite of where it had been grown. In those days, Morrison had been an optimist, and she had wanted to love him for that. She had, in fact, wanted to love him for a long time, but she hadn't succeeded. Even before he grew distant, and fell in with Smith's people, she hadn't been able to love him. He was too meager, too commonplace. There simply hadn't been enough of him to love.

Now, she wants to go out into the world and walk away. Or not walk away so much as just *walk*, without even that much of a sense of direction. One of these days, she will take too many pills, or her body will just give out, and she will die while Morrison is out somewhere doing Brian Smith's bidding. She will die alone in her claustrophobic little police house, with nobody there to tell her goodbye; though if you took Morrison's word for it, everybody died alone because, no matter who was there when they were going, the actual departure had to be a solitary one, and the destination—whatever it might be—was one that you alone could reach. But then again, supposing it was different. What about all those stories of people who entered a brilliant circle of light and saw other bodies, other faces around them, welcoming, sweet faces, bringing them home? What if, when you died, you didn't move away into the ultimate loneliness, the ultimate separation, but instead, you returned to some other state, a state you had known before? What if death wasn't a solitary thing, after all, but a point where everyone who had ever been separated out, everyone who had wandered a lifetime, separate, but trying to connect in some way with someone or something else, returned to the shining, communal oneness from which they had all originated, tiny fragments of light and consciousness merging into the whole? She had read about such things; there were people—millions of people in Asia or some such place—

who believed this. They thought there was one single mind that we were all a part of, and that we returned to it in death, to be separate no more, but to share in the one single, eternal thought that all of us had, and were. That thought was the universe, or being, or something like that. It was Buddhists, she seemed to remember, who believed this idea—Buddhists, or maybe Hindus—and they believed it as a matter of fact, the same way other people believed in gravity, or medicine. At times, the sheer mass of this belief, so many millions, almost persuaded her that it was true, and for giddy minutes she would sit wondering if any of those millions ever saw what a terrifying idea it really was.

ET IN ARCADIA

EGO.

Still there and gone away at the same time. Here and there, lost and found, in the everlasting present.

I can't help thinking that, if you want to stay alive, you have to love something. I used to have a friend, a boy called Liam Nugent, and I think I loved him, but now he's gone, and I don't know if I love anybody. Not Dad, that's for sure. Once upon a time, yes, but not now, because he's not really *here* now. He's lying in bed, silent, far away, and it's like he's dead already. Maybe I could love Elspeth, but I can't really see it. Sometimes I don't even think I like her, but then she does something funny, or she just says something outrageous, and I think I could almost be *in love* with her, like some character in a book. Though everybody says there's a big difference between being *in love* and actual *love*. It gets difficult around about there and I don't like it when things get difficult for no good reason. Complicated, yes; I can do complicated. The world is complicated, there's all kinds of stuff going on. Some books are really complicated. But love probably isn't that complicated, it's just difficult. And maybe love is the wrong word here, anyway, at least when it comes to people. People are hard to love, even if you're having sex with them, or good, funny conversations like the ones Elspeth and I sometimes have. People are difficult, that's just how they are made.

Still, if you want to stay alive, which is hard to do in a place like this, you have to love *something*, and the one thing I love is the chemical plant. Well, that, and books. I love books. In a place like this, that's almost as weird as saying you love the plant, but at least it's more or less normal. Because you're definitely *not* normal, you're definitely *weird*, if you love the plant.

The thing is, I know everybody says it's dangerous, that it's making us all sick, that they should have razed it to the ground years ago and cleared the entire eastern peninsula instead of just leaving it to rot—and that's all true, I know that, but you still have to admit that it's beautiful. Maybe there are more obviously beautiful places in Canada or California, maybe they have gardens and parks with clear lakes and honest-to-Betsy live trees with autumn leaves and all the stuff you see on television, but we don't have those things. All we have is the plant. We're not supposed to go there and I suppose most of the kids don't, but there are plenty who do.

I don't think anybody spends as much time out there as I do, though. When the storms come, I go out and stand at the entrance to one of the old kilns, to watch the rain pouring down. Or I sit up on a ruined crane above the docks and look out over the water, to a point on the horizon that seems to belong, not just to another place, but also to a different time, the past maybe, or maybe the future, when the derelict buildings rot away and the poison in the ground, the poison nobody can see, loses its deadly power. I'm not supposed to go there—nobody is—but it doesn't scare me and it doesn't scare some of the other kids, because I see them out there sometimes, moving like shadows among the ruins, not wanting to be seen, and not wanting to see that anybody else is there with them. I imagine they go out there for the same reasons I do: because it's peaceful, and it doesn't belong to anybody, and, maybe, because it's the only beauty they know. It's odd to say that, but it really, really *is* beautiful, the way those old horror films they show on TV are beautiful, or the way Annette Crowley in 4B is beautiful, with the white scar running across her cheek and neck where her face was cut open in a car crash.

This beautiful place is called the chemical plant because that's what it once was, though now it's just hundreds of derelict buildings and a network of abandoned railway tracks running past the edge of the Innertown to what remains of the old harbor. If you were to draw a map of this end of the peninsula, you'd have the Outertown first, all mock-Elizabethan and ranch-style villas with wide, miraculously green lawns and hedges. Then there's the former golf course, conveniently situated so as to divide the good people in the nice houses from the ghosts and ruffians of the Innertown, now nothing more than a ghetto for poisoned, cast-off workers like my old man. Finally, with virtually nothing to separate it from the town, what remains is an industrial wilderness where the plant used to be. It's called the chemical plant, because it never had any other name, even the land it stands on is almost nameless, a stretch of nowhere that people sometimes call the headland, though the adults rarely talk about it and, when they do, they mostly just refer to it as *out there*. If you listen to some of the great and good around here, the whole lot comes as one unit, which they've started calling Homeland, and they've got big plans for us all, what they call a "regeneration program." That's Brian Smith's territory, though, so nobody in the Innertown is holding his breath.

The chemical plant is always beautiful, even when it's frightening, or when you can see how sad it is, when all the little glimmers of what was here before—the woods, the firth, the beaches—show through and you realize it must have been amazing, back in the old times. Sometimes you can still get that feeling. Like when it's early on a summer's day: half-light, ruined buildings looming out of the shadows, the last owls calling to one another from hedge to hedge on the old farm road that runs past the east woods and down to the water. An hour later, and it's completely different. The farm road is straight as a rod and ash white, still ghostly at this hour, soft and uncertain, as if it hadn't quite recovered from the moonlight. The hedges are dotted with pale, brave-looking flowers. Sometimes you can see a boat in the channel, far out on the water and, sometimes, it will be a passenger boat, not the usual utility vessels that wander back and forth, bearing cargos of industrial waste or spent fuel to the lucky towns farther along the peninsula. You can't see anyone on the decks, but this boat is in good condition and it has little round porthole windows all along the side, where there might be cabins. Maybe the people are asleep down there, or sitting in cheerful little circles in the dining room, having breakfast and planning the day ahead. This end of the peninsula isn't a place they would want to see, not even for curiosity's sake. If they did look out at some point—farther along the headland, say, beyond the last of the concrete piers—they might see smoke in the east woods, thin yellowish wisps of it among the leaves like the smoke signals in old Westerns. That might be me, or some other boy from the Innertown, sitting out all night because he can't stand to listen as his father lies breathing in the next room, every breath a step away from total absence, a reason to be afraid, but also for celebration.

There are plenty of places to go out on the headland: the poison wood, the docks, the warehouses, the kilns. The old processing plants, where the smell is still so strong you can almost taste the poison you are breathing. There are places to go, and there are still places you can't get into, inner rooms within rooms that you don't know for sure where or what they are, though you know *something* is there. I like the strips of ground between one place and another, and all the places where you can go and never see anybody, the mudflat-and-oil smell of the farther edge, the old loading yards with their rusting cranes and that one crippled boat, eaten away by years of wind and salt water, deserted, of course, though I always feel that someone might be there, not a ghost, or anything of that ilk, but not a man either, or not a man from anywhere *I* know. It would have been immense once, that boat; now it's just a broken hull, the decks rusting, the lower levels a mass of rotting stairs and gangways, dangerous and unsteady under my feet, leading down to a reddish darkness, where the vast, stagnant tanks lie, heavy with salt and nickel. This was where everything led to once: the road, the train tracks, the walkways—their only purpose had been to fill huge boats like this with unimaginable quantities of poison and fertilizer and dark, oily liquors that would travel halfway around the world in the sealed hull while great oceans raged around them. When one of those anonymous-looking ships broke on rocks, or foundered in difficult waters, you can imagine all the government types and PR folks back home figuring out the angles—what lies to tell, what they think they can get away with, what they know for sure they can deny. And all the way down, in sweet water teeming with the cast of *The Blue Planet*, the ship would fall, split open like a coconut, pouring out gallon after gallon of its venomous cargo.

Sometimes I think the headland is at its most beautiful in winter, when everything you take for granted, everything you don't bother to look at during the rest of the year, all the hidden angles and recesses, the unseen pipework and fields of rubble, come back new, redefined by the snow and, at the same time, perfected, made abstract, like the world in a blueprint. Everything looks closer together and, at the same time, it's like there's more *space* than there was in autumn. When the first snow comes, you start to see new things, and you realize how much of the world is invisible, or just on the point of being seen, if you could only find the right kind of attention to pay it, like turning the dial on a radio to the right channel, the one where everything is clearer and someone is talking in a language that you understand right away, even though you know it's not the language you thought you knew. And then there's the way it's all transformed, how it all looks so innocent, as if it couldn't hurt you in a million years, all those drums of crusted and curdled effluent, all those pits with their lingering traces of poison or radiation, or whatever it is the authorities want to keep sealed up here, along with the dangerous mass of our polluted bodies. Under the snow, it all looks pure, even when a wet rust mark bleeds through, or some trace of cobalt blue or verdigris rises up through an inch of white, it's beautiful. Really, they should send an artist out here, some artist who isn't squeamish, but isn't just cutting sharks in half, either. A war artist, maybe. Because if this resembles anything, it's a war zone. But then, isn't a war zone beautiful too, if you look at it the right way?

Years ago, the railway still ran along the coast, bringing in freight cars full of raw materials at night, when the people were sleeping, so their dreams were laced with the noise of goods trains and the shifting of points, an undercurrent of shunts and whistles that continued into the daytime, reminding them that they belonged to this place, that it was in their blood and their nerves. That's what I imagine, anyway: for about as long as I have been alive, the plant has been closed—not only closed, in fact, but condemned, a government-certified zone of irreversible contamination that no one is officially supposed to enter. Not that anybody makes any great effort to keep us out, either. That would mean drawing too much attention to the place and people would start getting worked up again about what might be out there. Because, really, nobody knows what's out there. This is what makes it interesting, for me, and the others like me: for as long as I have known it, the plant has been empty and silent, a vast labyrinth of corridors and abandoned rooms, some open to the sky, others with glass or metal roofing and, above each kiln—we call them kilns, but there's no real evidence to say what they were used for—a giant chimney rises up into the clouds, a wide brick chimney that, in the wet months, fills with great cascading falls of rain, just as the glass roofs and the sheets of corrugated metal on the storerooms will break into a music that sounds repetitious when you first hear it, but soon begins to reveal itself as an infinitely complex fabric of faint overtones and distant harmonics that is never quite the same from one moment to the next. Maybe they should send a musician out here, not a painter. Turn it into music. That would be something. I can picture trendy people in warehouse apartments, people in public relations or something, sitting on their prayer mats and meditating to the sound of the rain bouncing off the corrugated roof of an old storeroom, all of it carefully sampled and filtered through a hundred synthesizers or whatever, with some Tibetan singing bowls and a dulcimer thrown in.

They don't make any huge efforts to keep people out now, but they don't really need to, do they? To begin with, we had scavengers and such, industrial beachcombers looking for something to sell, but they soon gave up. Now, nobody comes out here except a few kids, and I know that we all feel the same way when we are out on the headland by ourselves. I've stumbled upon others now and then, and I've felt something break, not just in my own mind but in theirs, too: a sense of being part of the quiet, of being outside time and, harder to put into words, and impossible to convey to someone else, a feeling of reverence for the place, whether for the clumps of wildflowers and grasses that grow amid the broken glass and rubble, or for how still it can be on a summer's afternoon—so still, it's as if nothing has ever happened, here or anywhere else. So still, it's as if no one had ever existed, and time was just about to start. Maybe it seems daft to talk about reverence, but this complex of ruined buildings and disused railways that runs as far as I can walk in any direction, whether along the coast, or inland through scrubby woodlands and fields of gorse, this apparent wasteland is all the church we have, and I know, when I meet someone out there, some boy with a kite or a box of matches, some girl I recognize from school, I know I am interrupting, not some childish game or one of those acts of supposed vandalism the adults are always complaining about. No: what I have chanced upon is a secret ceremony, a private ritual. When that happens, I can tell that the other person, this other boy or girl, is unquiet, unsettled, as if he or she has been caught out in some way: perhaps we stop and talk, exchanging a few pointless words before going on our way; more often, we exchange shy, almost guilty looks, then steal away, hurrying back to the safety of the long grass or a dank storeroom, out of the flow of time, and away from the gaze of others.

I used to come out here with Liam. That was before he disappeared—before he *went away*, as the adults always say, though I know they are hiding something. I know something bad happened to him, just as I know—we *all* know—that something bad happened to the others who have vanished. Five, now: all boys around my age, with parents and friends and school desks, vanished into thin air, leaving nothing but a tangle of sheets, or a book set facedown on a bedside table, to show they had once been present. Five boys from the Innertown, a place nobody cares about, a polluted, discolored town at the far end of a peninsula most people don't even know is there on the maps. Five boys: Mark Wilkinson, William Ash, Alex Slocombe, Stewart Riva—and Liam Nugent, the last to go, lost somewhere between his house and the sports hall, and nothing to show where he had gone, or when he was last here. No mark, no clue, no sign of a struggle, no note, no stain on the air at the point where he turned and walked away—if, as the adults tell us, he *chose* to go, of his own free will, tired, as the others were, of this dying town at the end of a desolate peninsula, a place where nothing good can ever happen, where boys like Liam, or Alex, or Stewart, have nothing to look forward to. Liam was my best friend. He was a long, thin guy, a good swimmer, not handsome or anything, though some of the girls liked him for his personality. He was fucking crazy, to be honest, and he didn't have much of a home life, but then there's not many of us have much of a home life. His dad was then and still is the peninsula's number-one piss artist, and the only way that Liam's disappearance has changed his life is that he occasionally gets bought a sympathy drink at the club that he mightn't have got otherwise. That old fucker has got grief down to a fine art: humble, stoical, but essentially a shattered man, he sits at the bar and waits for one of the gullible to wander by. He never had a good thing to say to or about Liam when he was still here. He even stole his paper-delivery money to buy vodka. Liam was pretty pissed off about that, and he'd taken pretty much all he was going to take from the old fucker, but if he'd been planning to leave, he would have told me about it. He would have wanted me to go *with* him, for God's sake. That was how things were with us: I can't remember a day going by when I didn't see him; we had secrets that nobody else knew; we did everything together. If he had decided to leave, there's no way he would have gone without me.

But he didn't go away. Nobody goes away. The kids talk about it all the time, but the truth is, none of us really knows what's out there, twenty, or fifty, or a hundred miles along the coast road, because nobody has ever gone that far. People from the Innertown don't leave, not even to go on holiday or visit relatives. They talk about leaving all the time, of course, but they never actually get out. So when the adults put about the story that Liam had gone off to seek his fortune in the outside world, just like those other boys before him, I knew something was wrong. Liam hadn't left the Innertown, he wasn't halfway along the peninsula, walking away in the evening rain, he wasn't standing by a road a hundred miles distant, hitchhiking to some city he had seen on television. He wasn't just gone from his desk in Room 5A, he wasn't just missing from the five-a-side team, he wasn't swimming somewhere in a big, Olympic-size pool or off some beach in Greece, he was gone from the world altogether. Lost. I knew it, because I could feel it. It was like when the snow melts, and afterward it seems that something is missing. Some essential piece of the apparatus of the world, some necessary presence has vanished overnight in the quiet patter of rain and wind gusting through the cracked pane in the landing window. That was how it felt to me when Liam disappeared: something essential was gone, and it didn't seem right that everything else should just continue, the way it had done before. I missed his voice, and the way he had of making faces at me in the changing-room mirror, just as I missed the white glare of the snow on the railings of the public library: it was the same thing, the same local flaw in the world that should have caused the whole system to crash. I think about him all the time, and I know he wouldn't have run away without me. It might be a funny old world, like my dad used to say when he was still talking, but it's not *that* funny.

———

When I say the plant is beautiful, I'm not saying that I think it was ever a good thing for the town. I know it's made people sick, and I can't imagine all the hours I spend out there will do me any good when I'm older. But then, who knows if I'll even get older. Some kids don't even make it to twenty, and when they die, nobody knows what was wrong with them. So I have to be realistic. I have lived here for fourteen years. Fourteen and two-thirds. I have breathed this air for more than five thousand days. I have breathed and swallowed and digested the smuts and tainted dust and blackened rain of the headland for around seven million minutes. How many breaths does that come to? How many pints of water? How much bread? How many eggs? With every breath I take the world into my lungs, with every swallow I take in, not just food and drink, but everything that it contains, all the traces and smears and soot falls, all the threads of copper and nickel and 2,4,5-T and who knows what else. People say we are what we are, the future is written in our blood—and you have to admit, there's no avoiding chemistry. If you lived out here, I don't think you'd argue with that.

A large percentage of the people who worked in production at the plant are either sick or dead now. My dad, for example. My dad has been sick for almost as long as I can remember. I don't suppose he ever was much of a talker, but now he doesn't say anything, not one word. Of course, folk from the Innertown don't like to talk anyway, not unless they're teachers, but at least they exchange greetings, a "good morning" here, a remark about the weather there, the little bits and bobs of conversation that allow people to get around one another peaceably. My dad doesn't do any of that. When he was first ill, he would sit in the kitchen listening to the radio, or he would go out into the garden if it was warm and watch the weeds growing. After my mother left, though, he just collapsed in on himself. These days, he stays in his room most of the time, living in utter silence. Sometimes he sleeps all day, but quite often he just lies on the bed and stares at the ceiling. When he does get up, he just sits in the kitchen waiting for the kettle to boil. It never does, though, because he keeps forgetting to switch it on. When Elspeth comes round, we go into my room and play games that we make up as we go along, but we do it quietly so he can't hear. I don't think he'd like it if he knew what we were doing. Not that he suspects anything, as far as I can tell, and he likes Elspeth. Sometimes he even smiles when he sees her. It's good when he smiles. I wished he'd do it more, and preferably not just when my cute girlfriend comes round.

Though I suppose I ought to be glad he doesn't talk much because, if he did, he'd probably just go on about my mother and how unhappy he was when she walked out. Or worse, how much he loved her and how great she was. In fact, I know that's what he would do. My mother wasn't really that interested when she was here, as far as I remember, but at least she was around. I remember when she left, she sat me down at the kitchen table and tried to explain what she was doing. She didn't try explaining herself to Dad, she just threw a few things in a bag and pissed off while he was upstairs sleeping, but she took a few minutes to give me the low-down on how difficult it was for her.

"I'm going to be gone awhile," she said. "So you'll have to keep an eye on your dad for me." She was doing that tone of voice she'd used since I was two, only now I was ten, and I knew exactly what she was doing. "Can you do that for me?" she said. "Can you look after your dad for a bit, till I get back?"

I shook my head. "You're not coming back," I said.

Her face crumpled a bit. I suppose she was hoping I wouldn't make this any more difficult for her than it already was. "Why do you say that?" she said, all pathetic.

" 'Cause you're not," I said. "You're going for good."

She started to cry then. Christ, it was so fucking *hard* for her all the time, looking after my dad, looking after me, no time to herself. She was still young, she had a life ahead of her. I heard her say that once to Jenny Allison's mum outside the Spar shop, and I knew exactly what she was up to. "I'm not," she said. "I just need to get away for a bit." She smiled through her tears. "You can understand that, can't you?" she said.

I didn't smile back. "Sure," I said.

She nodded and put her hand on my shoulder. "Of course you can," she said.

"I mean," I said, "you're still young. You've got your whole life ahead of you." I started to wonder, then, how old she was. I don't think I knew.

She looked at me as if I'd slapped her. "What?" she said, all innocent. "Where did you get *that* from?"

"You," I said. I looked her in the eyes. She'd stopped crying now and she wasn't smiling anymore. She stood up. Here we go, I thought. Time for the tough, what's-love-got-to-do-with-it routine. That woman could go from sweet salt tears to hard as nails in thirty seconds flat.

"Well," she said, "I thought you'd understand. I mean, you're not a little kid anymore."

"I never was," I said. "You just liked to *think* I was."

She didn't say anything. Her suitcase was in the hall and she headed out there then, hard bitch, nobody understands her, so fair enough, she'll just get on with it. She put her coat on, and those fancy leather gloves Dad bought her, then she opened the front door and picked up the suitcase. The last thing she said, before she disappeared forever, was, "Let your dad sleep. He needs his rest."

Translation: Don't go waking the bastard up till I'm long gone, I don't want him coming after me and making some big scene. Which, as it happens, is exactly what I didn't want either. I didn't want him humiliated, maybe on the street or somewhere else in front of a lot of people. Not by this selfish bitch. She didn't even close the front door behind her, she just walked off down the path and that was it. Haven't seen her since.

Thing is, when I think about it, I remember how she looked standing in that doorway, and I remember that she was pretty. Prettier than she had looked in a long time. She had lipstick on, and she was wearing that nice winter coat that made me think of Ewa Krzyzewska in *Ashes and Diamonds*. Plus, she had done her hair up, and she looked fucking amazing. At that moment, I had to admit, she was something special. A young woman with the rest of her life ahead of her. If she hadn't been my mother, I would definitely have fancied her. But she *was* my mother, and there she was going out the door, and I knew I'd never see her again. And all I could think of was how pretty she was, no matter what a hard bitch she was being. I didn't say anything to her when she was going. I didn't want her to think I was accepting anything. As the door closed, I was starting to pack things up in my mind and move on. You have to move on. After a minute, I stood up and went over to the sink. There was a little stack of dishes on the draining board and an ashtray, with one lipstick-smeared stub in it. She must have forgotten to wash that up before she packed. And I was standing there, staring at the little pile of ashes and the red of the lipstick, and the words of some old song came into my head. I don't know where I'd heard it.

> *Laura is the face in the misty light,*
> *Footsteps that you hear down the hall . . .*

That was her name. Laura. I fucking hated her.

After a while, I went upstairs and looked in on Dad. He was sleeping like a baby and I was about to leave him to it when I saw the envelope on the dressing table. Very quietly, my mind on tiptoe, I walked over and retrieved it. I wasn't sure what I intended to do, but I wanted to see what it said before I let him see it. I went downstairs, closing the door behind me so he could sleep in peace. When I got back to the kitchen, I opened it as carefully as I could. I could easily put it back in another envelope, I thought, before he woke up. But when I read what it said, I couldn't help myself, I just tore the stupid thing into small pieces. What it said was: *Gone away, can't say where. I'll send somebody for my things*. That was all she said. Two sorry little sentences. She couldn't even do him the courtesy of a paragraph.

———

They say I was a quick birth, that it was all over before they even got old Laura as far as the maternity unit. I'm not surprised really. Once it figured out whose belly it was in, my little infant brain probably decided to get the hell out of there and try its luck in the wild cold world. Trouble is, the wild cold world is mostly two things I'm not very good at, which is other kids and school. I mean, I don't mind other kids that much, it's just that the politics is so fucking boring. X is friends with Y, but he doesn't like Z, and Z is Y's mate. Cathy wants to go out with Tommy but *he* wants to go out with Kerry, who is Cathy's best friend. Meanwhile, Kerry wants to go out with *him*, but she doesn't want to hurt Cathy's feelings. God knows why anybody would want to go out with Tommy in the first place, because he's as thick as two short planks, but there you go, that's kids for you. Little adults, all hurt feelings and consideration. Then, suddenly, they all go crazy for a while, everybody fucks or fights everybody else and, before you know it, you've got history with all kinds of people you wouldn't even give the time of day if you could avoid it.

That's my view, anyway. But then, I'm not that keen on kids. Mr. O'Brien told me once that I was misanthropic, and the other kids in the class all laughed, though I can't imagine any of those fuckers even knew what it meant. I can't remember why he said it, what I'd said or done to provoke such an outburst on his part. Usually he was so positive, all JOY OF DISCOVERY and AMAZING FACTS and ISN'T NATURE BLOODY WONDERFUL. Ironically enough, if there was any kid in that class who could have agreed with him on all that, it would have been me. Up to a point, anyway.

"You're a nasty little misanthrope, Wilson," he said, standing over me, gazing into my face with a sudden and surprising air of loathing. I was quite taken aback. "Do you know what a misanthrope is, Wilson?" That was something he did, he always used our names. At the end of the sentence when he was asking a question, at the beginning if he wanted you to stop doing something. He was a big man, very tall, with lank grayish hair and a long, thoughtful-looking face, like a Swedish actor. Think Max von Sydow as the Knight in *The Seventh Seal*. All he needed was the accent.

I nodded. "Misanthrope," I said. "Somebody who, for good reason, doesn't think much of the human race. Also a play by Molière, the French dramatist."

Mr. O'Brien snorted. "Which you, of course, have read," he said.

I did smug for him. "As a matter of fact," I said, "I have."

"Well," he said. "We're *very* clever today, aren't we, Wilson?"

"*I'm* very clever every day," I said. Some of the other kids laughed. I could see Liam out of the corner of my eye, shaking his head and making cut-throat signs with his finger.

"Are you now?" O'Brien said. "Well, if you're so clever, Wilson, perhaps you could write me a nice long essay about—let me see . . . 'Great Philanthropists of History.' How does that strike you as a title, Wilson? *I* think it has a certain ring to it."

"All right, then," I said. I picked up my pen.

O'Brien laughed a sad, dry laugh. "Oh no," he said. "Not on my time. I have the education of your highly advanced little brain to attend to." He smiled graciously. "Give it to me tomorrow," he said. "You've got till lunchtime."

He looked around. "Do any of you know what a philanthropist is? Cunningham?" He walked over to the smallest boy in the class and stood towering over him. You find that with teachers: as soon as they have a run-in with somebody, they go straight to the weakest cub in the pack. It's how they restore order. Just like hyenas.

Cunningham looked up at him hopefully. "Is it a stamp collector, sir?" he said.

I didn't know what to write at first, for O'Brien's essay. I didn't want to do it the way he wanted me to do it, writing shit about Andrew Carnegie and stuff. I wanted to do what I needed to do, so I wouldn't get any more extra assignments, but I had to work in something else, too. Something oblique. Then I remembered this old story about three brothers. Or maybe it was seven. How, one after another, the eldest first, they leave home and go out into the world, to travel the gorse-scented roads in search of fortune and fame, or to perform some task, to find a horse that can run faster than the wind, or a bird with feathers of gold. The older brothers are strong and confident but, in the end, they fail the test. Perhaps they come close, perhaps they catch the bird, or they find out that the horse is concealed in some far valley where nobody goes, but each has a fatal flaw, not a vice so much as a failure of attention, a tendency to be pulled off course by the noise and warmth of a busy tavern, or the smile of a pretty girl. Only the youngest comes through. He is smaller and weaker than his brothers, but he is clever and modest and he is wise enough to know that good fortune comes from the least promising encounters. He understands that, when you meet a talking animal, you had better listen to what you are being told. He knows how to pass the door of a tavern and not be drawn in; he knows how to flirt with a pretty girl, then move on unscathed. At the end of the story, he captures the golden bird and he gets to keep the magic horse; sometimes he even marries the princess—and because of the cunning he has shown, and his readiness to accept the good luck that the world offers to those who come ready to accept it, he gets to help his wayward brothers. He drags one from some vile tavern, the other from the King's prison, he settles debts and pacifies wronged fathers and, at the last, he brings his brothers home to share in his happiness. Which does not please them in the slightest. They feel humiliated, they want to steal away the princess, they wonder why the pip-squeak of the family got all the luck. Maybe they try to betray him, but they do not succeed, and he forgives them even this sin, as he forgave all the others. It's the one thing he can do by *himself*, this forgiveness. Everything else was a gift: he was born small, and cunning, and modest, and all he did, as he traveled through the same adventures that ruined his brothers, was to follow his own nature. Except for the forgiveness, nothing really came from him. It was grace, pure and simple. A grace that, for one reason or another, his brothers never got to share.

So that's what I write about. Grace. Then I put in some stuff about the Innertown and its problems and how the self-appointed philanthropists in the Outertown aren't doing much to help us. I tell how the people who live here are trapped, how they can't imagine any other life. I give a little history of the place: how, two generations ago, there was almost nothing here, just a couple of farms and some cottages along the shore. How most of the people who live here are the children, or at most the grandchildren, of people who came from somewhere else. I say how it's a fairly young community, how, for example, Constable Morrison is only the fourth policeman to live in the police house, full time at least. We should be connected in all kinds of ways to the outside world, and yet we're not. The Innertown is a young settlement that grew old before its time, old and tired, the people bound to this soil, not by work or family or some more general fondness for the light or the weather, but by inertia. I even chuck in a bit of mystical stuff, about how it sometimes feels as if the headland has some kind of hidden power, drawing people in for no real reason and holding them there for what seems like an eternity. By the time I've done with it, the Innertown is starting to sound like hell. Still, it's not a bad essay and it says something, I think. Not about philanthropists, of course, because I don't believe in any of that crap. Guys like that, the ones who spend their whole time getting rich, they don't love other people. For them it's all tax deductions and PR. Still, whatever the essay might have said, however faulty its logic, O'Brien never got back to me about it. When I handed it in, he took it and said some mealy-mouthed stuff about me learning a lesson, though I'm not sure what lesson he wanted me to learn. He didn't mark the essay and give it back to me. In fact, he didn't say anything more about it. I wonder if he even read it. Not that I care, I'm just curious. It would say a lot about a teacher, if he could make you write something like that and then just chuck it in a bin, because he'd only set it as a punishment for cheek, or whatever. Like he threw out a challenge that he couldn't be bothered to live up to himself. Like he was a fucking wanker to be frank, and all that JOY OF DISCOVERY stuff was just plain bullshit. Something like that, it could make a kid cynical for life. Didn't bother me, though. After all, I'd kept my side of the bargain.

———

The one thing you can count on kids to do is talk. Round here, they talk about all the usual shit, but they also talk about what is happening to the boys who disappear, and speculate as to where they are. The boys get all sensitive, and the girls put on sentimental voices for the lost boys. Or they argue constantly about how to get away from this poisoned little town. It's the same argument Liam and I always had before he disappeared: he would tell me various plans he'd made for us getting out into the big wide world and making our way, but I would just shake my head and laugh, while he went on, making up more and more incredible stories about the possibilities the outside world might offer, if only we would dare to go and find out. To be honest, those stories of his made me feel a bit desperate: I couldn't understand how he could believe in stuff like that, all that stupid naïve crap, like the stuff you get on TV.

"We can't go anywhere," I would say. "Not without money."

"We could *get* money," he would say.

"How could we do that?"

"We could ask people to help us," he would say. "Like those sponsored bike rides. They could sponsor us to see how far we'd get." He thought about this for a moment and decided he liked the idea. "Yeah," he said. "A sponsored escape. We could go around door to door, put up posters, the whole shit." He marqueed his hands. "Sponsor a new life," he said. "Send these boys out into the world and watch them prosper."

I encouraged him. "Make the impossible possible," I said.

"Make the possible impossible," he said.

"Make the probable unlikely," I said.

He did a double take. "What the hell does that mean?" he said.

"Damned if I know," I said. "Anyway, you don't get the sponsor money till afterward. You have to *do* the bike ride first, that's how it works. First you *do*, then they pay."

"Well, that wouldn't work," he said. "Couldn't we do it the other way round?"

"It wouldn't be proper sponsoring then," I say. "How would people know you were going to do what they were sponsoring you to do?"

"Why wouldn't we?" he said. "Why else would we want the money?"

"They don't know that, though." I looked at him. He seemed genuinely frustrated, like the idea had been some kind of a go before, and now I was ruining it. "They don't know that, do they?" I said.

He was quiet for a minute, then he shook his head. "You

know," he said, "sometimes I look at you in awe and wonder." That was a quote from a film we'd seen on TV: *And the Band Played On.* It was just this little piece of badinage that runs through the film, between the Centers for Disease Control guys, played by Matthew Modine and one of my favorite actors, Saul Rubinek. Liam and I had sort of adopted it. Usually it was funny, but this time it felt a bit sad. A couple of weeks later, he was gone.

What I felt, when he disappeared, was grief. But it didn't start with him going, it started long before that, maybe on that day, or during some other conversation we had about getting out. After he disappeared, I wanted people to do something, to make something visible, to say something that wasn't already scripted. At the same time, though, I couldn't stand all that public stuff. Because the public stuff isn't grief, and it doesn't help anybody. It isn't grief, it isn't anger, it's just going through the motions, doing all the stuff that you think you're supposed to do. Anger might have given rise to something, it might have made a difference, but this was all uncertainty and constant second-guessing, that feeling you have that it's probably somebody you pass on the street who is doing these bad things, some pervert maybe, who just looks like a saddo, or maybe like an ordinary guy, maybe one of the Outertown people, somebody with a wife and kids and a big car and an office somewhere. Brian Smith, maybe. Because you have to ask yourself how a creep like that operates. Anybody who gets away with the kind of crap he's gotten away with for so long either has to be very clever, or he's got some kind of power. That's how the world works. The bad people win and the rest pretend that they haven't noticed what's going on, to save face. It's hard to admit that you're powerless, but you have to get used to the idea. That's why they have school, of course. It's there to train you in the vital discipline of being powerless.

Of course, the opposite of school is books. Me, I love books, but I can't afford to buy them. Nobody round here can, except maybe the business people over in the Outertown. But then, the Outertown kids all go to college somewhere, and they probably don't read anyway. I heard Suzie What's-her-name is doing Business Studies now, whatever that is, and little Steven Fuckface whose dad has the nice midnight-blue Mercedes is away at some fancy school where they dress up in funny clothes and toast muffins all day. I don't imagine it involves much reading in either case. It's so typical of how the world works: the people who love books, or whatever, can't afford to buy them, while the people with tons of cash do Business Studies, so they can get more money and keep the book readers powerless. All us poor folks has is the public library. Though I keep seeing in the papers that Brian Smith and the other bigwigs gave loads of money, tax-deductible, for that, so I suppose that trickle-down crap works after all. I mean, hardly a day goes by when I don't thank my luckies that the Brian Smiths of this world have enough money to spare to maintain the public library in the Innertown. Hardly a day goes by when people don't ask themselves how the Brian Smiths of this world got all that hard-earned in the first place, but there's a whole ecology of cash flow and accounting to ensure we don't work *that* out. And to keep us sweet, they build libraries and sponsor charities.

So they built a new public library, right next to the old snooker hall—and a very fine building it is, by Innertown standards. I imagine they even bought some new books but, for a long time, I didn't see them. Most of the books in the library are crap, romances and thrillers and cowboy stuff, because that's what the people of the Innertown like, right, moronic books about cowboys and nurses and spies that are all scuffed and old. What new ones they have are even worse: fucking self-help books and novels about rich people having mad passionate affairs with their tennis coach and shit, books about home improvements—really useful to us Innertown folk, what with all our disposable income—and folkloric hemstitching or whatever. How to make a patchwork quilt from leftover sweaters. Novels by former politicians who were never that good as politicians, or television celebrities who need a sideline to pay for their alimony settlements. Cookery books by ex–rugby stars and models, books about Pilates by former soap actors, books about traveling around France or Bolivia on a donkey or a motorcycle, books about plastic surgery, books about how you ended up hating yourself and why you should love yourself in case you, like the celebrity author, develop a cocaine habit and a seven-figure debt. These are the books we have in the Innertown library, mostly, because this is what morons like us like to read. This is what we need to know. How some celebrity did ten years of barbiturates and vodka, then saw the light. How some fucking millionaire made his money. How some government minister fought his way out of the inner city so he could take bribes with the best of them.

Almost, but not quite. Nowadays, there's this mad librarian called John, a big fat bloke with bad hair and worse glasses, who sneaks a few good things in under the radar every now and then. I didn't like John when I first met him. Now I think he's all right—though I imagine he could do with getting laid sometime in the next fifty years. I mean, I love books, but John is a pathologically compulsive reader, which mostly means that he can turn up for work in the morning with egg yolk on his tie and hair out of a Godzilla movie and he hasn't even noticed. To begin with, I thought he was wrapped too tight for the Innertown, but I more or less like him now. He loves books, and he knows everything there is to know about music. That's all the life he has.

When I first met him, though, I have to admit that he got up my nose. I'd been browsing the shelves, looking for something new and coming up stumped. I'd read all the Dostoyevsky they had, the complete fucking works in some ancient edition with red-and-yellow dust wrappers, so they looked like boxes of cheap sweets. I'd read Virginia Woolf's *To the Lighthouse*, which was the only book of hers they had managed to acquire. Not much happened, but I liked the way she looked at things, and I'd have liked to read more of her stuff. I'd have enjoyed knowing what she thought of the Innertown; that would have been an amazing book. I read *Nostromo* and *Heart of Darkness* and *Lord Jim*, and I'd try to imagine what it would have been like to have Joseph Conrad as a mate, or maybe an uncle, when you were a kid. I'd read F. Scott Fitzgerald's *The Great Gatsby* and I'd almost cried at the end, around about the point where Gatsby's dad turns up. I'd read fucking Hemingway's *A Farewell to Arms* and wondered why nobody ever bought the guy a dictionary. I'd read *Diary of a Nobody*, and all the Charles Dickens stuff they had, and they were great, but I couldn't get on with Trollope. I'd read the anthology of poetry from 1400 to 1945. I'd read some history books, some biographies, and a book about English folk music that looked like it had been used as a doorstop for fifty years. By the time John arrived at the library, I was running out of stuff to read, next step sniffing glue and juvenile delinquency. Or worse still, celebrity memoirs.

That was when I found Marcel Proust.

It was a nice edition, almost brand-new and nice colors, all dust-wrapped and smelling of the printers. Blue on the cover, like some French song about *la mer*. Weird titles. When I saw the complete set on the shelf I almost cried, it was so beautiful. I grabbed the first four volumes, the limit of books I could borrow on my ticket, and carried them off to the checkout desk. That was when I met John. He had just arrived, to take over from the stuck-up cow who used to be head librarian, and he was working what budget he had for the Greater Good of all. That's the wonderful thing with nerds: they're enthusiasts. Not having a life means you get to love things with a passion and nobody bothers you about it. And every now and then, you get to pass something on.

John looked at me a bit snooty, that first time, when I wandered over to the checkout desk clutching my prize. I think he was a bit of a snob; he probably figured he'd ended up working in the Innertown library because of some cruel twist of fate. "You'd do better to read these one at a time," he said, picking up the first volume, which was intriguingly called *Swann's Way*. "It's slow, but satisfying reading. Definitely not Rider Haggard."

Of course, I'd never heard of Rider Haggard, though it was a pretty good name for a writer. Too good really. Maybe he'd made it up. "Is it good?" I asked.

"Good?" He looked at me over his wobbly glasses. "Yes. It's good. It's better in French, though, it has to be said."

"French?"

"Yes."

"Do you have it in French?"

"Why?" He smiled slightly. "Can you read French?"

"Not really," I said. I was doing languages in school, but I was pretty sure Miss Lemmon's French classes hadn't quite equipped me for *this* yet. "*Un petit peu*," I added, hopefully.

"Not much point, then," he said.

I was a bit annoyed by that. "So," I said, "have *you* read it in French?"

He nodded. Smug fucking bastard.

"What, all of it?"

"It's a real page-turner."

"I thought you said it was slow."

"Definition of a page-turner," he said. Then he grinned, and I knew he was just mucking about, and I kind of liked him from that moment on. It was John, after all, who made me go back and read Herman Melville. I'd consumed some kids' version of *Moby-Dick* they had in the junior library, but not the real book. For some reason, the powers that be decided many years ago that *Moby-Dick* is some sort of kids' book, and they put it out in all kinds of weird editions, all abridged and illustrated and gutted to the bare bones of an "adventure." Worse still, they had Melville down as a one-book wonder, so I didn't even know about *The Confidence-Man*, or *Bartleby the Scrivener* or *Billy Budd*, until John came along. Nobody should ever forget the debt of eternal gratitude they owe to whoever it was who first got them to read Herman Melville properly. According to John, the real version of *Moby-Dick* was a page-turner, too—and he was right about that, just as he was right about Proust and all those others. The definition of a page-turner really ought to be that this page is so good, you can't bear to leave it behind, but then the next page is there and it might be just as amazing as this one. Or something like that. Of course, as right as he was about all things literary, John was wrong about pretty much everything else.

After that first meeting, I spent as much time as I could in the library. Before John arrived, I'd just gone in, browsed the shelves, picked four books, got them checked out, and ran home. Some woman my dad's age, with the same gray skin as his, only upright and walking about all by herself, would stamp them for me, looking like she'd rather call the police than let me borrow these particular fucking books. Once, she'd stopped midway and looked me in the face, possibly for the first time ever.

"Do you actually *like* Henry James?" she said.

I nodded. "Can't get enough of him," I said.

"You know, we've got some great books for teenagers in the Young Adults section," she said.

I shook my head. "Not really my kind of thing," I said.

She frowned then and stamped my copy of *The Turn of the Screw*. "I hope you enjoy it," she said. "Henry James *may* be just a bit old for you."

I smiled happily. "Well," I said, "I only read him for the sex scenes."

I thought she'd crack a smile then, but she didn't.

So I was pretty happy when the old cow suddenly retired and John showed up. I tried to imagine his life: where he lived, what he did. I thought maybe he wrote books in his spare time. If he did, I can't imagine they were any good. He liked books too much. Though I sometimes wondered what he liked them for. There was one night, for example: I was in late, and John was sitting at the desk, reading a book with a bright, gaudy-looking cover. It was quiet, and he was completely absorbed in whatever it was he was reading. That made me curious, so I went over and tried to sneak a closer peek at the cover, to see what the title was. But as soon as he saw me, John laid the book flat on the desk and started reading out loud.

"*When engaged in hand-to-hand combat*," he said, "*your life is always at stake. There is only one purpose in combat, and that is to kill your enemy. Never face an enemy with the idea of knocking him out. The chances are extremely good that he will kill you instead. When a weapon is not available, one must resort to the full use of his natural weapons. The natural weapons are—*" He looked up at me. "What are the natural weapons, Leonard?" he said.

I shook my head. I didn't want to interrupt the reading.

John shook his head likewise and went on. "*One*," he said. "*The knife-edge of your hand. Two: Fingers folded at the second joint or knuckle. Three: The protruding knuckle of your second finger. Four: The heel of your hand.*" He gave me an amazed-and-happy look. "Isn't it great, Leonard? This is a book that actually tells you how to kill people with your bare hands."

"What the fuck is it?" I said.

"*The Anarchist Cookbook*," he said. "Listen." He went back to reading from the book. "*Attacking is a primary factor. A fight was never won by defensive action. Attack with all of your strength. At any point or any situation, some vulnerable point on your enemy's body will be open for attack.*" He flicked the page, then went on. He'd obviously been reading this for a while. "This bit is good," he said. "*There are many vulnerable points of the body. We will cover them now: Eyes: Use your fingers in a V-shape and attack in gouging motion. Nose: (Extremely vulnerable) Strike with the knife-edge of the hand along the bridge, which will cause breakage, sharp pain, temporary blindness, and if the blow is hard enough, death. Also, deliver a blow with the heel of your hand in an upward motion, this will shove the bone up into the brain causing death.*"

Adam's Apple: This spot is usually pretty well protected, but if you get the chance, strike hard with the knife-edge of your hand. This should sever the wind-pipe, and then it's all over in a matter of minutes." He grinned at me. "Et cetera, et cetera," he said. "Isn't it fantastic?"

"Why's that then?" I say.

He looked at me. "This book teaches you how to kill and maim people," he said. "I mean, at last a book that is actually useful." He quoted again. "Ears: Coming up from behind an enemy and cupping the hands in a clapping motion over the victim's ears can kill him immediately. The vibrations caused from the clapping motion will burst his eardrums, and cause internal bleeding in the brain." He genuinely was excited. "I didn't know that," he said. "Did you know that, Leonard?"

I didn't say anything. I hadn't realized John had such a deep and abiding interest in fucking people up.

"Here's a good bit," he said. "Listen: There are many more ways to kill and injure an enemy, but these should work best for the average person. This is meant only as information and I would not recommend that you use this for a simple High School Brawl. Use these methods only, in your opinion, if your life is in danger. Any one of these methods could very easily kill or cause permanent damage to someone." He was so happy. "This guy tells you how to kill people, and then he tells you not to do it."

"Well," I said, "that's very responsible of him."

John snorted. "Hell, that's not going to make any difference," he said. "Once you've got stuff like this at your fingertips, you're going to use it, right?"

"I don't know," I said. "Who are you going to use it on?"

He laughed. "Well," he said, "I've started a list. I'm up to twenty-seven now."

"Am I on it?"

John looked hurt. "Why would I want to kill you, Leonard?" he said. "I mean, *you* of all people. The one other bibliophile in town?"

"Edmund Hillary," I said. I felt a bit grim, to be honest.

"Edmund Hillary?" He looked puzzled.

"Because I'm there," I said. Of course I knew that it doesn't matter what you read in a book, because you have to have the will to kill somebody to actually do it and you can't read up on *will*. It doesn't matter what techniques you master, you actually have to be prepared to do it. The surprising thing about most people, considering how much we all hate one another, is that they're not prepared for that. They fantasize about it all the time, but they couldn't *do* it. At some unspoken level, that fact defines everything that happens between us. It's that simple. Even in the most law-abiding place, what makes the difference is that one man is capable of killing and another isn't. You put those two men in the same room, and it doesn't matter what else comes into play. It's the difference between giving a shit and not. No matter how bad things get, most people still care about something. That's what makes them so fucking sad, and that's what makes them beautiful. Still, I don't say any of this to John. I just wait for his answer.

"I'd never kill *you*, Leonard," he said. He looked unhappy. As if he was hurt that I asked.

"That's fine, then," I said.

He gave me a wry smile. "Fucking *Anarchist Cookbook*," he said.

"*Mrs. Beeton's* what I go by," I said.

He nods. "Yeah," he said. "She's got a really good recipe for rhubarb crumble, I hear."

I made a face. "Now there's how to kill somebody," I said.

So. A pretty dubious character when all is said and done. A mixed bag. Still, it was partly because of John that I met Elspeth. After he arrived, I had permission, I could hang about for hours and that was exactly what I did, partly because I was curious about John, but mostly because he had all kinds of secrets tucked away there, in back rooms, in forgotten boxes that he'd pulled out and started going through. Sometimes he would be too busy to talk, but when he was free, he'd get stuff out of the archives or the Reference section for me to look at. Sometimes, he'd just pull out a pile of stuff and let me go through it while he did his work. So one afternoon, after school, I've been sitting for a while, head down, going through a dictionary of quotations—sometimes *that's* the way to read, in little snippets, the sushi version of food for thought—when, all of a sudden, I look up and I realize it's evening already. I can see the soft green of the evening trees and the splashes of orange between the leaves. I have this amazing sensation, then, a kind of quiet happiness, to think that everything—the park, the streetlamps, the little petrol station on the corner opposite—has all just arrived from nowhere, temporary, like a film set. Then I look into the space facing me and that is when I see her: a girl my age, but older-looking, in her short leather jacket and blue jeans, her hair cut short, like a boy, the plaid shirt under the jacket unbuttoned enough to show the thin gold chain around her neck. After a moment, she catches me watching her and shoots me a questioning glance. "Can I help you?" she says. She isn't being snotty, but she means it as a challenge. It makes me think she's been looking at me before I saw her, and she was just waiting for me to notice.

"What time is it?" I say. This is the best I can come up with.

She looks round at the clock on the far wall, then back to me. "Well," she says, "the big hand is at six, and the little hand—"

"All right," I say.

She laughs. "What's the problem?" she says. "Is there some-place you have to be?"

I shake my head. "No problem," I say. I'm trying to place her. I think she looks like somebody at our school, some girl in fourth year, but she also looks different. Then I figure it out. "You used to go out with Jimmy van Doren," I say. It sounds a bit like an accusation.

She smiles. "Oh my," she says, "don't I have the checkered past."

That makes me laugh, but I don't say anything.

"Well," she says. "I don't go out with Jimmy van Doren any-more. He's *archived*."

"Oh yeah?"

"Absolutely."

"So what are you doing here?" I say. On reflection, that sounds like a rude question, but she doesn't mind.

"Watching you read," she says.

"That must be interesting."

"It is," she says. "I like the way your lips move when you come to the big words. It's very touching."

"Ha ha," I say.

"Ha ha," she says. "So. Now that I'm free and everything, do you want to go out with me?"

"Why would I want to do that?" I say.

"Because I'm very sexy and very, very beautiful."

"Is that so?"

"Absolutely," she says. "So. What do you think?"

"I don't know."

"You *don't know* if you'd like to go out with me?"

"Don't rush me," I say.

"We could stay in, if you like," she says. "I'm not fussy."

"I told you," I say, "don't rush me."

"Well," she says, "suit yourself."

"I will."

"You don't know what you're missing."

"I can imagine," I say.

"Oh no you can't," she says. She smiles real beautiful then, and I know I'm wasting my time pretending.

"I didn't say no," I say. "I said don't rush me."

"Well, you better make up your mind quick," she says, "or you'll regret it forever."

"Oh yeah?" I say. "How do you know that?"

"*Believe* me," she says. "I know."

I have to smile. She's pretty, that's for sure.

"So," she says. "What's it to be?"

I don't say anything. Maybe, right at that moment, I am in love. Romantically, that is.

"I'll give you a blow job, if you like," she says.

I'm a bit taken aback by that, but I manage not to show it. Or not too much. "Oh yeah?" I say, trying to look nonchalant.

"Absolutely," she says.

"When?" I feel hollow deep down, like somebody has just scooped out my insides.

"Now," she says.

"Where?"

"We can go outside," she says. "Back of the library." She looks over at John, who is pretending to put away books under the Home Improvements section, but is really watching us. "Where John goes to smoke reefer," she says, just loud enough for him to hear.

By this time, she's pretty sure she has me, and she does, but not for the reason she's thinking. She's thinking I've never had a blow job before, but I have. Some old woman stopped me when I was going down the West Side Road toward the shore. She was in a car, and she just pulled up beside me and asked if I wanted to go for a little ride. I'd never seen her before, her or the car, which was odd because you don't get many tourists driving down the West Side Road. So I asked her what she meant and she said she would give me ten quid if I'd let her give me a blow job.

I wasn't sure, to be honest. She was pretty old, and she wasn't nice-looking by any stretch; if anything, she looked more like a bloke than a woman, with loads of makeup and dark red lipstick. But then, I thought, ten quid is ten quid. So I got in the car and she drove me down to the shore, which was where I was going anyway. It didn't take long, and she seemed happy enough. She told me I was a nice boy, and she gave me the ten quid. Then she gave me another five. "That's for your little brother," she said. "Have you got a little brother?"

I didn't have a little brother, but I wasn't going to tell her that. "Yeah," I said. "I've got two."

"That's nice," she said. "What are their names?"

"Liam and Benny," I said. It was the first names I could think of.

"Lovely," she said, but she didn't give me any more money and, I have to say, I was a bit disappointed for little Benny. "Well, now. I hope you don't mind if I drop you here, sweetheart."

I shook my head. "This is fine," I said.

"Thank you, dear," she said. She waited for me to get out, smiling sweetly all the while, then she put the car in gear and drove away. I didn't see her after that.

Of course, it didn't occur to me till afterward that I shouldn't have got in the car, or that she might have anything to do with the lost boys. That was what the town were calling the boys who went missing. The lost boys. Like in *Peter Pan*. Now, I don't know if anybody else around here has read that book—I mean, *read the book*, not watched the film—but I don't think it's all it's cracked up to be. All that stuff about Wendy being their mother is a bit sickly, if you ask me. And you've got all these people going around killing one another, but you never get any details and you can't help thinking it isn't real. It's like in "Little Red Riding Hood," when the Woodsman cuts the Wolf's belly open and Grandma comes out right as rain and ready to finish the next line of her knitting. I mean, what's all that about? People shouldn't be telling kids stories like that, where something bad happens and then it's all OK in the end 'cause Mummy kissed it better. They should be telling it like it really is in the big wide world, which is: when you're fucked, you're fucked. Kind of *Anna Karenina* for kiddies.

Anyhow, I don't think Elspeth will go through with it, but she does. Right there, behind the library, next to the bins. It's really good, too, not like the old woman. After that, I want to do something else, but she just laughs and says I have to wait till next time. Which is how we come to be going out. Not very romantic, but then we're not really that interested in romance. I think, on the whole, romance is something that should be saved for later, when you're old enough to deal with it. In the meantime, there's fucking. Kids are better at that than romance and all that difficult shit.

We've been going out for a few months now, and it's an eye-opener to say the least. I'd fucked a couple of girls before, but nothing like this. Elspeth and me, we play games, all kinds of stuff, things I never heard of. Elspeth is the one who thinks them up mostly, because that's not really my thing. Leave it to me, and it would be all blow jobs and mad shagging, because I'm fairly straightforward in matters of the heart. Still, I like the games, most of the time. It can seem a bit contrived, but when it's good, it's great, and when it's really good, it's scary.

It started with just little things, but then Elspeth read an article in a porno magazine about what some French kids were doing and she thought we could try it. It was called *jeu du foulard*, which means the scarf game, more or less. The first time, she hid the scarf in her pocket and only brought it out when we were safely past Dad and in the room; it was a long poppy-red and dark-blue silky-looking scarf that she'd found among her mum's stuff. What I was supposed to do was tighten it round her neck until she passed out from not being able to breathe. It was supposed to be an amazing sensation, she said. I thought it sounded a bit dangerous, but it was exciting too, and we did it twice. I did it to her first, then she did it to me. It really was an amazing feeling when you were blacking out, not what I expected, because it wasn't just a sensation of passing out and things going dark, there was this amazing light, a pure white light that happened in my head just before I lost consciousness. The actual blacking-out part didn't last very long, and it was a bit uncomfortable when the scarf was being tightened, but Elspeth wanted me to do it to her again and the second time we did sex afterward. That was beautiful. We left the scarf round her neck when we were doing sex.

I've always liked Elspeth for sex. I didn't think I'd enjoy it as much as I did when we first started, but it's really beautiful with her, really exciting and pleasurable. She likes to do sex whenever we can, mostly in my room, but also outside, in the woods, or out at the plant. A lot of the time, she wears this big dress and she just sits down on me and spreads the dress over us, so nobody would see what was going on if they stumbled upon us. Once, when we were out walking in the woods, she just lifted up her dress and she didn't have anything on under it. She held the dress up round her waist and pressed her back to me. She looked round and gave me a really nice smile, then, like butter wouldn't melt, "You can stick it in my arse if you like," she said. I thought that was a bit risky, out there on the footpath and everything, but we did try it for a while, before we had to give up. Later on, though, we worked out how to do it nicely, and we do that sometimes.

Of course, if Dad knew about any of this, he'd be pretty upset. He'd probably think we're too young, or that there was a risk of Elspeth getting banged up. He'd be wrong, though. We've done it plenty of times in loads of different ways and nothing bad has happened. Elspeth thinks it might be because a lot of men round here have dead sperm, because of what is in the ground around the plant. She says I might be one of them, which means I'll never have children, which is fine with me, considering how silly things are around here. She also makes it pretty clear she's not interested in love, or anything like that. Which also is fine by me, when she's saying it at least. Me, I sometimes think the real trick is to keep things like love and such abstract. Abstract can be complicated but, when it's all said and done, it's not difficult.

I don't know if what Elspeth says about the little white cells is right, but there might be something in it. The authorities go to great lengths to make it clear there's nothing wrong with us still living next to the plant, but they still do all kinds of tests on people—like when they go to see the doctor, for example. Some people, like Dad, are really sick for reasons nobody can explain, and he's had all kinds of tests. A week or so after Elspeth and I discovered *jeu du foulard*, I got a letter from the health center with three wooden sticks, like very thin ice-lolly sticks, a laminated-looking envelope with STRICTLY CONFIDENTIAL, FOLLOW INSTRUCTIONS CLOSELY printed on it, a card with colored writing, and a printed instruction book that told you how to take samples of your bowel movement. The steps were very clearly written out, so anybody could understand what had to be done, and the packet was addressed to me, not Dad, so somebody somewhere obviously thought I was at risk. I got a bit alarmed about that for a while, because it probably meant they knew something they weren't telling people. I didn't tell Dad, though, because I didn't want to upset him. I didn't do the test either. I was a bit curious, but when I read the instruction SUGGESTIONS TO CATCH YOUR SAMPLE ARE: FOLDED PIECES OF TOILET PAPER, YOUR HAND IN A SMALL PLASTIC BAG, OR ANY CLEAN DISPOSABLE CONTAINER, I couldn't go on.

Now, though, I do wonder if maybe there's something in me. Lurking. Some chemical trace, some cancer. Because after I got that test kit through the post, I started to have all kinds of minor symptoms: sudden nosebleeds, numbness in my fingers, swollen knuckles, bleeding gums, gut pain. It was as if my body was just waiting for a suggestion of sickness and as soon as that suggestion came, the sickness was already there, waiting to happen.

I didn't tell Elspeth about all this, of course. She seems to think that we've all been affected one way or another, and we can't do anything about it. We don't all have the same diseases, but there's abnormal groupings, she says—statistically rare clusters of problems to do with the nervous system, or respiratory diseases, or cancer of the colon. Some of us are still healthy, but it's only a matter of time. She doesn't seem that put out, though. She talks about it very matter-of-fact, like she was talking about catching a cold. That's how she is about everything, I suppose. Nothing seems to bother her. But then, she's different from other people. She's healthy and she doesn't give a fuck about anything. She just wants to cram as much life as she can into the time she's got, and after that, it's no big deal one way or another. She's not sentimental, about that or anything. Which I miss sometimes, to be honest. She's so tough and matter-of-fact, I sometimes wonder if she has any feelings at all, besides being more or less permanently horny. Not that I have any complaints about that. It's just, I wish she would be softer, now and then.

Still, you have to take the gifts the world gives you. There's nothing worse, in people like us, than ingratitude.

———

For quite a while after Liam disappeared, Elspeth was the only friend I had. What with having to help look after Dad for so long, I got into the habit of keeping myself to myself, more or less. Besides, when you lose someone like Liam, you're a bit cautious about new acquaintances. You don't want to hitch up with some weakling and suffer all over again. A couple of times, though, I'd see some kids out by the plant, or on the landfill, and I'd be curious about them. The only one I knew was Jimmy van Doren, Elspeth's old boyfriend, and I only knew him in passing. As far as I knew, his little crew were the only kids who ever went out to the plant in a gang. The rest of the gang didn't look like much, but I was curious about Jimmy because he'd had sex with Elspeth. It's always difficult to imagine the girl you're fucking as being with somebody else, even if it is water under the bridge. It always seems like bad taste, like she couldn't wait for the best, and had to waste her time with second-raters till you came along.

The way I met Jimmy was this. We'd had a school assembly, and the Head, Mr. Swinton, had had a sudden rush of blood to the brain and gone apeshit about the book of Job, reading to us straight out of the Bible, the King James version no less, which is always a mistake with kids, because if ever there was a book just begging to get the piss taken out of it, it's the Bible. Especially the King James version. Old Swinton, he's going on about Job's dead kids, and his boils, and how God's just handed him over to the Devil to do what he likes with him, even though Job has always been a bit of a Holy Joe. It makes you wonder what kind of a prick God is, on His off days.

Anyhow, I get out of this crap and I'm walking along feeling a bit mystified, thinking maybe Mr. Swinton is having a midlife, when I spot Jimmy van Doren walking next to me, matching me step for step, his head down, a perfect reflection of me in my reflective state. I stop dead then and get ready for whatever's coming—maybe he wants a go at me because of Elspeth, though he's waited long enough—but he just keeps on walking for two or three paces before he turns and smiles at me. As he does, another boy materializes beside him, shorter, not as broad, but similar enough to Jimmy at first glance that they could be brothers. They aren't, as it happens, and when you look close, you can see that the similarities are pretty superficial. I ignore the little guy and look at Jimmy. He just smiles, though.

"Boy, that Job," he says eventually, still smiling. As he speaks, I am aware of other kids too, standing off to either side of me. One I sort of know, the other I might have seen about the place. The one

I know is a gangly, pikey-looking girl who everybody calls Eddie. A lot of the kids round here know her, she's got the reputation of being a bit parboiled in the little gray cells. The other guy is fat, kinda ugly, not too bright-looking. Jimmy notes me scouting his little crew, though I've kept it all very minimal, but he just goes right on talking, friendly as ever. "Yeah," he says, "God really fucked *that* guy over."

"And then some," the little guy next to him throws in. He's not smiling. He looks like he'd rather perform delicate surgery on my tender parts than stand here gassing.

"Worse than living round here," Jimmy says.

"At least we haven't got Almighty fucking God to contend with," the little guy says.

The other kids aren't talking, they're just spectators. You can tell, they have absolute faith in Jimmy. He speaks for them. They would probably do anything he told them to do, no matter how stupid. All this for a kid with a joke name. He's called Jimmy van Doren because his dad changed it by deed poll from O'Donnell. Patrick O'Donnell, part Irish, part pikey, but he's got his own little landscape-garden business, so he changes his name to Earl van Doren, for more class. He's got letterheads printed with this and he's sending them out all over the peninsula, hoping that somebody will see the "Earl" part and think he's some kind of minor aristocrat. Apparently, minor aristocrats do well in landscape-garden design, which is sad in all kinds of ways that I don't even want to think about. Though, doubtless, this is what gives Jimmy his edge. He'll scrap with anybody, he'll take it further than anybody, he's a born leader and you don't mess with him. We're kind of in Boy Named Sue territory here.

Now, he's looking at the little guy in awe and wonder, like he's amazed, not just by the wit and wisdom of his remarks, but by the fact that he can actually speak at all. He looks just long enough to let him know he's been duly noted, then he swings back. "Hey," he says, mock-surprised, as if he's just noticed me standing there, "isn't your dad the guy who's got some disease nobody knows what it is?"

He fixes me with his eyes and stands there, grinning. I grin back. They're just playing, I know that. They don't bother me at all. It may be a crew of four, but it's only Jimmy really, and I think I could probably take him. So I just hunker in and wait to see what transpires. It goes through my mind that maybe I need the exercise. "Yeah," I say. "He's the one."

"Yeah." He looks around at the others, like he's about to tell them some big important secret. "He goes to see the Head Doctor and the Head Doctor says: Cheer up. It's not every day somebody gets a disease named after him."

The other kids laugh, all except the little guy. He snorts and gives Jimmy a disgusted look. "I suppose you think you made that up," he says.

"Sure I did, Tone," Jimmy says. The little guy's name is Tone, apparently. What an inappropriate fucking name for this short-arsed little twerp.

"No you fucking didn't," Tone says. "I read that in my brother's joke book."

"Your brother's got a book?"

"Yeah," Tone says. "Sometimes, when he's good, I read it to him."

They're going on like this, Jimmy and Tone, bouncing words

back and forth at each other like Ping-Pong balls, Jimmy good-humored and forgiving, Tone trying to see how much he can get away with, and I'm just standing there, watching, listening, like the others. Then, suddenly, right in the middle of it all, they stop with the banter and the whole gang looks at me.

"Well, *Leon*ard," Jimmy says, "what do you think of that Job story, then?"

"It's just a story," I say.

"Fuck, no," Tone says, indignant. "That's the *Bible*, Leonard. That's God's honest fucking truth, that is."

I put on a serious look. "Well," I say, "if it is, God's got a lot to answer for."

"Yeah?"

I nod. "Yeah," I say. "All those plagues. All that *smiting*."

Jimmy pretends to look impressed, kind of stopped in his tracks by the sheer weight of my knowledge. "You have to give it to him," he says at last, turning to the others for confirmation, "this boy knows his Bible."

Tone nods. "He sure does," he says. "Tell us, Leonard. Have you read the Good Book, like, all the way through?"

I nod back, but I don't say anything. I look at Jimmy.

Tone looks at the others, then he turns back to me. "Jesus, Leonard," he says. "Get a life, would ya?"

They all laugh, but they know it's all coming out pretty lame and I just give him a long look, like he was something I'd found floating in a toilet bowl. "Exactly my plan," I say, giving him the stare, only light, pleasant, couldn't-give-a-fuck style. "Just as soon as I wipe the mud off my boots." The gang laughs again. Tone glowers.

Jimmy comes over to me, puts his hand on my shoulder.

"You're all right, Leonard," he says, all Hollywood buddy movie. "You wanna be in our gang?"

I smile. "Not particularly," I say.

Jimmy smiles madly, a zany Mel-Gibson-on-triple-vodkas smile. "OK, then," he says. "Be seeing ya."

With that, he turns and walks off in the direction of the West Side, the others loping dutifully after him—only the two hangers-on, Eddie and the fat kid, keep turning back and waving, as if it was all some parting-is-such-sweet-sorrow deal. Tone looks back too, but he's not waving. I think we might have some silly stuff to work through later, if I'm not careful. I don't really need that trivial kind of hassle at the moment; if there's any nonsense to be gone through, I'd rather just do it with Jimmy and get it over with. Still, it hasn't come to that. Not yet. And it's a wise man who knows when it's better to keep the peace. Always better to keep the peace, if you can manage it, I think. And when you can't, get in quick and hit hard. Dog-eat-dog and all that.

———

I don't tell Elspeth about my run-in with her ex—I'm assuming this is what the run-in is all about—so things just go on as per. We fuck, we talk, we make it clear we're not in love. I don't go out of my way to avoid Jimmy's gang, but I don't go looking for them either, so the next time I see them is about a week later out at the plant. Which isn't a surprise because, as I say, I'd seen them out there before, a couple of times. Still, it's always a disappointment, that kind of thing. It's much better if people stay where you left them, and don't turn up where they're not supposed to be. I'd rather it would stay as it was out at the plant: no gangs, just the odd solitary individual slipping away through the bushes and rubble when they realize they've got company, or passing by in silence, furtive and awkward, like sad animals. A few days after that first encounter, though, I find the whole crew on a patch of ground near the old waste-disposal unit, in one of the few places I thought was mine and mine alone. Like it's my secret, private garden, only there's pipes and rubble and pineapple weed instead of roses. They're all there, crouched around a fire, poking at something in the flames with sticks. I would prefer to work my way around them and move on, but Jimmy looks up and sees me, so I haven't got that option. I'm not about to slink off when I know he's clocked me, so I go over, all casual and not that friendly.

Jimmy gives me a big welcoming smile, then he turns to Tone. "Hey, Tone," he says, "here's your mate Leonard."

Tone draws himself up to his full height and looks around, like one of those meerkats on the David Attenborough program. When he sees me, he puts on this ugly, vicious-sidekick smile. Biding his time. Waiting till the pack leader gives his say-so. The more he goes on like this, the more ridiculous he's going to look. He's about as scary as custard.

"Hiya, Leonard," Jimmy says. "You following me, or something?"

"Nah," I say. "I'm visiting a sick relative."

Jimmy grins dangerously. "I thought you had one of those already," he says.

I smile. "Can't have too many sick relatives," I say. "It's the healthy ones you've got to worry about."

Jimmy laughs at this, which is good of him. I'm feeling pretty lame, to be honest. I've been up all night, reading *Seven Pillars of Wisdom*. Fucking great book, once you get into it. I've come out to the plant for some peace and quiet, not to trade badinage with Jimmy and his scout troop. Jimmy looks around. "I don't think we've all been properly introduced," he says. "I'm Jimmy. This is Tone. That bloke over there who looks like a girl is Eddie. The one who looks like something out of *Jason and the Argonauts* is more than usually earnest."

The fat boy squawks at this. "My name's not Ernest," he says. He's got these odd eyebrows, one black and hairy, like he's got a caterpillar stitched to his head, the other almost invisible. It makes his face look all lopsided.

Jimmy laughs. "I didn't say it was," he says. "Can't you just *lighten up?*" He turns to me. "We've only just had lunch," he says. "There might be some left, if you're hungry."

I look at the fire. There's something there, in amid the flames, something that used to be furry, all blackened now, with dirty-brown skin and bone showing through the singed fur. A cat, maybe; it's hard to tell.

"No, thanks," I say. "I'm not a big fan of nouvelle cuisine, if I'm honest."

Jimmy looks nonplussed. "OK," he says. "Suit yourself." He glances at Tone. "We're going hunting," he says. "Tone here was wondering if you'd like to come."

I nod. "Love to," I say. This could be a mistake, but I don't have any choice. Back out, and I've got wuss written all over me. Not to mention another insult and injury to stoke little Tone's fires.

———

I'd heard stories about hunting before. Mostly bragging, the usual kids' bullshit, but I knew even before we got to where we were going that it was real with these guys. I wouldn't have expected anything otherwise with Jimmy, I suppose. I'll give him that much, he takes himself seriously. We head out toward the east side, Jimmy leading the way.

It's Eddie who takes it upon herself to fill me in. As we lope along, heading toward the landfill, she gets in step with me. "It's just rats, mostly," she says. "Not always, though. Sometimes you get a seagull, but they're usually too quick. Sometimes you get something special." She pulls out a big hatpin, the kind that old ladies used to have and you only ever see in junk shops nowadays. "This one is yours," she says. "It's my lucky pin." It is, too. I can see it in her face. She's doing me a special honor. "I've got some big fuckers with that one," she says.

I slow a little and look at her. I'm quite touched. "I don't want to deprive you of your lucky pin," I say.

She grins. "That's why I'm letting you have it," she says. "'Cause it's lucky. Your first time and all." Her face suddenly goes serious, as if she's just figured something out that she hadn't realized before. "Just this once, though," she says. "I want it back after." She stops walking altogether and looks a bit worried.

I stop walking too. There's a terrible sadness about this girl that reminds me of the sick people I've seen at the clinic when Dad goes in for his tests. "Absolutely," I say. I take the pin. I suddenly feel sorry for her. Maybe I even like her a bit. She's gangly and spiky and she's probably a borderline nut job, but she's not bad-looking when you get up close. She shouldn't be hanging around out here with Jimmy and his boys, though. She should be at home, watching re-runs of *Dr. Kildare* and swooning over Richard Chamberlain, or something. I can just imagine her swooning, and it's a strangely satisfying idea. I venture a smile. "Thanks," I say.

Her face brightens, and now I see that she's really quite pretty.

Sexy, too. I mean, I like Elspeth and all that, but if it came to it, I wouldn't mind a quick one with Eddie. I suppose my face betrays that thought, because she smiles real happy at me and blushes. Then she gets out another pin—a long, coppery-looking thing—and lopes off after the rest of the crew toward the landfill. The hunting ground.

The landfill isn't officially a landfill. It isn't *officially* anything at all. There was a farm out here once, a long time ago. Johnsfield Farm it was called. The farmhouse itself, and quite a few outbuildings, are still more or less standing, though nobody has lived there for decades. The fields are just weeds and rubble, with the odd bit of machinery here and there, rusting in a stand of tainted willow herb or nettles. The actual house is off to the south of where we are, a ruin among newer ruins, but nobody ever goes inside, or if they do, they keep themselves well hidden. I've gone in there a couple of times, but it's dank and ugly inside, even in the summertime, and I didn't linger. There's nothing to see. Nothing to find. People in the Innertown tell a story about a gang of blokes who dosed some girl up with rum then took her out to the old farmhouse and did stuff to her, but I think this is all just talk to scare the little ones. They say she was raped and tortured for hours before she died. That girl's ghost is supposed to wander about the place crying and begging for mercy, but it's all too storybook to take seriously. If somebody tells that story, all you have to do is ask what the girl's name was, or when all this occurred, or what happened to the blokes afterward, and they don't know a thing.

Still, that story might have something to do with Johnsfield ending up as an unofficial landfill, because it probably gives people permission to do whatever they like there and of course they've ruined it. It was probably a nice little farm once, but after the plant closed, and with that gang-bang story for backup, the people round about started driving out here years ago to dump stuff in the last field at the end of the dirt road that runs out to the Ness. They don't do it in the daytime, they only come at night, since officially it's illegal, what they're doing. Though I can't imagine that the authorities would ever prosecute them with the full force of the law for dumping more crap on a place that's already up to its eyes in poison and garbage. Better here than somewhere else. I don't know if the fly-tippers are locals, or if they come from outside; whoever they are, they know that it doesn't matter what they do. Nothing matters really. Those people probably tell themselves the place is past caring about, but it's still surprising to see what they leave out there, mixed in among all the usual household rubbish: rusted bird-cages thick with lime and millet, dead animals, bags of needles and plastic syringes, swabs, old power tools, body parts. It's fairly open country out at Johnsfield, no pits in the ground, no fences, just a long jagged hedge that stays black till well into the summer, when it puts out a few thin, painfully tender leaves and the occasional miraculous, sweet-scented flower. I once saw a picture of an old wishing tree, like they used to believe in around these parts, a gnarled and twisted old rowan covered in notes and cards and cheap decorations fixed to the branches with scraps of ribbon or baling twine. That's what the boundary hedge looks like, like one long row of wishing trees dressed with blown plastic and calico and hanks of what might have been dog or cat skin. It's almost jolly, like Christmas at the mall. If we had a mall.

Anyway, this is where we are and this is our hunting ground. These are our games. I'm pretty much in favor of the old Be Here Now way of going about things, so having got myself drawn into this particular folly, I decide I'm going to enjoy it. Maybe get to know Eddie a bit. Of course, it's just pointless scouting at first. Jimmy and his crew—with me along for the ride, though I'm keeping just enough space between us so they don't start imagining I'm one of them—all of us, together and individually, wander aimlessly across the piles of rubbish, sinking in, bouncing out, sometimes tumbling into a nasty pocket of mush and fumes, bearing our simple weapons, looking for any sign of life. We can use what other tools we like, though the hatpin is de rigueur. The hatpin is the weapon of the right hand, and has to be gripped just so, to avoid losing it in the melee, but the others all carry their own specially prepared weapons for the left hand: Eddie has a double-edged knife. Ernest, or whatever his name is, has a long, possibly Teflon-coated fork, like one of those implements people have at barbecues. Tone brandishes a vicious screwdriver carefully sharpened to a point, and I can imagine him working on this, with love and care and anticipation, in his quieter hours. Best of all, Jimmy has a Chinese-made clasp knife with a six-inch blade, double-sided, in nicely tempered dark steel. He says it's a flensing knife, but it isn't.

I have nothing, of course, having come unprepared. But I don't care. I don't really want to be chasing little furry animals around with a hatpin and a fake flensing knife, not at my age. We're not going to catch anything edible. There are rats, seagulls, hedgehogs, maybe a few feral cats living among the rubbish, and, to be honest, I'd rather just leave them to get on with it. They've been breeding out there for years, those cats. If you come down this side at night, you can hear them wailing, females in heat, toms fighting, and you'll see them wandering about, all scrappy faces and vicious scars, missing ears, torn fur. Some of the kids come down here to play games not that different from what we are doing now, just wandering up and down looking for animals and birds to torture with blades and matches and burning oil. The only difference is, those kids set traps and nets to get their prey, while we are *hunting*. All the same, it feels like a childish game, especially the hatpin rule, and I'm a bit embarrassed about it.

Finally, Eddie spots a big rat and we all set off in pursuit. Ernest isn't much use to anybody, he just jumps about waving his weapons and shouting tally-ho, but Eddie really throws herself into it, scrambling across the garbage, her hatpin hand lunging at the little furry body—and then there's more of them, a whole family of rats, big ones and little ones, all fat and healthy-looking, plump bodies full of blood and organs, just begging to be skewered. Only they're too fast, and nobody gets anywhere near them. They just disappear into all the rubbish and we just keep toppling in after them, getting ourselves covered in wet and slush, snagging on old bed frames and defunct Silver Cross prams, dangerous little nicks appearing on our knuckles and wrists. Pretty soon, I'm ready to give up, but Eddie keeps on, and she's more than making up in enthusiasm for what she lacks in stalking skills. Finally, she lunges and sticks her hatpin right through something that squeals and struggles, then hangs, well and truly speared, twitching, but silent now, the life running out of it a little too quickly. She looks at what she's got, then she shows it to me.

"It's just a baby," she says. I look at it too, but I'm not sure *what* it is. Up close, it looks pale and fake. "It's only little," Eddie says. She seems sad now, though I'm not sure whether this is from pity or disappointment.

"Not much meat on it," I say.

"Yeuch!" She looks at me like I'm some kind of crazy person.

"I wasn't going to *eat* it." Then she grins and holds it out to me. "You want it?" she says, and I can feel something starting now. It's like when a cat brings you a bird or a mouse it's caught. That's a sign of affection.

"So," I say. "What else do you catch out here? Other than baby rats?"

"How do you mean?"

"You said you sometimes got something special."

"Oh." She grimaces. "All kinds of stuff," she says.

She gives me an odd look and I wonder if she's offended about the baby-rats dig. I don't want her to think I'm putting her down, so I soften it up a bit. "Like what?" I say. The way I say it, though, it still comes over as a challenge, and I have to backtrack a little more. "Really," I say. "I'm interested."

She's been thinking all the time and she jumps in then, all bright and excited. "I got a mooncalf once," she said.

"A what?"

"A mooncalf," she says. She's not sure, now that she's telling it to me, but there's a part of her that wants to be and she gets all defiant. "It was huge. With these big saucery eyes, and a pointy snout." She looks back fondly at the image of whatever it was she once caught—and I believe right away that she's telling the truth. She's all tender and excited, so I'm absolutely certain that she caught *something*.

"What did you do with it?" I ask.

She thinks a moment, then shakes her head. It's like air going out of a balloon. "I killed it," she says.

"Really?"

"I didn't *mean* to. I just—"

"A mooncalf?"

"Yes." She gives me a sad look. "That's what it was," she says. "There's mooncalfs all over, out here along the shore." She gazes at me expectantly. When I don't say anything, she looks sad again. "I'm not making it up," she says.

I shake my head. "I know," I say. Everybody has a theory about the secret fauna of the headland. People tell stories about all kinds of real or imaginary encounters: they see herds of strange animals, they catch glimpses of devils, sprites, fairies, they come face-to-face with terribly disfigured or angelic-looking mutants from old science-fiction programs on late-night TV. And it's not just animals they see. You hear all kinds of stories about mysterious strangers: lone figures stealing through the woods, gangs of men roaming around at night, a criminal element who come in from the shore side to see what they can steal from the plant, troublemakers and pikeys, sex perverts and terrorists. John the Librarian says the buildings down by the docks provide a perfect hiding place for insurgents to lay up and store their weapons. Or maybe they're counterinsurgents, he'll say with a twinkle in his eyes: revolution-aries, *agents provocateurs*, terrorists, counterterrorists—who can tell and, anyway, what's the difference?

"They have them in books," Eddie says. "They used to be all over, but now they hide in places where nobody ever goes. Like squirrels."

I nod.

"They're in Shakespeare," she says.

I reach out and touch her arm. "I know," I say, softly. I want her to believe that I believe her, but I don't think she does.

We haven't seen Jimmy in a while. Ernest and Tone are just standing about on a firm island among all this crap, standing up on the highest point, scouting their little horizon, and my mind goes back again to that meerkat film on TV. Finally, Jimmy turns up, and he's got this huge rat on the point of his Chinese knife. He grins at us all as he waves it in triumph. "He shoots, he scores," he says. Then he looks back and forth to Eddie and me curiously. "You catch anything," he says to me, and I can see he's not talking rats.

I don't say a word.

"I got one," Eddie says. "It's just a baby, though."

"Never mind," Jimmy says. "You got *something*, at least." He gives me an amused look.

After we finish killing stuff, we flop down on a grassy bank and Tone and Ernest start building another fire. Jimmy has gone back out into the sea of rubbish, searching for bigger game. I can see he wants a special kill, or maybe an especially disgusting find to mark the occasion of my first outing, but he's not coming up with anything. I sit down with Eddie. I've noticed two things about her: first, she's got this really sexy mouth, real blow-job lips, but sweet with it, and her legs, in her tight black jeans, look almost impossibly long. I saw a John Singer Sargent portrait in a book once, where the girl had long slender legs like this, and I couldn't stop thinking about it for days. Still, I don't push anything. I don't think it would be wise to make Eddie blush twice in one day. Instead, I do the old conversation deal. Playing catch-up.

"So what happened to Ernest?" I say. He's just out of earshot, helping Tone with the fire.

"Who's *Ernest?*" she says. She's already forgotten the introductions. I nod at the fat kid. "Oh, Mickey," she says. "His name's not Ernest, it's Mickey." She gives me a puzzled look.

OK, I think. Not the sharpest toothpick in the box. Sweet, though. "So," I say, "what happened to *Mickey*, then?"

"How do you mean?" She looks over at the guy a bit worried, as if she's expecting him to have his arm hanging off, and she hadn't noticed it before.

"His eyes," I say. "I'm assuming he wasn't born like that."

"Oh," She puts her hand to her mouth and giggles, cute as anything. You have to wonder if she does things like this on purpose. "He got his eyebrow and his eyelashes blown off," she says. "With a firework. They haven't grown back yet."

"How did he manage that?"

"Oh, just mucking about." She looks back to the page in her head marked Guy Fawkes Night. It isn't a big book, but it is clearly labeled. "He lit a banger and threw it at Tone. But nothing happened. So he goes over and picks it up and puts it to his eye. Like he's trying to figure out what's wrong with it. 'This thing's a dud,' he says and then—BANG!—it goes off." She grins happily. "We all thought he'd blown his eye out."

"Nice," I say.

She settles down and looks a bit disappointed. "He hadn't, though," she says. "He just blew his eyelashes off. And his eyebrow." She thinks for a moment. "It hasn't grown back."

I nod. "You said," I say.

"Maybe it never will," she says, continuing in her reverie. She seems to be trying the idea out for size. Having one black eyebrow might be OK on a temporary basis, but it's obvious that, to her mind, forever is a different thing altogether.

"So how did you get to know him?" I ask. "Mickey, I mean."

"Mickey?" She looks confused again.

"Yeah," I say, softly. "Mickey."

"Oh." She shakes her head. "He's my brother."

"Really?" I say. I don't want it to be too obvious, but I'm wondering if she's got this wrong.

"Half brother, actually," she says.

"No shit," I say.

She looks at me and grins. Then she blushes again. "Don't take the piss," she says.

"I'm not."

She studies me for a moment. She's gone all serious suddenly. "Really?"

"Really," I say.

She looks pleased. I've made her happy, I suppose. It's quite touching. Then she jumps up and squeals. "Come on," she shouts, to nobody in particular. "Let's *kill* something."

━━━━━

When I get home, after a happy day's hunting, I'm starting to wonder where this is all going. I've already told myself not to dig in too deep with Jimmy and his crew, but I have to admit it, I like Eddie, and Jimmy's kind of a challenge. Still, better not to get too comfortable. If I do shag Eddie, it's bound to get back to Elspeth, and that will not only piss her off but it'll put a big smile on Jimmy's face, too. Maybe that's what this is all about, of course. I'm not saying Jimmy would actually *tell* Eddie to do me, it would have to be subtler than that. To begin with, he probably just wanted to check me out, then Eddie maybe said something after our first run-in and he just told her to go for it. Or something along those lines. Though whatever it is that's going on, I think I'd better watch my step. I remember old Paul Newman, when somebody asked him if he was ever tempted to cheat on Joanne, what with all those women throwing themselves in his general direction, and he said, "Why go out for burger, when you've got steak at home?" Which probably looked like a pretty cool answer at the time, him being put on the spot like that, but it doesn't make that much sense. You can't eat steak every day and they do say that variety is the spice of life. Besides, if Elspeth is steak, that doesn't make Eddie burger. I'd think of her more as pudding, to be honest. Angel Delight, maybe. Crème brûlée. Tiramisu. Definitely *not* semolina.

Jesus H. Christ, I tell myself, I'm going to have to snap out of this. What I need is a distraction. After I look in on Dad, I head off to my room and try to pick up where I left off with *Seven Pillars of Wisdom*. But I can't keep my mind on it. I keep thinking about Eddie's legs and those sweet, pouty lips. Eventually, I drift off, lying on the bed with the book over my face, and I have amazing dreams all the way through to morning, but it's not camels I'm dreaming about.

Still, the fates are kind, even if we do work hard to ignore their occasional mercies, and the next day I get the distraction I need, because the Moth Man is here and, for once, I am—as they say in the self-help books—*unconditionally* happy. It won't last long, but it's something pure, which isn't that common a phenomenon if you live in the Innertown.

But then, that's the big problem with life in this place: there's more to it all than the bad days of wondering when another boy will disappear, because it hasn't happened for a while and so, according to a logic we all know, is bound to happen again soon. And it isn't just those other days, when we all go around in a stupor of fear and anger because, having finally given in to the temptation of thinking that those bad days have come to an end, we receive the news that another soul has been lost, some boy you know at least by name, some kid who plays the trumpet, or picks his nose at assembly, or likes to go swimming. Of course, you can tell yourself that he's gone away, like some fairy-tale character, to seek his fortune in the big wide world. You can tell yourself that, if this is the story the police put out, then they must do it for a reason, but in your heart you know that the boy has been taken, maybe dragged off to some secret place and killed, maybe worse. Maybe alive somewhere and waiting for someone to come, in some pit at the plant, or chained up and helpless in some sewer. And then, even if it's been quiet on that front for a while, there's always the chance that somebody has just died from a disease that nobody's ever seen before. We're definitely not talking *Salad Days*, out here in the Innertown.

So it might be better if there was no relief, if there were no happy times. Like that bit in *Tom Sawyer* when Tom wonders if maybe Sundays are just a more refined form of sadism than the usual weekday run of chores and school. Every week, you get one day off, just to remind you how awful the other six are—and even that one precious day is marred by a morning in church, gazing out of the window at the sunshine while some old fart drones on about God. At least we don't have much church here.

Still, it might be better just to get on with the ordinary routine of Dad being sick, and me having to wash out the bowl that he keeps by the bed, all the vomit and bile and spots of blood running out into the sewage, into the water that I will one day drink, after it has been processed and treated, because water goes round and round, the same water all the time: the same, but different. Water is everywhere. You can't escape it. When Miss Golding told us, in Religious Education class, that God was omnipresent, I remember thinking, while she was explaining *omnipresent* to the nincompoops, that God must be water. Even afterward, when I had grown out of the idea, I was still afraid of water; or rather, I feared something the water contained. I found a magazine once, out on the landfill, with an article about how some French guy had worked out some theory about water having a memory: it keeps a record of everything it has ever touched written away in its molecular structure, a whole history of piss and sick and insecticide, laid down in a submicroscopic, illegible script that will take centuries to erase. Everything has its own clock, its own lifetime: stars, dogs, people, water molecules. Human beings only know one version of time, but there are thousands of others, all these parallel worlds unfolding at different rates, fast, slow, instantaneous, sidereal.

Anyhow, whatever else might crop up, you don't normally get unconditional happiness round here. It's always tainted by something: worry, or fear, or just the idiot feeling that it's something you don't really deserve, so it's probably some kind of trap. That day, though, I am happy, pure and simple—because the Moth Man has come, and I like it when the Moth Man comes.

I hadn't been expecting him, because you never know when he'll be here. He comes and goes according to some law that only he understands, and I only know he's back when I see his van, parked just off the road at the gate to the old meadows on the east side, or maybe farther toward the shore somewhere, his little green van, with faded lettering on one side from whoever owned it before, some guy called Herbert, who did some kind of repairs. The first time I saw the van, the Moth Man had just pulled in at the gate to the meadows, and I watched him take his gear out of the back, all the netting and lighting equipment, the tiny, ice-blue tent that he would set up in the middle of the meadow, the rucksack full of cooking utensils, the ancient camping stove. It was like watching a magic trick, the way he got all this stuff out of this tiny van, and then there was more, and still more, till he'd made a little settlement around himself, all the instruments and lights and piles of netting. He didn't say anything to me, all the time he was unloading, though he knew I was there. It was only when he was done that he turned to me and gave me a questioning look. He still didn't say anything, though.

I was thirteen then, if I remember. I bet, for him, I was just some *gosse* who had turned up, one of those local kid spectators he probably got all the time. I didn't want him to think of me like that. "What's all this shit for?" I said. Big kid, blasé as fuck.

He laughed. "What do you think it's for?" he said.

"Dunno. You some kind of photographer?"

"Nope."

"Scientist?"

"Sort of."

"Well, if you're here to measure the pollution, you'll need more stuff," I said.

He laughed again and shook his head. Then he explained about the Lepidoptera survey, and what you could tell about a place by the number and type of different butterflies and moths you found there. Finally, he stopped talking and looked at me, to see if I was getting bored. "So," he said, "what's your name?"

"Leonard," I say. "Leonard Wilson."

He nods and stores the name away in his head, but he doesn't tell me who *he* is. He just starts getting some stuff out of a bag to make himself some lunch. As he does, he asks me if I'm hungry. I say I am, and so I get into it with him, fetching stuff and helping him get it all together. Finally, when we're sitting down to baked beans and sausages, he looks at me. "Some people say there are no mysteries anymore," he says. "Do you think that's true, Leonard Wilson?"

I don't say anything at first. He's treating me a bit too young, maybe, but I don't mind. Later on, I'll let him know that I read books and such, and he can talk normal. Besides, right now, I'm enjoying being treated like a kid. Most of the time, I'm fixing Dad's food, or his medicine, or I'm doing stuff around the house, or shopping. It's fun to be a kid for a while, so I play along, just a bit. "I suppose," I say.

The man grins. He's beginning to work me out, maybe, but he's started, so he's going to finish. "You suppose?" he says. "OK. What about that tree over there? What kind of tree is that?"

I don't move my head, just glance over with my eyes. "It's a sycamore," I say. Pretty dumb question: it's all sycamore round here.

"OK," he says. "No mystery there, then."

"Nope."

"OK. So how did it get there?"

I know this one, I think. Any minute now, he'll be talking about God and eyeballs and all that Divine Craftsman stuff, like Mr. O'Brien in full-on MYSTERIES OF NATURE and THE BENEFICENCE OF THE DIVINE ORDER mode. Still, I'm happy to go along. I like his voice. It's all soft corners and friendly, but it's in its own place, it doesn't intrude. "Well," I say, "I don't know for sure. But I imagine a seed blew there on the wind and—"

"And how did the wind get here?"

"What?"

"How did the wind get here? How did *you* get here?" He's

making a point, but his voice doesn't change. He doesn't do the JOY OF DISCOVERY like old Mr. O'Brien. "How did *any* of it get here?" he says.

I shake my head. Here comes the God part. "*I* don't know," I say.

"So *that's* the mystery," he says. Then he just sits there, smiling.

He sits there smiling, then he looks up into the leaves overhead, like there was something he'd forgotten to check, before he turns back to me. "Let's go," he says. He gets to his feet in one quick movement and starts off into the trees to show me something that, for him, is of vital significance. I mean, here is a guy who can *read* the landscape. I thought I knew a bit about the headland, from coming out here so long and checking things up, birds and flowers and such, in field guides at the library—but I'm just looking at the pictures, while this guy is reading the fine print. Over the next several months, as he came and went, he showed me all kinds of stuff, from downright silly to little pieces of natural magic. He showed me how to nip the back off a flower and suck out the nectar inside. He showed me what henbane looks like and told me about how the witches used to smoke it in a pipe when they had toothache. He told me more than I will ever need to know about various obscure moth species. What I get from him is that he likes kids, and he listens to what you are saying. Sometimes he gets all enthused about something, and when he's like that, he can talk for hours. And sometimes he's a bit too grown-up-to-kid, but you can see he really cares about this stuff and he wants to share it with you, not to make himself look smart, but because he loves it all so much. Sometimes I think he might be lonely, because I get the impression he hasn't got a proper home, he just seems to drive from place to place in his van, camping in fields and setting up his nets, his only companions the moths he catches then releases, or curious kids like me that he attracts along the way. It must be a fine life, sometimes, just camping out in one place for a while, then moving on, like some nomadic tribesman, at home, not in one place, but everywhere. But he doesn't seem to have a wife or a girlfriend or anything like that, and I sometimes wonder what he does for sex. Maybe he's got some floozy he sees someplace, as he passes through. Maybe he's got a few. I think, though, that he's really married to his work. Which means that the Innertown probably isn't his favorite spot, because the results he gets here can't be all that satisfying. Not that he doesn't catch anything. On the contrary: he nets thousands of moths every night, but they're all the same, small, peppery creatures that blunder into the net so readily it almost seems they're doing it on purpose.

So he's a bit of a mystery, in some ways. I like him, though. That first day, I knew he was going to be a friend to me, even though he was old—he's probably about forty, maybe a bit younger. He'd been talking about moths and mysteries, and about his work, then he realized it was getting on for evening. "Right," he says. "It's probably time you got home to your family, Leonard Wilson. You do have a family, don't you?"

"It's just my dad now," I say.

"Oh?"

"My mum left," I say. "When Dad got ill she just fucked off and left us to it."

He shakes his head. "I'm sure there was more to it than that," he says.

"Maybe," I say. I don't really believe it, but I'm not going to argue about it and spoil things. I've argued with myself for long enough about it. "So," I say, "what about you?"

"Me?"

"Well," I say, "I suppose you have a family too?"

He laughs. "Not really," he says. "But I'm all grown up. I can look after myself."

"So can I," I say. I like him, but he's a bit insulting sometimes, with all this grown-up stuff. He might not be all JOY OF DISCOVERY but he's treading a fine line right now.

He smiles. "I didn't say you couldn't," he says. He seems sad, now, as if he's thought of something that he'd rather not remember.

"So where's your dad, then?" I ask him, just to break the mood, but then I see from his face that it's thinking about his dad that made him sad in the first place.

"He's dead now," he says.

"Oh," I say. I feel awkward. "Sorry," I say—which makes me feel even more awkward, and fucking stupid too. What am I sorry about? What difference does that make?

"Don't be," he says. "He was getting on. And he wasn't himself at the end, there." He looks away, off into the trees, like he's trying to picture something.

I read once, in this really terrible book, that you have to talk to people about things like this. I don't know why, but I suppose it's good for the dead to be remembered. Maybe not when they were sick, but how they were before, when they were still young, or happy, or something. And I can see the logic of that. It bothers me that I can't remember Dad from before his illness. It would be useful to be able to remember him as a young man—dancing, say, or at a football match, shouting for the home team. Or maybe sitting in the pub, just after opening time on some warm summer morning, sitting there on his own before the crowds come in, with a paper and a pint of bitter, the bluish smoke from his first cigarette of the day spiraling up in a long thin streamer through a fall of golden light. That would be good and maybe it would be good for the Moth Man to think about something like that. So I give it a go. "So," I say, "what was he like, your dad?"

He looks at me, the kind of look that says: Do you really want to know, or are you just being polite? I'm not sure I know myself, but he seems satisfied. "My dad was an engineer," he says. "That was how he earned his living, and that was what he loved. That's why he came here, to do a job of work. Later, though, when he came back, he was supposed to be retired. A lot had happened to him between his first visit here and his last."

"What happened to him?"

"My dad was a bighearted, innocent man," he says. "He was an enthusiast, which also made him something of a fool. He trusted people, which can be fine, but he was too open, too easy to reach. He also liked a drink. In the end, he was just wandering about the world, bumping into the furniture. He would fall over from time to time, but he always got up again. Sometimes, I wished he would just quit and stay down."

I listened. I didn't have a clue what he was talking about, but I could see how sad it all was. Still, I couldn't help being surprised at the way he talked about his old man. It was like he was talking about somebody he hardly knew, or some character in a book.

"Your father worked at the plant," he says.

"Yeah," I say, surprised at the sudden change of tack. "Till they shut it. Then he got sick."

"My father helped build the plant. He worked on the first

plant, back in the early days. At that time, there was a whole group of companies working for the Consortium, divvying up the first, highly lucrative contracts. Arnoldsen's. Nevin's. Lister's. My dad knew them all, they were like family to him. Sometimes, when he was talking about those days, he would be saying the names, and you'd realize how much they meant to him. They were familiar, like the words he used in his work, all the technical stuff, which he would also talk about, even though he knew nobody understood it. But those names were special, too. They were his litany. All the deep words that he treasured, the way somebody might treasure the words of prayers or old songs." He stopped and looked back to where his dad was inside his head, saying his private litany.

"So what went wrong?" I said. I hadn't expected to say this, but when I did, it was like I'd been waiting years to ask somebody this exact question.

He snapped out of his reverie and looked at me. I think my question startled him, but he did his best to give me an answer. Not the one I was looking for, but an approximation, a good guess. "Dad was proud of the work he did here," he said. "People were proud of the plant back in those days. Even later, people would reminisce about the time when old George Lister himself came out there, when they finished the first phase and the plant was officially opened, but that wasn't so. People like my dad—and yours—never saw those people. *They* made their money from far away, and they spent it far away on things that working men couldn't even imagine." He looked off into the distance and I thought I'd lost him again.

"So," I said, "the big boss didn't come to the opening?"

"No," he said. "He would have sent some deputy, or maybe one of the younger sons. There were four sons, if I remember."

He looked at me curiously. "Come on," he said. "It's time for you to go. Your dad will be worried."

I shook my head. "If my dad's even awake, I'll be fucking surprised," I said, and he shook his head in mock disapproval at all this obscenity in one so young.

That was the only time we ever talked about that kind of stuff. Later, it was all about the work he was doing, or maybe stories of the places he'd been to, or little tips for going around in the world and not having too bad a time. That's how it is. He doesn't come very often, maybe once every couple of months, and I never know when to expect him. So that morning, when I catch a glimpse of his van, half hidden behind the big hedge out by the meadows, I'm happy. I don't want him to see it, though, so I just drift over to where he is working and stand watching. He doesn't make a big fuss, either. He's setting up a big net, a high thing taller than he is, and it's obviously got all his attention, getting it just right. Still, he takes the time to register the fact that I am there. "Leonard Wilson," he says. I think there is a pleasure in the way he says my name, like he's been looking forward to seeing me again. He pauses for a moment and looks at me sideways. "So how are you?" he says.

"I'm fine," I say. And I'm happy because it's almost true. True enough to be able to say it without thinking I'm pretending.

"That's good," he says. "You want to come over here and help me set this thing up?"

"Absolutely," I say.

He nods. "OK, then," he says, and we go to work, careful and competent and good-humored, as if we'd been doing this forever. It doesn't take long with us working together, and once it's all done, he sends me off to get some wood for a fire, which I do, but by the time I get back, my arms laden with twigs and fallen branches, he's sitting on this huge fallen log by a fire that has obviously been burning for some time, brewing something in a little saucepan that sits amid the flames, all blackened and scabbed with years of heat, like a miniature witch's cauldron. When he sees me, he looks up and gives me a big smile, one of those smiles that imply a world of shared secrets and a future that only he and I know about.

"You're back," he says. He gestures to the place next to him on the log. "Take a seat," he says. "I'll fix you some of my special tea."

I laugh. I'm not annoyed that he sent me off on a wild-goose chase. "Oh yeah?" I say. "What's special about it?"

He smiles and gives the pot a careful little stir. "You'll see," he says.

———

It takes a while for the tea to brew the way he wants it. It smells terrible, a bit like those traces of greeny shit a caterpillar leaves when you keep it in a jar or a matchbox for a while, or the slurred nubs of rotten cabbage stalk in a rainy field after the machines have been over it. The Moth Man doesn't seem to mind, though; he crouches over the pot, stirring and breathing great whiffs of it, humming to himself absently all the while, completely absorbed in the alchemy of it all. Finally he's satisfied. He looks over, gives me this big grin, and picks up one of the cups. He holds it to his nose for a moment, then he drinks it down quick. I follow suit; the stuff tastes even worse than it smells, but I manage to gulp it down without choking. The Moth Man laughs, then he slips down and sits on the ground, so his back is leaning against the log. I do the same. For a long time—maybe ten minutes, maybe longer—we just sit there like that, two campers out in the woods by their fire, communing with Nature and all that shit. After a while, though, I start to feel odd, kind of warm from the inside, but not feverish, and things look different. The trees have more detail, the colors are subtler, everything looks more complicated and, at the same time, it all makes more sense, it all seems to be there for a reason. I don't mean it's designed, I'm not talking about some isn't-nature-wonderful shit. I mean—it's there, and it doesn't have to be explained. It's all shall be well and all manner of thing, and all that. I look around. The green of the grass is like something out of Plato, every twig and leaf is perfect, but it's not just that, it's not just that the objects I see are perfectly clear and logical and right, it's something else. It's wider. From where I'm sitting, I can see everything around me in perfect, almost dizzying detail, but I can also feel how one thing is connected to the next, and that thing to the next after that, or not connected, so much, but all one thing. Everything's one thing. It's not a matter of connections, it's an indivisibility. A unity. I can feel the world reaching away around me in every direction, the world and everything alive in it, every bud and leaf and bird and frog and bat and horse and tiger and human being, every fern and club moss, every fish and fowl, every serpent, all the sap and blood warmed by the sun, everything touched by the light, everything hidden in the darkness. It's all one. There isn't a me or a not-me about it. It's all continuous and I'm alive with everything that lives.

Then, almost before it's there, that oneness breaks, and I see someone. A boy. He wasn't there before, and now he is, standing at the edge of the clearing, like he's just come out of the woods, and he's staring at me, not surprised at all, but more like he'd expected me to be there and has been trying to make me notice him, trying to get my attention with that piercing stare. There is something odd about him that I can't figure out, something about his face that seems familiar, though not so much the features as the expression; it's like an expression I know from the inside, an expression I've tried out at some point then given up on, the way an actor might try to get in character by looking at the mirror in a certain way, psyching himself into happy or wise or deranged by changing the way his face works. The expression in this boy's face is faraway, not distant so much as remote, not proud or cold or offended, more plaintive than anything, as if he wanted to call out to me but has momentarily lost his voice. He wants to call out, that's it, and the look on his face is the result of that failed desire to speak. He wants to call, for help maybe, or maybe because he thinks I need help—and I'd felt that plaintive appeal before I saw him, I'd felt the stare that he'd been directing at me a moment before I turned, even though I was happy, or not so much happy as fully alive, totally connected to everything around me, to everything I could see and everything I couldn't see, to the woods and the sky, to the warm blur of headlamps running away along the coast road, or over the hills and away, to the life beyond, the roads and cities, the lights in the office blocks, the paintings in museums and galleries, the Flemish courtyards I've seen in art books, the piazzas and canals, the rice fields and snowcapped mountains, the skies that same blue I've seen in picture books for years, but never in real life, never here: a blue like forgetting, the deep, cool blue of the room where the newly dead are absolved of their names and memories. When I see him, though, I am suddenly *back*: a local, isolated thing in the woods, a little cold in my own skin and trapped in the slow run of time like a swimmer caught in a current that's too strong to resist, too strong even to tread water—and after a moment I see what is odd about him. It's his face, yes, but it's not just the expression, it's who he looks like. I think, for a moment, I'm seeing one of the lost boys but at the last minute, before he slips back into the green shade under the alder trees, he turns and gives me a long, questioning look— and he doesn't look like Liam, or any of the other boys I know about. For what feels like a long time, I stare at him, trying to hold his eyes, but he's gone before I can even register in so many words that, if he looks like anyone I know, it's *me*. The same face I see in the mirror every morning: the same face, the same questioning look, the same doubt in his eyes, the same defiance. He looks like me. He was staring at me, and I was staring at him, and now it's as if I've been split in two, as if the whole world has split, one part of it flowing away to the harbors and cities I'd seen in my vision of a moment before, the other fixed, cold, predestined.

A moment later, this me/not-me vanishes into the woods and, when I turn to the Moth Man, I see that he is also staring at me, with a friendly, slightly questioning look on his face—questioning, but with just the hint of a smile behind it, a good smile, I think, a smile that says everything is fine. From the look on my face, I suppose, he realizes that I've seen something that bothered me and he looks off in the direction I'd been staring into a moment before. His eyes search the trees quickly, then he looks back at me, but he doesn't speak. My face is sad now, I can feel that, I can feel how my expression looks to him, and it's sad, maybe frightened, the face of someone who's been going along on what feels like some big adventure and suddenly gets scared. Like a kid on his first roller-coaster ride who realizes, too late, that he's afraid of heights. But the strange thing is, I'm not sad at all, I'm not scared, I've just fallen back into the flow of time too suddenly, after that beautiful stillness of before. I've come back too abruptly and, for a few seconds, I'm so disappointed that I want to cry.

That's when everything changes again and the Moth Man's face suddenly lights up, like he's understood everything and he's seen what a stupid mistake I've made, only he's not judging me, he's not pointing out my error, he's seeing the funny side of it, and he's laughing, a silent, fond laugh, *with* me, even in my folly, because he knows that, once it dawns on me, I'll see how wrong I was to be frightened, or worried, or sad, all things being good and cause for celebration, no matter how bewildering or terrible they seem.

———

The news comes on a Friday, at the end of the afternoon. This time it's Tommy O'Donnell's parents who have found their son's room empty that morning, the bed not even slept in, the boy gone. He must have disappeared sometime in the night, because Mike O'Donnell—who is Jimmy van Doren's uncle—had popped his head round the door at around ten on the Thursday night to see if everything was OK and he'd found Tommy at his desk, listening to his Walkman. He'd asked Tommy if his homework was done, and not believed the answer, but he'd not had the heart to nag. Then he'd gone to bed early, leaving his wife downstairs watching a documentary on cosmetic surgery and his only son safe in his room, happily skiving. No, there was no reason for Tommy to go out, he knew the rules about going out on his own at night and, anyway, if he wanted to go somewhere, he only had to ask and Mike would drive him there. Mike O'Donnell worked with his big brother in the landscape business, but he wasn't a partner in the firm. The general view was that, while Earl van Doren swanned around the place pretending to be one of the elite, Mike did all the real work, which meant he often came home exhausted. But that wouldn't have stopped Tommy asking for a lift somewhere, and the temptation to say no wouldn't have occurred to Mike. Everyone knew Mike O'Donnell for a good sort: hardworking, dutiful, absurdly loyal to his brother, a kind husband to a rather ungrateful wife, and a doting father—he would rather have died than deny his son anything. Now the boy was gone but, because there was no sign of forced entry at the house, or any evidence to suggest that he hadn't simply run away, we all know that this is going to be another of those cases that gets quietly buried, while the authorities, including the police, go on with the real business of promoting Brian Smith's Homeland project.

After that, on the Monday, it's supposed to be school again, but nobody goes. It's one of the small gestures that we have available to us: on the school day after one of our kindred disappears, we wander around the town or the wastelands, stealing anything that looks valuable and breaking everything else. It is a mark of the authorities' shame that, no matter what we do, there are no repercussions. They are guilty, because they know they have failed us. We should burn down the town hall and the police house on days like this and maybe force their hands at last. But we never do. We smash windows. We steal cheap wine from the Spar shop. We go out to the plant and sit around sniffing solvent or getting pissed on the wine we've stolen, then we roll home out of our heads and sit around in all our separate bedrooms, plugged into our separate sound systems, crying our hearts out, or just sitting on a windowsill or a roof somewhere, looking at the sky. Some of us—the lonely ones, the outsiders—just go out to the plant and look for something dangerous to do, some death-defying stunt that will go unwitnessed by others, but will always be there, in the flesh, and in the spirit, a living testament to how willing we are to be done with the world.

———

After his cousin disappeared, Jimmy started harping on about Andrew Rivers. Rivers lived alone in an old cottage by the poison wood; everybody said he was a child molester and some of the kids were scared of him, but to me he just looked like a sad inadequate who preferred to keep himself to himself. A smart move in the Innertown. Still, Jimmy couldn't get it out of his head that the guy had something to do with the lost boys and he would talk to the others about how somebody should do something. I was pretty sure he was wrong but I didn't think it would do any harm to let him talk. Get it out of his system. "He was always out there, mucking about in the woods," he'd say. I didn't even bother to point out that I'd spent a fair bit of time out there too, and I'd seen Rivers in his garden, or twitching the curtains in his front room. I'd passed him right by and I'd seen him looking at me, but he'd never tried anything on. I mean, there wasn't that much to him. Maybe he was a bit of a perv, but I think he probably just liked to look. Besides, I couldn't see someone like that overpowering anybody. Certainly not anybody Liam's size. But I didn't say anything, I just let Jimmy run on. And run on he did. "That fucking pervert was probably just waiting for the right moment," he says.

Tone sees this as his cue. "He's a known pedophile," he says. "He's on the sex offenders list at the cop shop and everything."

"Oh yeah?" I say. "Who told you that?"

Tone gives me a dangerous look. "Everybody knows about it," he says. "He's got stacks and stacks of gay porn in his house. He just sits there looking through sicko magazines all the time, he never goes out, he hasn't got any friends or anything."

"Well, Tone," I say, "that makes him sad and lonely, but it doesn't make him dangerous."

That's where Jimmy jumps back in. "Same thing, sometimes," he says. "The fucker thinks about it till he can't stand it anymore. Or there's a full moon or something. Then he goes out and grabs somebody."

"I can't see that bloke grabbing anybody," I say. "I've seen more muscle on a fart."

Jimmy shakes his head. "He's probably got chloroform, stuff like that."

"What's the chloroform for?" Mickey asks.

Jimmy gives him an impatient look. "It's an anesthetic," he says. "You put it on a rag and hold it over somebody's mouth just for three seconds, and he's out like a light."

"Really?" Mickey thinks this is great. "So, is that like the stuff you get in plants?"

Jimmy is getting annoyed now. "What the fuck are you talking about, Ernest?" he says.

Mickey looks miffed. "Well, that's what you get in plants," he says. "Chloroform. We did that in biology."

"That's chloro*phyll*," Jimmy says. "Chloro*phyll*, not chloro-*form*. You stupid fucker."

Mickey doesn't say anything. He's looking hard done by, because it was a perfectly legitimate mistake, right? They sound more or less the same. Chlorophyll, chloroform—how is he supposed to keep up when they keep making it so difficult?

"Anyway," Jimmy says, "like I was saying. We should look into this guy. This Andrew Rivers."

Immediately, this sets alarm bells ringing in my head. But I have to be careful. There's a bit of the if-you're-not-with-us-then-you're-against-us going on here. Not just with Jimmy, but with the whole town. Everybody wants to *do* something. "What do you mean, 'look into this guy'?" I say.

Jimmy gives me a look, but he doesn't answer the question. Instead, he turns to Eddie, who's been sitting there all the time, not saying a word. Which doesn't necessarily mean she's been listening, either. "What do you think, Eddie?" he says.

"What?" She grins, like she's missed the joke or something.

"Do you think we should look into this guy Rivers, or what?"

Eddie thinks for a minute, all serious. She sneaks a quick look at me and I can see she has no idea what we're talking about. Finally, she nods and grins. "Absolutely," she says.

Jimmy purses his lips and looks around. "OK," he says. "Eddie's in. Who else?"

Tone doesn't miss a beat. "Deffo," he says.

Jimmy nods appreciatively, then turns to Mickey. "What about you, Ernest?"

Mickey is still sulking, but he sees his chance to rejoin the pack right here. "Let's *do* him," he says.

"All right," Jimmy says. Finally, he turns to me. He's saved me for last deliberately, of course. He's probably expecting me to wuss out. I notice Eddie's watching me closely now, too.

"We're going to check him out, right?" I say. I want some terms of reference set, so it doesn't go pear-shaped. Which it will anyway, but I still want some terms of reference.

"Right," Jimmy says.

"Ask him what he knows," I say.

"Ask him what he knows," Jimmy says, his eyes fixed on mine.

I consider it for a second, but really, there's only one way I'm going to go. It's pretty dumb, and I know it, but I'm not going to let them go without me. Not Eddie, anyway. "All right," I say.

Jimmy wants full confirmation, though. "You're in?" he says, his voice all quiet-but-firm.

I look at Eddie. She's watching me hopefully, like she doesn't want me to screw up. Like some mother at the school sports watching little Herbert in the egg-and-spoon. I can't let her down. "I'm in," I say.

Jimmy nods. Eddie grins happily. Tone isn't sure he likes it. He'd probably prefer it if I'd wussed. I look at Mickey. He's sitting there off to Jimmy's left, still nursing hidden wounds, but he's looking at me with an odd expression on his face, as if he's just discovered a new possibility that he hadn't known was on offer. It's a scary moment, that, I have to admit.

Because, looking at Mickey, sitting there in the half-light with that weird expression on his face, I have an overwhelming sense that something very bad is about to happen. And I'm totally signing up for it, right on the dotted line, though I have no idea why. Once I am in, though, I know there can be no turning back.

———

The next day, when I see Elspeth, I'm in a bad mood. We don't go back to my place, because some professional type is round there, doing stuff around the place for Dad, some nurse-cum-home-help type. He gets that off the social, or somebody, because of his condition. So we can't go back there, and we can't go to Elspeth's for the same reason we never can, which is that her parents are there, and she fucking hates her parents. Plus they watch her like a hawk, and they'd know right away what we're getting up to. So we go out to the plant, but it's raining and it's wet everywhere, so we just sit in a corner in one of the storerooms, where there's an old table and some crates. It's dry in this corner, more or less, but rain is dripping through a hole in the roof on the far side, and it's not that warm. I just sit there, moping, not even trying to get anything going.

"So what the hell's wrong with you?" she says.

"Nothing," I say.

"Oh, right," she says. "Doesn't look like nothing."

"I'm tired," I say. "I had to get the house all tidied up for Jenny or whatever her name is coming round."

She comes over to me then and leans against me. "Tired? Lacking in energy? Can't seem to concentrate?" she says in this voice-over tone.

I nod.

"Need a pick-me-up?" she asks.

"Probably," I say.

She steps back and gives me a wounded look. "Well, don't put yourself out," she says.

I don't say anything. I do need a pick-me-up, but I'm not in the mood for her brand of pick-me-up. What I want is something more—I don't know. Personal. Like the other day, when I was talking to Eddie, just talking and mucking about.

Elspeth isn't a quitter, though, I'll give her that. She waits a moment for her point to register, then she leans back in and puts her hand up my sweatshirt. It feels cold, which is nice, actually. She moves her hand in slow strokes over my chest and then slides it down to my belly. Then she leans in closer and starts nibbling on my ear. I have to give it to her, she has a very special gift. A talent. She sticks her tongue in my ear, then she draws back a little. "Resistance is futile," she whispers, then she bites me, very gently, in the softest part of my neck.

So we end up on the floor, getting all dusty and damp, fucking like bunnies. It's pretty amazing, because it always is with her, no matter how unpromising the venue, but afterward, when we stop and roll just that little bit apart, I feel like she's miles away and it all feels stupid and pointless. I sit up then, and start doing up my belt.

"Where you going?" she says. "I'm not finished with you, sonny."

"I'm not going anywhere," I say.

She sits up too. She's about to speak again, some saucy and smart remark no doubt, but she gets distracted by something she's seen over on the far side of the room. I follow her look and I see it too: it's some kind of animal, lying on the floor, barely moving, though even from here we can see it breathing, or maybe not breathing so much as gasping for breath. "Fuck," she says. "I got a fright there."

I pick myself up and go over to where the thing is lying. It's quite big, but I don't know what it is. I've never seen anything like it before. It's about the size of a small dog, with a piggy-looking head and big, staring eyes. It's obviously in a bad way because, even when I get close, it doesn't do anything. It just lies there, staring at me and panting.

"What's wrong with it?" Elspeth asks. She is up now too, but she's standing a little way off. "Is it sick?"

"Worse than that," I say. "I think it's dying."

She gives an odd little shout then, and turns away. "Oh shit," she says. Then she turns back, her hands half covering her face. "Leonard," she says. She hardly ever says my name. In fact maybe this is the first time she's ever said it in earnest. "You've got to do something."

"What?" I say. "I can't help it. I'm not a vet."

"Put it out of its misery," she says.

"Why?"

"'Cause it's *suffering*," she says.

"How do you know?" I say. I know how ungracious I'm being, but the idea of killing something just because it happens to be dying in Elspeth's general vicinity strikes me as wrong. The animal isn't wailing, or screaming in agony, it's just lying there, trying to breathe. Maybe it's saying goodbye to the air. Maybe it's making its peace with the god of its small world. I have no idea what it's thinking, but I have no intention of killing it just because Elspeth is feeling squeamish.

"Come *on*, Leonard," she says. "Do something."

I shake my head. "No," I say.

She shivers. "Christ!" she says. "It was probably lying there all the time we were fucking."

"Probably," I say.

"You bastard," she says. She's really upset about this now.

"Probably," I say. I'm just being stupid, I know that. And this is just an excuse. I know that too.

Anyhow, that's it for Elspeth. She starts straightening her clothes out. "If you don't do something, right now, I'm going," she says.

"OK," I say. I'm watching this animal and trying to figure out what it is. It's not a native species, that's for sure. Maybe an escapee from some wanker's private zoo. You hear about that, sometimes: some jerk gets together a whole collection of exotic wildlife, then he forgets to lock up one night and the countryside is overrun with boa constrictors or bobcats. Maybe that's what's happened here. At the same time, while I'm trying to figure it out, I'm also trying to send out an aura of compassion and concern, because I don't want the thing to be scared. It will be better when Elspeth goes. Right now, she's just scaring it.

"That's it," she says. She storms toward the door, giving the dying creature the widest possible berth. "By the way, Leonard Wilson. You're chucked."

I don't say anything. I don't really care right now. I just stand there, a few feet away now, while the animal slowly dies. And I know it's probably fanciful to say this, but I think, toward the end, it knew that I didn't mean it any harm. I think it knew that I was a friend, and I think it might have been glad I was there, to keep it company in those last minutes. Because there is something about its eyes, a kindness, a softness, that I think I understand. It's like a person's face when they smile: the way you know it's a real smile is by the eyes. Not that this animal was smiling, but it had that look in its eyes. The look that makes a smile genuine in a person. Only it's an animal, and it can't smile. Or maybe what I mean is, whatever this animal does to smile is something that I could never recognize, because the only kind of smile I know is a human smile.

Afterward, when I know for sure it's dead, I go out. I'm expecting Elspeth to be long gone by now, but she's not. She's standing out by a patch of willow herb about ten yards away. I go over to her and she gives me a slightly tearful look. "Is it all right?" she says.

"It's dead," I say.

She starts to cry, then. For a moment, I think she's going to walk out on me again, but she doesn't. She throws herself against me, and just cries on my chest, waiting to be held. It's like the young Elizabeth Taylor in one of those movies where you can't believe how beautiful she is, even at that part in the movie when her horse has just died, and she goes to some man and her body language silently says, "Hold me." So I hold her. Not Elizabeth Taylor, of course. I should be so lucky. Young Elizabeth Taylor is gone now and, as they say, they don't make 'em like that anymore. So I suppose nobody's ever going to be *that* lucky again.

———

I was trying to find a way of getting Eddie away from the rest of the crew. It was all going fine with her, but I didn't want to take it any further with the others watching. That might be exactly what Jimmy is waiting for. Then, a few days after the animal-in-the-storeroom incident, I receive a gift. Sometimes that happens. The world just turns around and gives you a gift, and the only thing to do is accept it. Not that gifts don't sometimes have consequences you could have done without.

I'm sitting in the front room with Dad. He is stony silent as per, sitting in the chair by the fireplace staring at a fashion magazine he's found somewhere. It's a really old magazine with those washed-out pictures that look like they've been left out in the rain. I have no idea where he found it. That's what he does, he goes around the house looking for stuff that reminds him of the old days. That face in the misty light and all. It's not healthy. I just wish he would forget about the so-say beautiful past and make the best of what's left to him.

He's so absorbed in reminiscing, he doesn't even look up when the doorbell rings. I look at him. "Somebody at the door, Dad," I say, but he still doesn't look up. I wait a few seconds. "Might be for you," I say. Still nothing. I get up quietly then and go see who it is.

It's Eddie. She's looking really good, like she's cleaned herself up nice and done her hair a bit less spiky. She's wearing a white blouse and this really short pleated skirt, kind of school uniform for prize day. "Hiya," I say.

"Hiya." She stands there on the doorstep looking at me, with a sweet but slightly absent smile on her face.

"Want to come in?"

"Yeah," she says. She steps inside, but I hardly move, so we're really close together now, and I can smell her hair and her skin. I close the door, and it's just us, standing in the hallway. "I've got a message from Jimmy," she says.

I shake my head. "No you haven't," I say.

She looks confused for a second, then she figures I'm mucking her about. "I have, though," she says, and she grins.

I put my hands on her shoulders. "Tell me later," I say. Then I kiss her. At first she doesn't do anything, then she kisses me back, and it's really wet and sweet, not like Elspeth at all. I mean, I like Elspeth, and she is amazing in all kinds of ways, but there's something a little bit hard about her. Something too deliberate, as if she's thinking things up all the time instead of just letting them happen. With Eddie, it's all soft and wet and sweet and a little bit helpless, like we're just falling into each other. I like that. I could stand here all day, just kissing her, but then I think about Dad. He's just behind the door and I don't want to disturb him. I'm not that keen on his stardust-memories routine, but I can't really begrudge him his one small pleasure. Besides, he might be decades away in his own mind right now, but that doesn't mean he won't snap out of it and come wandering through, on his way back to bed. I peel myself away from Eddie for a moment. "Let's go upstairs," I say.

"What about your dad?"

I nod to the front room, and she makes a little aha face, then she smiles. "You're not going to lead me astray, are you?" she says, but she doesn't wait for an answer. We just go up the stairs, very quiet, and shut the door behind us. Dad never comes into my room, so I've finally got Eddie all to myself. "Alone at last," I say. She giggles and we start kissing again. Everything else disappears, Dad, Jimmy, the plant, the town, the lost boys and, for a moment there, I think I am in love. Just like in the movies.

Over the next three hours, I find out a few things about Eddie. First, that she's not really as dumb as she acts, it's just that the way she thinks is a bit different from how other people think. She's not that good at attention, so everything is all over the place. She starts a thought, then she goes off somewhere else in her head and she doesn't often come back to the same place she started. A really straightforward little question will get all twisted till it's some big complicated thing and she just gives up. She has this little squeal she does when she's happy, and this giggly little laugh that makes people think she's not right in the head. Maybe she isn't. But she's not dumb, either.

She's a bit like me, in some ways. She's in a lone-parent household too, only it's her mum who's at home, not her dad. She doesn't have any real brothers and sisters; Mickey is almost exactly the same age as her, just a couple of months younger, and he's the child of her dad's first marriage. What happened was, he ditched the first wife and got together with Eddie's mum, who's got this beautiful old-fashioned name, Dorothy. I've never see Eddie's mum that I know of, but I've got this picture of Dorothy Lamour in my head and I can't let it go. I don't suppose she's anything like Dorothy Lamour, but it's nice to imagine her like that, because then I'm in bed with Dorothy Lamour's daughter, which is more than kind of sexy. Anyway, Dad, who sounds like a bit of a rascal, gets Dorothy pregnant with Eddie, but he meets the old wife and they have a bit of a tumble, for old times' sake. This is just a few weeks later, before Dorothy even knows she's expecting, so it's probably a bit of a shock when Dad gets the news from both wives about the patter of tiny feet. While Eddie's telling me all this, I keep remembering that Groucho Marx bigamy gag and I'm trying to keep from laughing, because now I've got Groucho Marx and Dorothy Lamour having it out about all this, with the first wife—I'm thinking Maureen O'Hara—standing by with this big seen-it-all-before look on her face. Anyway, Groucho decides that he's going to stay with Dorothy, but he's going to keep both kids, and Maureen O'Hara doesn't mind, because she doesn't really want any big connection to Groucho, what with all she knows about him from the first marriage. Which is acceptable, if not exactly hunky-dory, in Dorothy's book, only now Groucho changes his mind and pisses off with some other woman he's met—Veronica Lake, let's say—and leaves Dorothy with both kids. Meanwhile, Maureen O'Hara has vanished, last seen walking out along the West Side Road with a cardboard suitcase and a hatbox. When Eddie's telling all this, she's really funny and she strings it all together somehow so it sounds like a really daft movie script. "So that's how I get to have a brother who's the same age as me," she says.

"Ernest," I say.

She laughs. "Mickey," she says. "After his mum."

"What? His mum is called Mickey?" Actually, this is OK, when I think about it. It doesn't change anything, in fact. I can see Maureen O'Hara as a Mickey. Some John Ford thing, where she's a tomboyish beauty waiting for some man to come and find her. John Wayne, probably.

"No," she says. "Michaela. It's Mickey for short."

"Oh," I say. "So what's Eddie short for?"

She looks at me like this might be a trick question. "How do you mean?" she says.

"Well, how did you get to be called Eddie?"

She thinks about this. "I dunno," she says.

"It's not short for anything?"

"I don't think so."

"You don't think so?" I say. "You mean your parents called you Eddie?"

"Yeah," she says.

I'm not convinced. She's hiding something. "It's short for something," I say.

She gives a little shrug and looks worried, but she doesn't say anything.

"Edwina," I say.

That makes her squeal. She gives a half-disgusted, half-incredulous laugh. "No!" she says, all indignant.

"Edina," I say.

She shakes her head.

"Edaline? Edwardiana? Éditions Gallimard?" I say this with the best French accent I can manage and she rolls her eyes.

"You made that up," she says. She's not annoyed, though.

"Theodora?"

"No."

"*Th*andra?" I say, lisping it.

"No."

I jump up, and do an Archimedes. "I know," I say.

She looks excited, like I'm about to tell her something she's needed to know her whole life. "What?" she says.

"It's *Rumpelstiltskin*!"

She punches me then, in the upper arm, and she hits hard. "Fuck you," she says. Next minute we're laughing at each other and a minute after that I'm fucking Dorothy Lamour's daughter again, and it's just like it was the first time, all salty and sweet and close-up-and-personal, just like before, only better. When we stop again, and I'm thinking I could do this forever, she leans up on her elbow and looks at me. "Did you know," she says, all grave and didactic, "that if you pick a Chihuahua up by the scruff of its neck, its eyeballs pop out?"

When I sneak Eddie out again, Dad is still in the front room, only now he's got the radio on, which is actually quite a promising sign, because at least he's listening to something. I mean, something is going into his head. Sometimes he watches TV, but he always has the sound turned down low, or even mute, and you can see from his face that he's not really making any sense of what's going on, he's just looking at the colors and movement in between sleeps. So the radio is good. It's Radio 4, some arts program, and some new young American director is talking about a film he's either made, or wants to make, where he and Janet Leigh—he's put himself in the film—are building this sculpture in the desert from pieces of magnetic rock. Only the work keeps getting interrupted, because some guy with a huge silver knife is after them, and then there's a gang of kids in leather jackets, with switchblades and stuff, who are also after them, so they have to keep escaping and starting again, over and over, just him and Janet against the world. I stand and listen for a while, then I give up trying to follow it. Obviously, here's a guy who's seen too many movies. I look at Dad to see what he's making of it all. He looks absolutely rapt, his head turned to one side, like a bird, just sitting in the big armchair, listening.

I decide to leave him and go upstairs and tidy up. I'd wanted Eddie to stay longer, but she'd said she had to go. So, just before we say goodbye, I ask her about the message.

She looks at me all confused. "What message?" she says.

"The message from Jimmy." I'm grinning at her. "Remember?" Her face is a blank. "You told me, when you got here, that you had a message for me. From Jimmy."

She shakes her head. "I dunno," she says. "I forget."

I laugh. "Well," I say, "it can't have been *that* important." Now, this being Eddie, I don't know if there really was a message and she forgot it, or if she just made it up as an excuse to come round and see me. Either way, I'm glad she came, and I'm sorry she has to go.

I'm lucky she did, though, because twenty minutes after I've finished sorting the room out, Elspeth turns up. And she is not happy. "Where the fuck were you?" she says, as soon as I open the door.

I make desperate hushing signs, but she just ignores me.

"I was waiting for you, you bastard," she says. I'm looking to the front-room door, thinking Dad will be out any minute to find out what's going on. As if. "Did you forget, or what?" Elspeth says.

"Come on," I say. "Let's not argue. Dad's in there having a rest."

"Sounds like he's watching telly," she says.

"Well," I say, "he's listening to the radio. But we should let him get some quiet." She's giving me this totally pissed-off look, but I'm not sure it's for real now. I think she's starting to remember that I'm not that good with time, plus I've got him next door to look after. Plus—well, she likes me, doesn't she? "So," I say, "let's go for a walk. We can talk about it, right?"

She gives me this incredulous look. "A walk?"

"Yeah. A walk."

"You want to go for a *walk*?"

"What's wrong with that?"

"I'm not going *for a walk*," she says. "I'm too upset to go out for a bloody walk." She starts up the stairs, not even bothering to look back to see if I'm following. Which means, of course, that we're going to fuck. And after that, everything's negotiable. Almost before we get through the door, she turns round and starts working at my jeans. "Come on," she says. "I'm in sore need of a good seeing-to."

I just stand there and let her get on with it. "You wanton hussy," I say.

She looks up and smiles. "That's me," she says. Then we're on the bed, sideways, doing it in our clothes and I'm feeling a bit guilty about Dorothy Lamour's daughter, though not *that* guilty. Tiramisu and steak in one day. All I got wrong was the order. Then, when we've both calmed down and started taking it slower, she looks up at me and laughs. "A *walk*," she says. "He wants to go for a bloody *walk*."

———

It turns out Eddie did have a message for me, but since she'd forgotten what it was, I don't find out till the next afternoon, when Tone catches up with me outside the library.

"Jimmy says to ask if you're ready for tonight, or what," he says, barely concealing his distaste.

"Why?" I say. "What's tonight?"

Tone sneers. "I thought you'd fucking back out," he says. "I knew you wouldn't go through with it."

"Ready for *what*?" I say.

Tone gazes at me in awe and wonder. "I suppose you're going to tell me you didn't get the message," he says.

The penny drops then. "Oh," I say. "Eddie told me she had a message for me, but she forgot it."

"Yeah, right."

I give him a look to let him know if he doesn't cut this crap I am going to break his fucking neck. He gives me the same look right back. I have to hand it to Tone, he isn't the one to play statistics. I've got height, strength, and speed over him, and he probably knows it. He just doesn't give a damn. If ever we get to the point when I have to fuck him up, it won't make any difference to him. He'll just keep coming right back till he gets something over on me. It's a fairly chilling thought. "Yeah," I say. "Right. So just calm down and tell me the when and the where."

"You mean you're in?" he says.

"I said I was, didn't I?"

Give him his due, he does look slightly penitent then. Not much, but enough. "Ten o'clock," he says. "At the old substation on the West Way. You know the place?"

I nod. "I'll be there," I say, and I can see that he believes me now. I can also see that this is going to be one big mistake from start to finish. Hammer Horror time, or some kind of sad farce. Or maybe a little of both. I ask myself what the fuck I'm doing all this for, or how I ever got involved with Jimmy and his crew in the first place, then I shake my head and turn for home, to get ready.

RIVERS

When he hears the first noise, Andrew is in the middle of writing a letter to Patricia Franz. It's not a good noise, but he doesn't pay much attention, because this is a difficult letter, the last he will ever write to her, and he's looking for the best words to put down on the paper so she will understand why he has decided not to stay in touch. He knows all the noises in this house, and every sound that happens outside, in the garden or along the road, which is usually empty, though sometimes people walk by, on their way to pick blackberries. Though he can't imagine that anything growing around here would be good to eat. Sometimes a kid from the

Innertown drifts by on his own, a nice-looking boy with dark, curly hair, and Andrew watches him go wandering along the path from behind the curtain. That one boy looks good-hearted, someone whose father could be proud of him, but they're not all like that. A lot of the boys are mean. They call him bad names and put stuff through his letter box. Dog shit. Old condoms. Fireworks.

Sometimes, when he sees that one boy on his own, he goes out and does things in the garden, so he can look up and catch the boy's eye, all natural and easy-seeming, like it had just happened by chance. He likes to look at children, especially when they are on their own. He likes the way they get all wrapped in their own thoughts when they think nobody else is watching. They walk along with their heads down, or they stop and gaze up through the trees at something, or maybe they sing to themselves. He knows what they say about him in the town, but it's not true. He doesn't mean any harm. He just *likes* children, that's all. He's borrowing moments, borrowing looks and smiles and the odd word from people who are luckier than he is. He's not the kind of person to get married, or have kids of his own, not with him being so shy. Anyway, how would he ever have met anybody, when he'd had his dad to look after all those years? And even if he had met someone, who would want to live out here, on the edge of a poisoned wood? No, the truth is, he'd never even dreamed of anything like that. In fact, he doesn't think he's ever actually *talked* to a woman. He wouldn't know what to say.

Still, he *had* hoped to make some kind of connection with Patricia Franz. Because if ever anybody needed a friend, it was her. That's why he wrote to her in the first place, to be her friend, because he'd read about what she had done. By that time, his dad couldn't see at all well, so Andrew would read out loud to him from newspapers and magazines. His dad loved magazines. Whenever he got a chance, Andrew would go out—in the early morning, say, when there was nobody about, or maybe when it was raining—to search in people's bins all across the Outertown, and he'd bring home any magazines or decent-looking papers that he found. They were clean, though; he didn't take any that were crumpled or dirty. Most of the time, in fact, they were like new. He would read stories that he thought his dad might like to hear, maybe something funny to cheer him up, but it didn't seem to make much difference toward the end. His dad was in too much pain. Which is a funny thing to say, when you think about it, because if there can be such a thing as too much pain, that means there could be just enough, or too little. But then, when you think again, maybe that's exactly right. Maybe you can have too little pain. Maybe you can be condemned to have just enough.

The stories he liked best were the spectacular murders, whole families killed in their beds or on their living-room floor, rooms of blood and silence in the spooky police photos they sometimes printed. That was what started him thinking about Patricia Franz. He read about her in a long article with lots of pictures—the killer, the victims, before and after, the detectives—and even though what they said about her was horrible, he knew it wasn't the whole story. He could see in her face that she wasn't all evil. He studied those pictures a long time. Some of the dead people on the floor of their living room, a collection of knives and guns that were used in the various killings, and then, larger than the others, two images of Patricia: one, as an eighteen-year-old with long dark hair and a pretty face, the kind of picture they usually say was taken "in happier days," and another as she looked after she was arrested, in her orange overalls and her hair cut short. Those court pictures are never very flattering, of course, because the person is being portrayed to the world as a brutal criminal, and they are probably upset and angry. Even in that picture, though, there was something innocent about her. She had the look of a little girl thinking about something else to make all this ugliness go away, or maybe just trying to work something out. Andrew thought she had a good face, in some ways. It seems now that he was wrong, but at the time he thought somebody ought to give her the benefit of the doubt.

Not that he didn't understand that what she did was wrong. It was a terrible crime, one of the worst mass killings by a woman in history. Patricia killed seven people: three men, four women. One of the women was just a girl of fourteen. She murdered the first three in one house—it was her uncle and his second wife, along with her stepcousin—then she drove four miles to another house and killed the others. At the trial, she said her uncle had abused her as a child, but they didn't believe her. She didn't offer any reasons why she killed the second family. According to most witnesses, she hardly even knew them. In one interview, she said she was prone to fits of confusion and helpless fear, so that, even though other people seemed to think she was functioning normally, she barely even knew what she was doing. She called these fits her "clouds"; when she was in one of her clouds, she started drinking, and doing crazy things, but nobody seemed to notice until she did something really terrible, like killing people. Andrew thinks she intended that as a joke. As soon as she started talking about clouds, though, the prosecution took it as the first step in an insanity defense and brought in experts to say there was nothing wrong with her mentally.

Which meant that they thought it was a perfectly normal, sane act to kill seven people before teatime.

She didn't reply to his first letter, or the one after that, but he wasn't surprised. She probably decided he was just some weirdo with a thing for murderers. Or maybe she thought he was a journalist trying to get an angle on her. By the time he wrote to her, the press had made her into a monster. They said she was cold and calculating, but Andrew told her that he had seen the good in her face, and he wanted her to know that somebody, somewhere in the world, was on her side. He was quite proud of those letters. He showed the first few to Dad, but he wasn't that interested. It might have been more interesting for the old man if Patricia had replied, but she never did. Andrew kept trying, though. He imagined she would take her time to work out if he was genuine, and then she would write back. When she did, she would be really friendly and kind, not saying that much really, but apologizing for taking so long to reply and explaining what had been going on with the case. She would also thank him for the birthday card he had sent her, or she would say some of the things she wanted people to understand about her, maybe ask him to help her tell her real story. She would want people to know that she wasn't cold, like the papers said, she was a person with feelings like everybody else. In her long interview with the first journalist, the one she probably trusted because he was going to tell the story from her point of view, she said she only killed those people because they had abused her. That's not what the guy said in the newspaper, though. He spoke to Patricia and then he spoke to other people, and he decided that she did it for money. Patricia Franz denounced him after that, but it was too late.

Andrew was disappointed that she wasn't replying to the letters, but he kept on writing. That was his life for over a year: looking after Dad, and writing to Patricia Franz when he got some time for himself. He had to give the old man his painkillers, and try to get him to eat; he had to clean up after him and tidy the house, so it was a busy time, but whenever he had a free moment, he wrote a letter or sent a card. But Patricia still didn't reply, not to any of them. He didn't even know if she had read any of the things he wrote. So, after a while, he got a little annoyed. He wanted her to know what an effort it was, to keep the faith, and to go on writing to her, when there was no dialogue, it was all just one-sided. Of course, when his dad died, Andrew had a lot of stuff to arrange, and he was never very good at that kind of thing. It was hard, and he thought he could use a friend, too, but she was all tied up with her appeal, and she didn't have time for him. They've put back her execution date three times so far, but she's still going to die, unless she can get her sentence commuted. Andrew doesn't really understand these things, though—and Patricia is on record as saying that she doesn't care that much about dying. She says that she got used to the idea long ago. The only thing that makes her mad is that she will die from being poisoned, when she would rather be shot. To be poisoned is so disgusting, she says. That was the word she used to journalists, when she talked about her own death. *Disgusting*.

People drive by here, though not usually at night, and when he first notices the noise, he's surprised to see that it's already dark. He looks up, he notices the blackness outside, and he should be working out that something bad is going to happen. He should be registering, but he's not, he's all caught up in the constant whirring of *self*. This noise isn't a car, as it happens. He's not sure what it is and he doesn't really focus, because he's distracted, thinking about

Patricia. He wants to tell her that he isn't going to write anymore, and it's a hard thing to say. He doesn't want to add to her problems. He's sitting in the dining room, with all Dad's decorations around, the wall of cuttings and photographs and stamps off old letters that the old man kept for years to make this room what he used to call his study. This used to be his favorite room and now it's Andrew's favorite room, because the two of them spent so much time together here, reading books and doing puzzles, or watching television. His dad had made the room by himself at first, pasting pictures onto the walls, images he'd found in magazines, or scraps from soap or jam labels, stamps, anything he could lay his hands on, really. After a while, though, Andrew had started helping him. They'd made books, too. They would build them over days, or weeks sometimes, from cuttings and stamps, then they would write or draw in them, little mottoes and sayings they had found. When his dad became too ill to continue, he moved upstairs permanently, but Andrew kept the room going and he would tell his dad about it sometimes. For a while the old man took a real interest; eventually, though, he couldn't remember anything, and his mind started to wander. He liked to sleep, and that was about it. But Andrew kept alive the man he really was, in his mind and in the room, and even in his letters to Patricia, mentioning him from time to time and putting in little reminiscences and facts about his life.

His dad was self-taught. He probably could have been very clever, if he'd had the opportunity. So, when Andrew didn't want to go to school, his father had decided to teach him at home. The only thing he knew about was logic, but he said that was enough. All that really mattered was to be able to think for yourself and make the right connections between one thing and another. Knowledge wasn't about facts, his dad said. It wasn't about *things*. It was about the relationships *between* the things. It was about *systems*. They didn't have textbooks, or anything like that, but there was one big book that his dad had built up over the years, a huge scrapbook full of newspaper clippings, some of them faded to yellow, some almost ghostly white and fragile as a moth's wings. Every time they opened up that book, it was like opening the door to another room, a lighted space whose orderliness had acquired an almost living form, the logical fauna of some distant yet still perceptible world. Andrew trusted that world more than anything else he had ever seen, even though he knew it was a kind of dream.

The rest of his education came from television and films. His dad told him what to watch at first, mostly documentaries and old films, films in a slightly milky black-and-white, films that looked so much like memories that, eventually, it seemed that they really did belong to his own past. For instance, he remembers Fred Astaire in a car, driving on a beach at the end of history, maybe the last man alive in the whole world. Farther along the coast, the people are gone; all that remains are faint palm prints of water and oil on a kitchen window, or the singed pages of a school Bible, or maybe just the moon peering in at the door of an abandoned cabin, finding a lamplit room, a deck of cards, and the remains of something that might once have danced, in a top hat and tie, to the music of some old Hollywood film. Andrew loved to watch old films on television, to see the real people who only exist in celluloid. They are the only ones who are free, because in their world, time does not apply, you can do what you like with it. He liked watching other programs too, but for the opposite reason: there it was all about time, because time is fast and relentless on television, nobody can stop it or slow it down. It's always there, threatening. The best thing, though, is when you see a woman with a torch, going through a building and either she's going to find something terrible, like a dead body, or someone is waiting for her there, in the darkness. He loves watching a woman walking slowly through a building at night with her torch panning across the unknown darkness, Agent Scully in a warehouse, looking for a suspect with superhuman powers, Catherine Willows in a suburban mansion or a sorority house, finding one body after another as she works her way through the building.

Now, sitting in the room, with his letter almost finished, he hears a new sound, closer this time, and he knows for sure it's a bad sound, but it's too late because whoever is there is already inside the house. He can hear them: there's definitely more than one, maybe four or five, and they are gathering just outside the door. And they are there, and he can't believe that he didn't register the danger, because he always hears everything, inside and outside. He can't sleep for it, sometimes. He hears owls moving in the trees, he hears a sound and goes straight out to it in his mind, so he can tell, without even seeing, that it's a fox, or a deer, or one of the feral cats that live out on the headland, coming through the bushes at the edge of the garden. So it comes as a shock when he reckons how close this danger has come without his knowing. A shock, yes; but more of a shock when he sees them coming into the room where he has been alone for so long. They are not cautious, like burglars. No, they are confident, casual, strolling into the room like it was their own house: three boys, then a girl with spiky dark hair, four of them—no, four at first, but then another comes, hanging back a little, looking like he doesn't really want to be here. He's in the shadow of the others at first, but then Andrew realizes that it's the boy he's seen before, the boy with the curly black hair who comes along the path sometimes, on his way to God knows where.

At first, he thinks they will speak. He imagines they will explain why they are here, at least, but they don't say anything, they just come into the room and surround him, casual as you please, thinking about what they are going to do next. He can see that they don't have a plan, they are just *there*. He can also see that the dark-haired boy wants to say something, but Andrew doesn't imagine he actually knows why they are here, and anyway, the boy is afraid of the others. Afraid, or maybe ashamed. It's the same thing sometimes. When Andrew was a child, he couldn't go outside the house, and he thought it was because he was afraid, but it wasn't just that. It was shame—and he thought it would be easy to say that he was ashamed of *himself*, though it wasn't even just that. He *was* ashamed of himself, when he went out into the world, but he was only shamed by being *there*, among others. He never felt that way at home. It was the shame of being with other people. He was afraid, too, but it was his shame, mostly, that frightened him. And it seems to him now that the dark-haired boy feels the same way. Maybe not all the time. Maybe he feels like one of the gang, most days, but tonight he is afraid, and ashamed, and Andrew feels afraid for him, because the others—the gang—will easily be able to smell that shame, that's what a gang is good at, smelling out the ones who are not altogether convinced, the ones who are ashamed. So Andrew thinks it will probably go very badly for the boy, if he isn't very careful. Of course, he knows it will go badly for himself.

It's the girl who starts things in motion. Everything is an event, everything *begins*. Sometimes you don't see that beginning, or you find it in the wrong place, but this time it's easy. The girl, who is not as pretty as she thinks, comes over to where Andrew is, standing up now, though he doesn't remember getting out of the chair. She pulls something out of her pocket. Andrew doesn't see what it is at first, and he draws back, then he looks and sees that's it nothing, just a little penknife. He almost laughs at that—but then she jabs him with it and, slipping it sideways, draws it along his bare arm. It stings like hell and he realizes it might have been a penknife, once, but she has sharpened it at the point and on the edges, so now it is a weapon. She is about to cut him again, and he tries to back away, then a voice comes, one of the boys. "Come on, Eddie," the voice says. "Leave something for somebody else."

What he says makes Andrew realize how scared he is. He hasn't been frightened before, he's been more angry, annoyed that these people had come uninvited into his dad's favorite room, into where he kept all his stuff, his maps and pictures and the Book. He turns to the boy who has just spoken, because *this* one is the ringleader and Andrew knows he needs to speak to the one in charge. He wants to tell them to get out of this room. But when he sees the boy's face—so hard, so amused by all this—he realizes there is no hope. They are all standing together, or all but the girl: the Leader, who is big and square and heartless-looking, a fat boy with spiky hair and one very dark eyebrow, the dark-haired boy, who is still hanging back, looking uncertain and maybe a little bit scared, and another boy, dressed in a grubby old Picasso "Dove" T-shirt and tie-bleached shorts, who looks oddly like a smaller version of the Leader, a likeness that is half natural and half worked on. The girl is still standing next to Andrew, and for a moment nobody is moving. They are all just standing there, looking at one another—and it is that, that stillness, that silence that resembles the moment just before everybody looks round at one another and laughs, it is this that makes Andrew desperate, so that he runs straight at them, trying to slip past the Leader and through, to where the dark-haired boy is, next to the door. Andrew thinks, if he can get to him, this boy will allow him to slip through and, though he may not get away, then at least they will all be out of his dad's special room.

It's an almost risible act, though, even Andrew sees that. The Leader simply lunges out and grabs him as he tries to get by, then he shoves him down to the floor and kicks him, hard. This is a signal to the others, and they all wade in, kicking, punching, one of them—the girl probably—sticking him with something small and sharp. Then someone takes hold of his arm and drags him up against the wall. Whoever it is props him up there—and Andrew sees that it's the Leader, the thickset boy, and he's talking, only Andrew can't hear what he's saying, because his head is singing, it's all noise inside his head like bells ringing, not church bells, but like the bells in old town halls in travel programs, those *sonneries* they always make a feature of in documentaries about Belgium or Holland. So, by the time he comes back to the room, he's missed what the Leader is saying. He can't really see the boy's face, either, it's mostly a blur close to and then, farther away, on the wall opposite, something comes into focus. Andrew sees it, and he realizes that this is something he has predicted, maybe something he has brought upon himself. Because his dad always said it: words are cheap, but pictures are a different story. You take a picture and you put it in the room, then you are taking on something magical, you are opening yourself to a possibility.

The picture he sees is one that he put up after his dad died. Even then, he knew the old man wouldn't have approved. It was too strong, too powerful. What Andrew saw in it was a fragment of history, a detail from a forgotten war, but he hadn't understood the power of the image, not until he looks up now and sees it, as if for the first time. It is a picture of a soldier, probably a young man not much older than these children, standing over the body of his enemies. He is wearing a mask, of the kind that anyone can buy in a joke shop, a Halloween mask with a skull-like face and stringy gray hair, a scary mask. He is carrying what might be an automatic rifle, dressed in a combination of army fatigues and casual clothes, trainers or tennis shoes on his feet, like any boy out for a Saturday afternoon, only he is looking down at what remains of a man, a ruined mess of a corpse, sprawled barefoot on the tarmac, his limbs absurdly twisted. The boy is glancing down at this man in passing, but he is still walking: it is a casual moment of appraisal; there is no emotion here, just a mild curiosity. Andrew had chosen this image for the wall because he liked the mask, and he was awed by the notion that this was a historic and terrible moment, captured on camera—by whom?—in the most casual manner. He'd wondered about the photographer, about how close he was and whether he was afraid the boy might shoot him. He'd wondered if the boy felt anything behind the mask, and if the mask allowed him to go about the business of killing with a sense that it wasn't really his doing, that he was simply performing a role. Maybe it gave the boy courage, too. Maybe this boy had been afraid, all the time he was growing up, that he might end up like this, killed by a scary monster and left to rot on an anonymous road, so he'd put on this mask and become the scary monster himself, the victor, not the victim, the one who keeps moving, killing everything in its path, rather than the one who is mown down before he even knows it. Andrew knew it was a terrifying picture, a terrible moment, and he had thought long and hard about using it for the wall, but he hadn't recognized the true power of this image, a power his dad would have seen right away. "It's all right to be afraid of dreams," his father had told him once, when Andrew woke up after a nightmare, crying and calling out for help. It was good to be afraid of dreams, if the dreams were scary—and it was good to be afraid of certain pictures, because pictures had just as much power as dreams.

Now, Andrew can see this picture, and he thinks at first it is a sort of prophecy, or premonition. But it's more than that. Someone is cutting his hands with something and he wants to scream, but he doesn't make a sound, he just keeps his eyes fixed on that picture. He wants these children to see it, to find their way to this picture through his attention, so he keeps his eyes fixed on that masked face. He keeps his eyes fixed on the picture and he tries to consider what they are doing to his hands as something other than pain, or rather, a different kind of pain, a shared pain, a courtesy. A courtesy and a bearing witness. A testimony, a testimonial, a testament. Not his particular pain, but all pain, everywhere. Not just this soldier's death, but every murder, every killing, every human life lost in war and genocide. Every human life, in its living and in its death. He keeps his eyes fixed on the picture and he considers how pain changes, when it is a courtesy and a testament, he notices how the body stops and listens to itself, in response to this pain. They are slashing at him now and he keeps his eyes fixed on the picture, and he lets his body listen to itself, going outside time, bearing witness, moving away from these children by surrendering to them. Because he cannot change this and he cannot end it. They cut his hands and his arms, they stab at his face, but he keeps his eyes fixed on the picture. These children are going to kill him, he knows that. Like this dead soldier, he will die for no reason, other than cruelty, so he keeps his eyes on the picture and he bears witness to that.

After a while, though, something breaks through his fixed gaze and he hears a voice, a pleading voice, a boy's voice. It's the dark-haired boy, and he is trying to get them to stop what they are doing.

"I don't think it's him," the boy says. "I don't think this is the guy."

"Why *not*, Leonard?" the Likeness asks—and there is danger in his voice. Leonard had better watch out for himself.

"He's not the type," Leonard says. Andrew is touched by this. He's grateful to this boy for coming to his defense, if that's really what he's doing. Though maybe it's himself he is defending. Maybe he is bearing witness to something too. "Come on," Leonard says. "Let's just leave him and get out of here."

The Likeness whips round now and turns on him. "Why don't you stop fucking whining?" he says. He's really angry with Leonard, and this isn't a new thing.

Leonard stands firm. He's quiet, maybe a little mournful. "He's not the one," he says, pretty well knowing that it doesn't matter now what he says.

"Who gives a fuck!" the Likeness screams, his face angry and barking, like a dog at the end of a chain.

Something in the room snaps then. They've all stopped what they have been doing, all gathered around him, hemming him in, but they have run out of steam now. It had started to get repetitive and they'd got bored. They'd wanted to do something bigger, something final. After this exchange, though, they back away, circling round Leonard, leaving Andrew on the floor, though the fat one, the one with the Eyebrow, keeps his eye on him, fixing him there with his attention. Or so he thinks—only nobody is fixed, nobody is holding anybody down. Andrew's not going anywhere, not because he's being held in place by some fat kid's staring eyes, but because he's suddenly tired of it all. Or maybe he is just tired of himself. We do tire of ourselves, he thinks, and if we can't find something else to take an interest in, then it gets pretty tedious, being human. We tire of *the self*, of the shape of it, and its slightly exaggerated colors; most of all, we tire of its constant noise and just long for a little quiet. Andrew thinks he remembers a time when *his* self was smaller than it had become by the time those kids turned up in his father's little study. He seems to remember a different shape, more muted colors, like the colors you catch glimpses of through snow on a winter's day. But most of all, he remembers something smaller and quieter. That would have been before his dad died. Afterward, he'd just sat around the house watching television or going through his dad's old stuff and he had lost contact with the world. All the same things were there, all the same machinery was there, but he didn't know how it worked. He didn't know how other people worked and he'd lost any real interest in doing things so that his lonely self just grew and grew, like some exotic hothouse plant. Those kids didn't know how it worked either, but they still wanted to do things and that was why they had come to his house, so that they could see themselves doing something. Andrew can imagine them poking sticks at an animal in a cage, or tipping baby birds out of their nests, and he knows he is nothing to them but bigger, slightly noisier game. When they hurt him, they do it with the same odd, almost tender curiosity about themselves, and what they are capable of, that they would have felt tormenting a kitten. *Look at me, this is what I can do.* It's a dangerous thing to get started on, because you don't know where it might end until it's too late. How it will end now, tonight, is easy enough to predict. It's a simple, almost logical progression, a progression from fists and feet to an old gas lighter for the cooker they found in the kitchen, then the knives in the drawers and the razor blades in the bathroom. Andrew had been angry when it all started, but by the end he was just hopelessly sorry about what they were doing.

The Leader intervenes in the dogfight, but he's not trying to make the peace. He's face-to-face with Leonard now, the Likeness backing him up, bristling and craning his neck, ready to kill. "How do you know he's not the type?" the Leader says. For a moment, Andrew wants to know what they are talking about, he wants somebody to go back to the beginning and explain why they are all here, and what is going on, but then he's too tired and maybe too scared for that. He just wants this to be over.

"How do *you* know he *is?*" Leonard asks. "We haven't even asked him anything. I thought we came here to question him, to find out what he knows about Liam and the others."

This is a challenge to the Leader, Andrew can see that, and the boy doesn't like it. "We didn't come here to question anybody," he says. "We came for revenge on this ponce."

"Nobody told me that," Leonard says.

The Leader does a little incredulous, music-hall turnaround for his troops. "Well," he says. "Did you hear that, boys and girls?" He spreads his hands out. "Nobody told *Leonard* that."

The Likeness is loving this. "Nobody told him what, Jimmy?"

"Why we came here," Jimmy says.

"And why did we come, Jimmy?" the Likeness asks.

"Ain't telling ya," Jimmy says, flaring away from the group with a mad laugh, and they all burst into activity again, rested from their labors, looking around for some new fun, some new trick. The girl goes out and rummages around in the kitchen; a moment later, she runs back in again with the big scissors, the ones with the red handles. She's really excited, jumping up and down almost on tiptoe.

"Let's cut off his pee-pee," she screams.

The Eyebrow snorts. "Pee-pee," he mutters, looking at Andrew like he is in on the joke.

"God, Eddie," the Leader says. "What is it with you and scissors?" He looks sad now that he has faced down Leonard's challenge, and Andrew thinks the boy is beginning to understand that Leonard is right, that maybe they are in the wrong house, but he can't let it register, in his own mind, or in the minds of the others, that he is wrong. He has waited for so long to do something, and now that all this has started, he has to see it through. Andrew understands that. But he can also see there is another reason for his sadness, and it has to do with Leonard, who is standing apart from the rest, watching, not prepared to do more to help, but no longer willing to be a part of what's happening. It has to do with Leonard, not just because the unexpected challenge is upsetting to the Leader—he *is* only a boy, after all—but because he likes Leonard, and now he knows they aren't together anymore, they're on opposite sides, totally separated. Meanwhile, the Likeness has been going through the stuff on the table and he's found a spike; Andrew doesn't know what it's for, maybe for sticking documents. He doesn't know where the boy found it; he didn't even know his dad had had one of those. "Let's do his eyes," the Likeness says, grinning savagely. He looks at the Leader. "Let's do his eyes with this."

Suddenly Andrew starts screaming at them, shouting and screaming like an animal, like a mad person. At the same time, Leonard starts shouting too. Andrew thinks at first that Leonard is going to try and stop the others from hurting him anymore, then he realizes that his defender is angry with *him*.

"Shut up!" Leonard shouts. He pushes Andrew into the corner

again and starts raining blows on him, kicking, first with one leg, then with the other, and shouting all the time. "Shut up! Shut the fuck up!" He goes on like that for a long time, maybe a minute, and then, with a horror that gradually gives way to gratitude, Andrew begins to understand what is happening. The boy is trying to rescue him. He's inflicting a smaller pain to avoid a greater, he's buying time, or maybe he's trying to make a more merciful end of it all. He keeps kicking and stamping, and nobody does anything to stop it, and then Andrew is swimming, his body is moving, rising, buoyed up, as if he had fallen into water and, after descending briefly, had started to rise, borne up on the tide, suddenly light. And all at once he is far away from the room, and he is dreaming, he thinks, drifting through something that feels like sleep, even if it isn't. He's dreaming something that, even as he watches it unfold, doesn't seem to be *his* dream at all, but something he remembers from somewhere, a story that belongs, not to someone else so much as to the air, like radio: a vision of a world that anyone might enter if he chose, or if he knew how. In the dream, Andrew is in a large country house, a vast, rambling mansion full of dark, dank-smelling rooms. Everything is in shadow, there is almost no furniture, the walls are bare, the smell of damp and rot is everywhere. He moves through the house and he smells it, on the staircase, in the hallway, in the huge, still rooms, but he doesn't mind it at all, because he is there for a reason, he has a purpose. He is moving quickly, searching for something, determined, though he is not quite sure what it is he is looking for, and the more he searches, the emptier the house seems, till there is almost nothing, no stair-case, no walls, no windows, only a space that is still the space inside a house, and a sensation of weightlessness as he goes on and on, searching, searching, a sensation of weightlessness that belongs, not to him but to the house, and then not to the house, but to everything. The whole world, the entire universe, is empty, weightless, without form or substance. Everything is melting away, becoming insubstantial, and the only solid fact that remains is whatever it is he is searching for. And then he finds it, and it's nothing, or it's light, not *a* light but light itself, just a shimmer of light that grows and brightens as it surrounds and then includes him, till he slips entirely into its great, wide whiteness. And it's peaceful, now, peaceful and a little silly, like the games Dad used to play, back when he was well. And he remembers an old rhyme his father used to say, something he had read somewhere, or maybe he made it up himself, because he did that sometimes, he made up silly little stories and rhymes from time to time. It was a stupid rhyme, just pure silliness, but Andrew had liked it for some reason. He couldn't remember all the words, just the ending, and first it was just himself remembering it, then he could hear his father saying it, as if he were there, sitting at the table in the room and they were safe again. Time had gone away and nobody could touch them. And he could hear his dad, it was his dad's voice, with a bit of a smile in it, repeating the words:

> *The planet turns*
> *From day to night*
> *And a marvelous planet it is!*
> *And sometimes the Devil*
> *Looks over our shoulder*
> *But who is it looks over his?*

Andrew has to laugh then, because he can just see the old man there, being silly the way he liked to be sometimes, and it was beautiful, because his dad looked fine, like he was when Andrew was a little boy, a happy man with dark hair and blue eyes, not sick, not dead. And Andrew laughed and laughed because his dad could be so funny back then, when he was still well, before he had to go away.

THE
FIRE
SERMON

UNDOING

I COULDN'T STOP KICKING HIM. I SUPPOSE I WANTED HIM to die, so the stupid game couldn't go on anymore, or maybe I was angry with him for being so pathetic. He just lay there, screaming and making weird animal sounds, till I thought I was going to go mad, and I knew Jimmy and his crew would never let him go now. Tone was dancing around with some kind of spike in his hand, talking about sticking the poor bastard's eyes and Rivers was lying on the floor, wailing. So I couldn't take it anymore. I just laid into him. It was all red, like you hear people say. I saw red. That was how it was. I saw red and I couldn't see anything else, though I knew I was moving and kicking him, using the wall to balance myself and keep him in focus without really noticing it, just using the walls the way a boxer uses the ropes in a corner, when he's got the guy hemmed in and doesn't want him to escape. I could feel myself breathing, gasping for air like a freestyle swimmer. I was really aware of that, which was odd to me, because I'd been in fights and things at school and I didn't remember anything about breathing. This was different, though. I don't know how long it lasted, but when I stopped kicking him I felt sick to my stomach and totally exhausted. I didn't really register much for a minute, I just reeled away from him, feeling dizzy, but I think he was still moving when I stopped. Then I came out of the redness and saw the others, all of them standing together in the middle of the room, watching me. They looked shocked—or maybe not shocked, but bemused, a bit bewildered, as if they thought it was me who had gone too far, and not them. There was blood all over the place. There was blood on me, too, even on my hands and face, and I felt them watching me like they were watching an animal that had just got loose from its pen. I think they were scared, too. All but Jimmy. Jimmy wasn't scared, he was just puzzled.

I knew what he was trying to work out, but I didn't care about that now. I didn't care about his gang; I'd never asked to belong to it anyway. I'd wanted to find out about Liam and the other boys and that was all. Now it was finished. I looked back at Rivers and he wasn't moving at all. Maybe he hadn't been moving before, maybe I'd just imagined it.

Finally, Tone breaks the silence. "You fucking killed him," he says, though not really to me. He looks at Jimmy. "He's fucking killed him, Jimmy."

Jimmy shakes his head. "Nah," he says. "He's not *killed* him." He walks over to where Rivers is lying motionless in the corner. "*You're* not dead, are you, mate?" he says. He prods Rivers with his foot. The guy doesn't move. Jimmy shakes his head and ponders the scene for a minute. "You know what?" he says, turning back to Tone.

"What, Jimmy?"

"I think he's fucking killed him," Jimmy says, then he bursts out laughing. Only it isn't funny ha-ha laughing, it's funny peculiar. Like he's just seen some sketch on TV that he isn't sure is funny or weird, or maybe just stupid. He looks at me. "Look what you've gone and done, Leonard," he says.

Eddie laughs then, just one daft laugh, more nerves than anything else. "Bugger me," she says. "I just worked out who he looks like."

Jimmy turns to her. "What do you mean, you just figured out who he looks like?" he says. "He doesn't look like anything now, does he?"

"Hamburger," Tone says.

"What?"

"He looks like hamburger," Tone says. "That's what he looks like."

Jimmy looks scandalized. "Well," he says, "that's not very nice, is it?"

"What do you mean, that's not very nice?" Tone says. "It wasn't *me* what done it."

"No," Jimmy said, giving me a quick, sideways look. "It was *Leon*ard. Still, you shouldn't speak ill of the dead."

Eddie laughs again. "No," she says, "I don't mean what he looks like *now*. I mean, who he *used* to look like."

This makes Jimmy and Tone laugh. I don't know what Mickey is thinking. He's just standing there, looking at Rivers. He looks a bit disappointed, though it might be dismay. Maybe he thinks he's going to get into trouble. "All right," Jimmy says. "Who did he used to look like, before he looked like hamburger?"

Eddie turns and goes over to the far corner. She points at a picture on the wall, above the little desk. "Him," she says. "*Psycho.*"

Slowly, with genuine curiosity, Jimmy and Tone move over too, leaving Mickey still staring at the body. They stand with Eddie, examining a tatty magazine photograph that's been glued to the wall among all the stamps and shit. "Oh yeah," Tone says.

Eddie is pleased. She does a tiny dance, like she wants to go wee-wee, then she lets out a microscopic high squeal. "I *told* you he looked like somebody," she says. "It's the *Psycho* guy. What's his name?"

"Anthony Hopkins," Tone says.

Eddie squeals again, a little higher up the scale. "That's him," she says.

"That's not Anthony Hopkins," Jimmy says. "He's the *Silence of the Lambs* bloke."

"Who is it, then?" Eddie says. She looks disappointed. I think for a minute she is going to cry. But then, I think we are all on the verge of tears, or something, by now.

"Anthony Hopkins is the Welsh bloke," Jimmy says. "This guy isn't Welsh." He turns to me. "Tell them, Leonard."

I think about just going then, but I feel too sad to go. I want to cry. I hadn't meant to hurt the bloke. I just wanted it to be finished. I hope he understood that. "It's Anthony Perkins," I say. "He was the guy in *Psycho.* Anthony Perkins."

"That's right," Jimmy says. "Anthony Perkins." He turns to

Eddie, who still looks like she needs cheering up. "You're right, though," he says. "This guy looks just like him."

Eddie grins.

"Looked, you mean," Tone says.

"Yeah." Jimmy stares at Tone for a minute, with the air of having just realized something then he turns and looks at Rivers. "Poor bastard," he says.

Tone nods. "Poor bastard," he says.

Jimmy walks back to the far corner and stands over the motionless body. "This bloke didn't deserve this," he says. He bows his head as if in prayer. Mickey joins him. Eddie and Tone hesitate a moment, wondering if this is a spoof or something, then they bow their heads—at which Jimmy immediately looks up. "You know what," he says. "I think Leonard was right. I don't think this is our bloke. Was." He looks at me. "You killed the wrong bloke, Leonard," he says; then, without waiting to see what I will say in reply, he looks back to Rivers.

The others stand watching, waiting to see what he will do next. They are all tired and sad now and they look lost, as if in shock. Or maybe remorse has set in. Jimmy stands silent a moment longer, head bowed; then he turns to the others with a strange new light in his face. "We'll have to raise him up," he says.

"What?" It's me speaking, it's my own shocked, maybe disgusted voice that I hear, though I'd had no intention of saying anything.

Jimmy looks at me; his eyes are shining. "Like Jesus," he says. "I mean, you're a Bible reader, Leonard. Everybody knows that."

"What are you talking about?" I say.

"We'll raise him up," Jimmy says. "Shouldn't be too hard. If we get it right, he'll be good as new in three days' time."

Eddie jumps up and down and makes her odd high squealing sound. "What do we do?" she says. "What do we have to do?"

Tone looks a bit lost. "Yeah, Jimmy," he says, his voice low and worried. "What do we do?" I think he's afraid it might work and that Rivers will rise up in three days and go straight to the police about what we've done.

Jimmy is really getting into this now. I'm not sure what he thinks he is doing, whether he really believes what he is saying, or whether it's all just a windup. Maybe he thinks he needs to give the rest of the gang something to take away with them. Maybe he needs something he can take away for himself. "All you got to do is lay him out right," he says. "So he looks like a cross." He studies the body. "Like Jesus."

They are all involved now, Jimmy and Tone, Eddie, even Mickey has come out of his stupor and is getting into it. I can't, though. I can't go through the motions, and I can't stay in that room any longer, with the faces and stamps and little birds looking down at me from the walls, as if in accusation, and the smell of blood, dark and sickening now. I don't think they'll miss me, anyhow. This is their thing, not mine. So I quietly make my way to the door, and start to leave. Jimmy notices, but he doesn't try to stop me. None of the others see me go. When I leave them, they are laying out Rivers's body, Eddie with one arm, Tone with the other, trying to get them into the right position, while Jimmy stands over them all, murmuring the words he's heard in a film, or maybe read in a book. "I am the resurrection and the life," he says. I slip through the door silently and his voice rises slightly, so his words follow me out and down the stairs. "I am the resurrection and the life. I am the resurrection and the life." It's obvious that he doesn't know any more of the words, so he's just saying them louder and putting more stress on what he thinks are the most important ones. "I am the Resurrection and the Life. I am the RESURRECTION and the LIFE."

His voice follows me out into the windy night, into the darkness, till I want to run to get away from it.

———

I don't really know how much of that resurrection stuff was real. Jimmy certainly made it sound real at the end there, when I was leaving, but that was done mostly for my benefit, I think. I didn't imagine for one moment that I had heard the last of it with Jimmy, but I wasn't much bothered about that. I was hoping nobody would see me, as I left the house, and then, when I got home and started taking off my bloody clothes, I was hoping nobody would see Jimmy's crew either, because if they got caught, I got caught, and they would say it was all me, everything, the cuts, the stab wounds, the kicking, the crushed bones, whatever else we had done to the poor bastard. I didn't want to get caught. I took my clothes off just inside the back door so I wouldn't trail evidence all through the house, then I put them in a black plastic bag and left it under the sink. I knew right away what I was going to do with it, but that would have to wait for later. Then I ran upstairs and straight into the bathroom. The shower was pretty cold, but I didn't care about that. I soaped myself well and washed three times, scrubbing hard, rinsing long; then I dried myself off, took the scrubbing brush and the towel, wadded it all up, and carried it downstairs. I put the washing things into a separate plastic bag, and put that bag next to the other one, under the sink. Then I went straight back upstairs, got dressed, and went to check on Dad. It was late, not that far off dawn, but he was still awake. He hardly ever slept at night. I think, maybe, it gave him some small, lingering pleasure, to lie awake in the early morning and listen to the birds. I don't know, though. You don't know what people like unless they tell you. All I could know was what I liked and maybe if I liked it, he might like it too. Some people like model trains. Some people like crazy golf. People are a mystery, when it comes down to it. I mean, how can anybody *like* crazy golf?

I didn't think Dad saw me, but if he did, it didn't matter. He wasn't going to say anything to anybody and, anyway, I was often up and about at night, in my clothes, doing stuff, or just sitting in the kitchen, watching it turn from dark to light, listening to the birds, maybe reading a book. That's what *I* like; I like books. When it comes down to it, maybe all you can really trust about a person is what they like. If you meet a crazy-golf fanatic, then you've got one kind of person. If you meet somebody who likes books, then you've probably got another kind of person. I can't imagine there would be much overlap between the two, but you never know. Maybe Marcel Proust used to sneak off from his cork-lined room and go for a few rounds of crazy golf in the Tuileries, or wherever they have crazy golf in Paris. When you think about it, that's quite a nice image: Marcel Proust in his frock coat and top hat, out on the crazy-golf course, early in the morning, when nobody else is about, indulging his secret vice. Maybe he'd play a few rounds with Gustave Flaubert, or André Gide. I don't know who was alive at the same time and I don't know if there is any mention of crazy golf in *À la recherche du temps perdu*. There might be, but I can't imagine it somehow. Still, I wouldn't know, because I haven't read the book all the way through yet. It's not that long since I got it out of the library, though it's probably overdue already. I've never really seen the logic of that: you lend somebody a copy of Marcel Proust's magnum opus, or *Moby-Dick*, or one of those big, industrious books by George Eliot, then you tell them they only have three weeks to read it. Really, they should have a sliding scale, so if you got Proust out, you'd get three months, or better still, three years. That would have made so much more sense.

I decided to take the black bags out on my bike to the landfill before it got too light. I wanted them gone as soon as possible and I couldn't sleep till that job was done. Dad was fine, he would just lie in bed listening to the world waking up for the next hour or two and, with the bike, it wouldn't take long to go to the landfill and dump the stuff. Then I could rest. I was supposed to see Elspeth later on that day, but I didn't think I would go. I had the black bags to do, and I needed to get some sleep after that. Besides, I didn't really want to see her. I thought, if I spent any time with her, she would figure out something was wrong and get it out of me. I was tired and I didn't feel like doing sex, or any of that stuff. I just wanted to stay in my room and sleep. After that, I could fix some food for Dad and me, and just stay around the house and read. I didn't want to be out in the world, where people could see me. I knew all about that *Crime and Punishment* stuff. It wasn't that I was feeling very guilty, or anything like that—I hadn't exactly killed some saintly old lady for no good reason, like the guy in the book, and I always felt the other one, the moneylender, pretty much deserved what she got. I wasn't the bad guy in any of this, or not as much as some people, though I had to admit, that morning, that I'd made a mistake going along with Jimmy and his crew. Still, even if I wasn't altogether to blame, I had done something bad, and you can't read Dostoyevsky without knowing how that worked. All I'd have to do is start walking down the high street and the guilt would be pouring out of me for all to see. Before I knew it, I'd be weeping like a baby and confessing to the Lindbergh kidnapping. Better to stay home, keep my head down, and figure out what to do next. Do some reading, maybe. Maybe I could make some progress with *Seven Pillars of Wisdom.*

After a day or two of this, though, I couldn't stand being in the house anymore, plus we'd run out of all the basics so it was time to get out there and shop. I do like shopping. I always want to buy expensive or decadent shit, like asparagus in tins, or those tiny pots of crème brûlée or Sicilian Lemon Cheesecake, but I mostly manage to confine my choices to sensible stuff, like potatoes, rice, sausages, frozen peas, all the reliable, filling basics that we've always lived on. Give me two days of dressed crab out of a tin and Asti Spumante and I'd be a happy camper, but I'd probably be shitting bullets, or throwing up all over the garden. People like us evolved to eat steak pie, mash, sausages, chips, roast chicken, peas, tinned veg. Feed us on anything else and we are magically transformed into big, sickly babies, all burping and farting and diarrhea. So I stick to what I know. Maybe what I like. I know Dad couldn't handle anything else, though it's not as if he eats that much anyway. He likes Angel Delight. He likes chips. As he slides down the hill toward death, he's getting a second childhood in before it's too late. Good for him. He's one of the few people I can make happy, and it doesn't take any more than whisking some pastel-colored powder up with some milk.

I'm thinking about Dad as I make my way home, dragging my bags of shopping along with me, my mind wandering. It's that old don't-want-him-to-die versus merciful-release argument, and there's still plenty of mileage in that one, so I'm a bit distracted when Jimmy and his crew turn up. So distracted, in fact, that I don't even see them till Jimmy pops up in my path, in my *face*, and starts on his shtick.

"That Rivers bloke didn't rise again like you said he would," he says.

It doesn't take more than this to wake me up. I put my shopping down to keep my hands free, then I slip one hand into my jacket, where my knife is. I've been carrying it ever since the hunting trip. All I can do now is keep my eye on Jimmy. I know, if anything's going to happen, he'll be the one who decides, so I want to see the sign. When I see it, he's the one I'm taking with me. I think he's working this out for himself too. "I didn't say he would," I said.

"Well," he says, "it's in the Bible, Leonard. You're the Bible expert in this gang." I ignore that. I'm not in this gang, or any other gang. "So, what do you think went wrong, Leonard?" he says. I can see that he's thinking as he says it. He's trying to guess what I will do, if he lets things take their course. I'm not sure, because he still has his gang to back him, but I think he might be scared.

"Him not being Jesus of bloody Nazareth might be the place to start," I say.

Jimmy smiles. He wants me to know that he genuinely thinks this is funny. I don't take my eyes off him. Eye to eye, and forget the rest of the crew. It's just me and Jimmy. Anybody makes a move and I am going to cut him up bad. "Well," Jimmy says, his voice slow and deliberate, "maybe you should have thought of that when you killed him."

"I didn't kill him," I say. "We all did."

Jimmy thinks about this for a minute. I can feel Tone getting restless, off to one side. I look for Eddie. Not that I expect anything from her. I think it scared her when I did what I did to Rivers. She's not sure of me now, and probably Jimmy has had something to say to her in the background. So she isn't doing anything, she's just watching. I think, if it came to the bit, she won't pile in with the others, but she won't try to help, either. This doesn't mean she is betraying me, though. If she isn't sure about me, I can't really blame her. More than any of them, she is one of the wild things—a bit formless, maybe, but beautiful too. All she needs is a bit more definition, a bit of focus. Anyhow, I'm hoping she knows that I'm not blaming her. I know she doesn't really know how she feels right now, but maybe later, when she has time to think, she might see that, in spite of who and where we are, I almost got to love her.

Finally, Jimmy decides. He is very deliberately not looking at my jacket pocket. "Nobody blames you for what happened," he says. "It was just one of those things."

"That's awfully white of you," I say.

He laughs at that. I'd read it in a book somewhere, maybe F. Scott Fitzgerald, and I'd thought it might come in useful. He turns to Eddie and smiles. "Sometimes he goes too far," he says, doing Dennis Hopper out of *Apocalypse Now*. "He's always the first to admit it, afterward," he says. He has his eyes on Eddie. She smiles. It's a touching moment, really. He's pretending to let me off for her sake. As if she really is in love with me, or something. Maybe she is, in her way, but he put her up to it in the first place, one way or another. That's the thing about people who don't know their own mind, you can leave them to the tender mercies of others and it doesn't matter. Give her a week, and she'll forget everything. Jimmy turns back to me with a sad or maybe a compassionate look on his face. "It's all right, Leonard," he says. "We won't rat you out."

"Jimmy!" It's Tone, missing his pound of flesh.

"Shut up, Tone," Jimmy says. His anger looks momentarily genuine. "Can't you see Eddie's upset?"

Tone looks at me, then he looks at Eddie. He thinks for a minute, and finally the penny drops. "Aw, fuck," he says.

Jimmy laughs. "You can say that again," he says. "Come on, boys and girls," he says. "Let's go kill something."

And that is that. Jimmy turns and walks away, a sad look on his face, like I've betrayed him or something, and the others follow. First Mickey, then Tone. Finally Eddie. She looks back at me, which is nice. She gives me this silly, hapless, who-knows-what-might-have-been look, and I want to give her a big hug and say some kind of proper goodbye, but I don't.

———

That night I went down to the docks and climbed into one of the old cranes above the loading area. All I wanted was to sit out and look up at the stars. From up there, you could see them all, and when you looked down toward the coast, you could see where the lights twinkled and winked across the water like the lights in old movies, perfect geometric patterns that stopped for a moment, when you first looked, then started shimmering again, white and cherry red and the odd point of gold from farther away. That night, though, the weather decided to turn and, by the time I got to the top of the crane, a massive thunderstorm was breaking above me, lightning, then a crash of thunder, then lightning again—not just flashes, but the whole sky turning a livid gold over the water, everything reflected and instantaneous. It was beautiful and dangerous, and though I caught myself wondering if I was going to be fried to a crisp up there among all that metal, I couldn't have imagined coming down. Better to die like that than from some petty ambush at the hands of Jimmy's crew, a blade stuck in my gut, maybe Eddie's blade, and me flopping around on the floor like Rivers, bleeding and cursing and weeping for myself, a lost animal, dying in the eyes of others. If you have to die, die alone, at the top of a crane, and let Nature kill you, with grace and beauty and the gorgeous cruelty of chance. Only, I didn't die; I just sat up there and watched the best light show anybody could ever see, the lightning inches away, it seemed, the thunder echoing in my bones and my muscles. It was beyond description. By the time it was over, I didn't give a fuck about anything. If I had to, I'd pick off Jimmy's people one by one, including Eddie, or I'd seek Jimmy out and cut him to ribbons in front of his own crew. I didn't care. I would have killed anybody that night, because of the storm. Because I knew, if I belonged to anything, it was to this. Not to them, but to the lightning and the thunder. To the black rain. To the cold metal. To the sky.

When I got home, there was a note from Elspeth saying I'd been a naughty boy, and she was coming round at lunchtime to chastise me. I picked it up off the mat in the hallway, and I was still reading it when I walked into the kitchen and found Dad on the floor, next to the table. He was half kneeling, half sitting, with a puzzled look on his face, as if he'd been perched happily on his chair a moment ago and didn't know why he was on the floor now. I thought, at first, that was all it was, that he'd had a fall; then, when he saw me coming in, he opened his mouth and blood came out. I had thought he was going to say something, but it wasn't words, it was blood, a great mass of it, spilling out of his mouth. Then he did the same thing again, like somebody repeating a spectacular trick, and a whole lot more spilled out. He looked even more surprised by this, then he toppled over and fell flat on the floor, on his side. More blood came out. I ran over and knelt down beside him. He had a sad look now, a look that took all the disappointments he'd ever had in a whole lifetime and brought them together in one final foregone conclusion. I put my arms around his shoulders and tried to raise him up, but I couldn't do it, even though he'd got so thin over all the years of being so ill. He was too heavy for me. A dead weight. Now his lips were moving, and he looked like he wanted to speak, but he was afraid to open his mouth again. Finally, he whispered something, but I couldn't make it out.

"What is it, Dad?" I said. Then I realized that I shouldn't be asking him to speak, I should be telling him to be still, to take it easy. "Don't try to talk, OK?" I said.

He looked confused at that, but he opened his mouth again, and this time words came out, along with an odd, seal-like cough and a spray of tiny droplets of blood that landed on my face and neck. "Time to come in, son," he said.

"Don't talk, Dad," I said. I didn't know what he was talking about, but he was scaring me with it.

He struggled, then, straightening his legs and trying to haul himself up, but he just skidded and sprawled on the floor like that cow you always see in the films about CJD. He couldn't get up, but he couldn't stop struggling. "Time to come in," he said again, and he tried to get up, while I tried to keep him down, to get him into the recovery position or something, while I thought what to do. "It's getting late," he said. Blood was bubbling out of his mouth now, and I could feel that the skin on his hands was cold, but it was the wild look on his face that frightened me more than anything. I had to get a doctor, I knew that, but I couldn't leave him like that alone. Then, after about a minute of this, he was gone, the life ebbing right out of him. Just gone. It was like when you take a bucket of water and carry it over to the sink and pour it away, all the weight just goes and you're left standing there with this sensation of emptiness and lightness. That was how it felt then. He just emptied.

"Dad," I shouted. He couldn't be doing this. He couldn't be dying, just like that, after all this time. There had to be more to it than this. "Come on, Dad," I said. "Come on. You can do it." For a moment, I even believed he could, then I stopped believing that and sat quiet, cradling his shoulders. I stayed like that for a while, not long I suppose, but it could have been, I don't remember. I was away somewhere, maybe going with him some of the way on his journey, in my mind, or my spirit, or whatever, then I came back to myself and struggled to my feet, letting him slip gently onto the floor. There was nothing to him now. I could have carried him any-where. I remember, when I came back to myself, I was trying to think how old he was, but I couldn't.

That was when I saw what he'd been doing in the kitchen, before he started bleeding. There, on the table, an old album lay open at a picture of Dad and her, some time before I was born, the two of them smiling, a bit shy, maybe, of whoever was taking the photograph, the gray of trees behind them, no place I knew, maybe a honeymoon photograph, or a picture taken when they first met, when they were happy and the future was laid out before them like a blueprint for children and money and happiness. I felt sad then, and I started to cry, because it wasn't fucking fair that it had come to this, him sitting in his old clothes, looking at pictures of his lost life. His lost love. Because he'd loved her, that was for certain, and she'd just walked out on him when he needed her most. Bitch. That was my mother there, in the picture, all smiles, posing for the camera, in a pretty summer dress and her hair all nice, just the way she looked when she left us, pretty and young, with her whole life ahead of her, beautiful, even, if you pushed it. A beautiful woman with her whole life ahead of her. I wished, then, that I knew where she was, so I could write and tell her how her husband died, still thinking of her, his lost love. His lost fucking love.

Give me some time to think, and a few clues, and I can usually work things out. And on my first day of being completely alone, wandering around the headland, not sure what to do about Dad, I get the first real clue. That's what the world does, sometimes: sometimes it gives you a gift, pure and simple; other times, it gives you a clue. Which is like a gift that you have to work for. Though you could say that the world is full of clues, if only you know how to read them. Clues, gifts. These are what we use to make sense of the world. Otherwise there's nothing. You don't got to have faith, like Miss Golding says in Religious Ed. Faith isn't a gift. Gifts have to come from the world, not from inside your own head. Clues too. It all has to come from somewhere. I mean, there are perfectly respectable people, philosophers and such, who think that the world is something we imagine, that it's all just an illusion we make up as we go along. Which means I'm making up the plant, and the murders, and my dad sicking up blood all over the kitchen floor. Of course I am.

My clue is a complete accident, a one-in-a-thousand chance. I'd spent my last night sleeping in the attic, just shacking out on the floor with a duvet and some pillows—I didn't want to sleep in my own bed, because I'd started thinking I would be the next of the Innertown boys to go, and they would be coming for me soon, just lifting me out of my own bed, like they did Tommy O'Donnell. I didn't want to sleep out on the headland either, though, because I wanted to be near Dad, that first night at least. I don't know why, it was just a sentimental thing. I couldn't do anything for him, and I knew I'd have to leave him soon. I'd wanted to lay him out neatly on his bed, but then I thought that would remind him of that face in the misty light, old Laura, young woman with all her life ahead of her, etc., etc., and I didn't want that. Besides, it would have been too much of an indignity to cart him up those narrow stairs. So I set him in the big armchair, more or less sitting up, as if he was reading, or listening to the radio. I thought about burning that album he'd been looking at, but I couldn't bring myself to do it. I thought about giving it to him to look at while he sat there, waiting for his heavenly reward or whatever, but I couldn't do that either. So I just sat him up in the chair, and turned on the radio. Quietly, but loud enough so he could hear, if there was some wisp of something left in there, some trace of consciousness or memory or spirit burning out silently in his head, like a dying ember. You get people who think that death isn't the end of your life, it's the beginning of the next stage in the journey, and maybe the soul hangs about for a while, taking stock, or whatever. I'm not sure I'd go along with that—probably not—but you have to allow for every eventuality, especially when it's your father you're dealing with. You only get one father, and the one I got wasn't that bad, he just wasn't lucky. On the other hand, maybe he got the luck he wanted. Before that night, I'd always felt sorry for him. Because, his entire life, all he'd wanted to do was love somebody. That was the one gift he had, a strange, quiet talent for loving. The person he loved was Laura, and if she had loved him back, he would have been happy, no matter what else happened. But that night, I wasn't sorry for him at all because, in a way, he'd got what he wanted. He got to love somebody, which meant that he'd been able to use his one good gift. Maybe it didn't matter whether Laura loved him or not. Maybe, for him, that wasn't what it was all about.

So I slept on the floor of the loft, then I packed a bag with a few bits and bobs, food and coffee and such, so I could make myself little camping meals, like the Moth Man does. I figured, if he could do it, so could I. Maybe I'd get myself a van, nick one from the Outertown sometime and drive off, be a nomad, get away from here. First things first, though. I said goodbye to Dad, and I took all the money I could find around the house; then I headed out. It was a fine summery day, warm already, even at that early hour. I made my way across the back garden and out, through the gate in the fence, then down along the little alley behind, all the wheelie bins there, one at each gate, solemn and secret, full of clues and stories, like black tabernacles. At the end, I looked out to check if anybody was up and about, but the only living thing I saw was Mrs. Hatcher's white cat, the one all the kids referred to as Mrs. Hatcher's Pussy. The Innertown kids had a lot of virtues, but originality wasn't one of them. I suppose Elspeth was a bit of an original, though it would have been better if she hadn't tried so hard.

Elspeth. When I'd stood her up, she'd left that note saying she would come round later. I'd forgotten about that. What she had said in her note could only mean one thing, which was very tempting. Very. Still, I'd have to be disciplined and stick to the plan for a while. I could get in touch with her later, explain about Dad. Use him as an excuse.

So I'd got safely out of the Innertown and I'd stowed my bag of stuff in my special secret hiding place, like all kids have, even when they're getting a touch long in the tooth for special secret hiding places, then I started out for the West Side, so I could hole up in the woods for a while and get some time to think. That's when I come across Morrison, the policeman, standing all by himself in a little clearing among the trees, all quiet and thoughtful-looking, all preoccupied. So preoccupied that he doesn't even see me, though he looks up just a moment after I duck into cover, like he's felt me there or something. Sensed my presence. Or, maybe, *a* presence. Because, as odd as it seems, I think he must have been praying, or something like it, when I came across him. He'd just been standing there, looking at something on the ground, his head bowed down, like somebody who's standing beside a grave, saying goodbye. That's what I should be doing, of course. Standing by my father's grave and saying goodbye. Saying a prayer for him, maybe.

Anyway, I must have disturbed Morrison because, even though he doesn't see me, even if he doesn't think anybody else is there, his concentration is shot, and he just turns round and walks away—quick, like all of a sudden he doesn't want to be there anymore—and I have the place to myself. I wait awhile, a couple of minutes, maybe more, before I come out from where I am hiding. I have the idea that this *is* something. I even think it might be a clue. I don't want Morrison coming back and finding me, because if he does, the clue might be lost forever. Sometimes a clue is that slender: you catch a glimpse of someone when he thinks he's on his own, and you see another side to him. Something you didn't know about before.

When I am sure he's gone, I wander out and cross over, all innocent, like some kid just farting about in the woods, to see what it was he had been looking at. It had been low down, on the ground, over by the edge of the clearing. It takes me a moment to find it, or not so much to find it as to figure out what it is. Because at first I think it's just some garden stuff that somebody has dumped out there. It's only when I get close that I can see that it's an actual garden, with carnations and poppy plants and a little rosebush that looks as if it has just recently been planted. All around the plants, around the roots, somebody has set out pebbles, like the ones you get on the beach, all smooth from the sand and the water, bright shiny pebbles and pieces of colored glass and bits of broken china. It's like a magpie's garden, or maybe those nests that bowerbirds make, the ones you read about in nature books and such. I saw a program about them on TV once—probably one of those bird programs David Attenborough used to do. One of the few complete sentences I remember Dad saying—it must have been when I was still pretty small, maybe even a toddler—was during one of those Attenborough programs. Or maybe at the end, when the credits were rolling. That would have been more likely. It would have been a respect thing. Suddenly I remembered it like it was yesterday and I remembered the exact words he said.

"When you get a program like this," he said, "it's almost worth paying the license."

So here's this little plot of ground, half garden, half Isn't-Nature-Wonderful, bowerbird, hushed-Attenborough-tones natural mystery—but I'm asking myself what it's for. Why is there a garden out here, in the poison wood? A little garden of flowers, like some graveyard plot? And what is Morrison doing here? Is it him, planting flowers out here, in the middle of nowhere, like some nutter?

Even then, it takes me a few moments to see how stupid I'm being. It isn't a garden, it's just what it looked like when I first saw it. Sometimes, you have to trust those first impressions. Even if they're not quite spot-on, they can be clues. This isn't a garden, it's a grave. Something is buried here. Something, or somebody.

And then it occurs to me that Morrison isn't a nutter, he'd gone there for a reason and that reason had to do with the lost boys. He was there to tend a grave. But whose grave? Could it really be that one of the boys is buried out here, where our mysterious policeman has made his little garden? Is Morrison the murderer? Because all the boys are dead, that's obvious. Morrison is the one who's been saying otherwise, he's the one who put it about that the boys had all gone off on a Dick Whittington, with their little knapsacks and their ten-league boots, their talking animal friends by their sides. You have to wonder why he puts so much effort into that. Does he believe it himself? Or does he have something to hide? Somebody killed the lost boys, and he's getting away with it all these years. Who else to commit a whole series of murders, and then get away with it, other than a policeman? Who else could cover it all up and make sure there wouldn't be any kind of investigation? I mean, he looks capable. He's a bit of a mystery, everybody says so. Even if he isn't the killer, he has to be in on it. The question I am asking myself at that moment, though, is why?

Then I know. It isn't Morrison, of course. It isn't him doing the killing, or kidnapping, or whatever; he's just covering it up. He knows the real killer and he's protecting him. Or maybe there's more than one killer. Maybe there's a whole gang of them. Maybe the boys aren't dead, but somebody has them somewhere, for who knows what reason. Maybe the people in the town are right and it really is some kind of experiment. I feel sick when I think of that, not at the thought, because I've heard it often enough before, but at the idea that it might actually be true. We can calmly entertain the most terrible thoughts, if we're not sure they are true. But then, suddenly, they *are* true, and we feel sick to our stomachs. Morrison probably feels sick too, and maybe he's feeling guilty about what he's got himself into, and that's why he's made this little garden in the poison wood. But then, why here? Why not in his own garden at home? His secret plot. Out here, where anybody might come across it, this pathetic little garden is vulnerable. I can just imagine what would happen if Jimmy and his crew found it. Why not put it somewhere else, where he could protect it?

But I know why. I look off in the direction where Morrison disappeared, but nobody is there. It's just me, in that silent part of the poison wood that even the kids avoid. Long ago, the first boy disappeared in these woods, and after that his best friend vanished too, so the place is a bit jinxed in some people's eyes. Not in mine, though. Nowhere on the headland is bad or unlucky, and everywhere has its own history. This wood has poison running in its veins, in the sap of every tree, in every crumb of loam and every blade of grass under my feet, but it once was a place where lovers went to be secret, girls whose dads wouldn't let them go out with boys, husbands whose wives didn't give them love, wives whose husbands were never there, sneaking off in pairs to hide among the trees and bushes, fucking and talking and making plans about how they would get away. That's part of the history too. This garden is part of the history, and my finding it is part of the history. So it's also part of the history when I kneel down and start to dig, pulling out the plants and scattering the glass and pebbles, digging down into the dark earth to find what is hidden below. Because something *is* hidden here. I'm not saying I've found a body, I just know that there is a clue somewhere in all that dirt and grass and poison. I have to dig a long time: deep, deeper, deepest. I'm afraid that the policeman will come back and find me, but I can't stop; it's part of the history of the place that I should dig, and keep digging, till I find my clue. Though when I do, it isn't what I had expected—but it is a clue, nevertheless. A tiny, significant clue.

A watch. A boy's prized possession, a good watch, fairly expensive by Innertown standards. It's all gummed up with rust and dirt, and the crystal is broken, but I know it's still a clue, not just some piece of rubbish somebody has thrown away out there. So I rub off the dirt and scratch at the rust and, after a while, I see that there is an inscription on the back of the watch, an inscription I can just about make out. It says: *To Mark from Auntie Sall.* It seems to me that this is a loved thing, something a boy would only have lost if he couldn't go back to look for it, and though it isn't conclusive, though it wouldn't stand up in court, Your Honor, I know what it is and I know who it once belonged to. Mark Wilkinson isn't buried here, but this is where his ghost has remained, because this is where what he most loved was broken. Morrison knows that. That's why he made the garden. He is praying to a ghost—but why?

Then I guess it. I have no way of knowing for sure, but I know I am right. It's forgiveness. He is praying to this ghost for forgiveness. Yet, surely he knows that forgiveness does not come without repentance? Surely he knows that, to be forgiven, he must confess his sins, if only in his heart, and so make his peace with the world? And how can he do that, if nobody helps him?

After that, I leave the grave site, or the memorial garden, or whatever it's meant to be, and I head back into the far reaches of the plant. I'd been thinking, before, about going back to see Elspeth, but I know that will have to wait, for later, or maybe forever. For the moment, I have to be alone. For the moment, I have work to do.

ELSPETH

AT THIS POINT IN THE STORY, ELSPETH IS THOROUGHLY pissed off. If you asked her about it, she'd say she was annoyed because her boyfriend has stood her up again, and she really needs a shag, but the truth is, she's worried. And pissed off too, of course. If he had any sense at all, she thinks, Leonard would come to her with his troubles, not Jimmy van Doren. If he needs someone he could trust, then surely *she* is the one—but as far as she can tell, he's gone off somewhere with Jimmy and that gang of his, out to some sewer on the headland, probably, to live with the rats and the mutants. Or maybe it's the girl he's gone off with. What's-her-face? Eddie. As she heads out to the old plant, not quite sure why she's going and with no real hope of finding anyone, Elspeth is telling herself that she wouldn't be surprised if Leonard was shagging that weird little bitch because, let's face it, he's the type—can't walk past a sick puppy without petting. Still, if *that's* what he's up to, it's not as bad as getting all comfy with Jimmy, because Jimmy van Doren is *not* the kind of person you go to when you're in trouble. Of course, if you haven't got any troubles to speak of, he'll be happy to make some for you. Elspeth had asked him about that, when she was still seeing him. Why he liked to see people suffer. Why he hurt them for no reason.

"It's a gift," he'd said. He had a big grin on his face. "A gift— and a public service."

"Is that what you call it?"

"Sure," he said. "People feel comfortable when they're unhappy. They know it's as much as they deserve." His eyes twinkled. "When things are good they start to worry. They don't know what to do with themselves. The world suddenly seems strange and frightening and they long for something they know. Something familiar— like pain."

Now, unless Leonard is going for some kind of care-in-the-community shag, Elspeth is pretty certain that he and Jimmy are out on the headland, getting into more trouble, and maybe comparing notes. You should always judge a person by the company he keeps. After all, that was what first drew her to Leonard, because he didn't keep company with anybody—he was his own person. He had his books and his films and such, and that was it. Elspeth had never really gotten into that, but she was happy he had something, 'cause it must have been hard for him, looking after his dad by himself all those years. His mum had been a really nice woman—a real looker, too—but after a while she just couldn't take it anymore and she'd run off with some guy she met at the dentist's or something.

Leonard never likes to talk about her, of course—which is fine, because Elspeth has never been very big on the empathy thing. She's not that into reading or films, either, though she did give it a try. Leonard would borrow videos from John, the dope-smoking nut job at the library, and they would watch them in his room, on some old video recorder Leonard had rescued from the landfill, but Elspeth couldn't see the point. There was never any plot, the dialogue was all in French or Japanese or whatever, and the subtitles were all fuzzy, so you could hardly make them out. All the time they were watching this stuff, she would be wondering what was so wrong with good old-fashioned Hollywood movies, real stories with real people in them, like that Bill Pullman in *While You Were Sleeping*. Elspeth likes Hollywood, she doesn't think there's anything wrong with just sitting back and letting yourself be entertained. TV is good too—even some of the soaps are well acted. But these films Leonard got from John? She still has nightmares about the one where some guy is walking around on a piece of wasteland with a big black dog, and the camera just closes in slowly on a piece of glass or a book or something, while somebody you can't see talks offscreen and there's water everywhere and that's it, only it goes on for four hours—in *Russian*.

Leonard had been trying to educate her, of course. He'd try to get her to read books. The classics: *The Brothers Karamazov*, *Anna Karenina*—there we go with that Russian shit again—and *Moby-fucking-Dick*. She just took one look at *Anna Karenina* and laughed. "Are you kidding?" she said. "Look at that thing. If you dropped it on your foot you'd break your toe."

He almost laughed at that, but he kept on at her anyway. That was the thing about Leonard, he really cared about all this stuff. He was worse than John the Librarian. "It's one of the best books ever written," he said. "You should give it a try."

"It's one of the *longest* books ever written," she said. "I'll give it a miss."

She did try D. H. Lawrence, but the smart money said he only did one good book, and that wasn't in the library. When she asked John why, he just snorted. She told him she wanted to read the classics, to improve her mind and all that. She'd said how she thought she'd start with *Lady Chatterley's Lover*, 'cause of the psychology and stuff. That made John laugh. "We don't have that," he said. "We *have* got *Valley of the Dolls*, though. If it's classics you want."

Elspeth doesn't want classics, though. Not really. What she wants—what she really *likes*—is porno magazines. Not just the hardcore stuff; the polite, *Forum*y type of thing is good too. Because, as she's tried telling Leonard a few times now, you can learn a lot from porno mags. You learn about different positions and things you can do to make sex more exciting, obviously. But you also learn a lot about people. Which is what Leonard could do with. If he'd stuck to reading porno, or *Story of O* or something, he might have more common sense, and he wouldn't be out somewhere with Jimmy van Doren and his little gang getting into trouble.

Still, she thinks, that's his problem. Hers is that she needs a big fat seeing-to. But that's not available, so she decides she'll take a wander down the old farm road on the East Side to walk off the frustration. It's a nice day, all sunny and clear and, for once, the air smells sweet, like summer in a normal place probably smells, so she heads on down along the hedge line, past the landfill, and out along the dirt road that runs down to the shore. She doesn't expect she'll see anyone out there, but she's not half a mile down the track when she comes across this bloke she's never seen before, some pikey by the look of him, cooking something over a bonfire. She stops a minute and gives him the once-over: and it turns out he's not a pikey at all, he's actually quite nicely dressed, for country-style anyway. In fact, from this angle, he looks quite handsome, with nice light-to-sandy-colored hair, not quite blond, though she can't see his eyes and she knows you should always go by a person's eyes. Still, he looks nice and she can also see that he's got a vehicle, a homely old green van parked over on a patch of wasteland, not far from where he's making a fire. He doesn't have a dog, which is good. Pikeys always have dogs. Usually the dog is nicer than the bloke, especially if it's a lurcher. Though she has to admit that she's generalizing a bit now. Anyway, she goes down the track a few yards, till she's just upwind of the bloke, and she sees that he's making some kind of stew. He's got a big bottle of Fanta or suchlike on a little mat, and a cup and some bread and he's making this stew, maybe rabbit stew, though if he's got any sense, he won't go eating any of the rabbits round here. He's completely absorbed in what he's doing, so he doesn't see her till the last minute. She gets to sneak up on him and deliver her best line before he knows what's hit him. "Want a blow job, mister?" she says, just as he turns round. He really is handsome, with a kind face and clear, blue-gray eyes.

He looks a bit startled by this, or maybe it's just because he's looking up into the sun. Then he laughs and stands up, wiping his hands down on his jacket. "Well," he says, "if I'm honest, I probably do. But not from you."

She's a bit offended by this, of course, but she acts casual. "So what's wrong with me, then?" she says, putting on her best who-gives-a-shit-what-you-think-anyway face. Only she does give a shit, of course, because she really is in bad need of a fuck, and if Leonard's not up to it, this guy can happily stand in.

The man laughs again. "There's nothing wrong with you," he says. "It's just that you're only a little girl. You're just a kid, and you shouldn't be wandering around the countryside offering your services to complete strangers."

"I'm eighteen," she says.

He shakes his head. "I doubt *that* very much," he says.

"You want me to prove it?"

"How would you do that?"

She grins. "Come over here and I'll show you," she says.

He laughs again. "No," he says, "you don't need to prove it." He takes a quick look to check on his lunch. "Are you hungry?" he says, hunkering down to give the pot a stir.

Now that he mentions it, she is hungry, 'cause she didn't eat before she came out, being in such a rush to meet Leonard, but she's too randy to think about food. This guy has got her all restless and wet, it's like something out of D. H. bloody Lawrence. Probably. Still, she's glad to accept what's on offer and they can take it from there. "I'm *starving*," she says, with a bit too much emphasis.

He looks up at her and shakes his head. "Sit down, then," he says. "I'll not send you away *starving*."

———

She doesn't know who he is. Not at first. But when she asks him what he's doing here, he tells her about the moth survey thingy, and she realizes that he's the one Leonard told her about. Which wouldn't stop her from shagging him, of course, but he genuinely isn't interested. She pushes the envelope a bit on that, but he just keeps laughing her off. She tells him he can do anything he likes—she's never met a bloke who didn't go for that. If you say to them, all soft and submissive-looking, *you can do anything you like*, they usually just go straight to automatic and then you can just about do what you like with *them*. Not this bloke, though. He's a nice guy, and handsome and all, but he's a bit dim. It's not like she wants to *marry* him or anything, and she's told him she's eighteen so he's fully insured against any legal comeback. Of course, he could be gay. Maybe he likes Leonard. Or maybe he's just some simp going about the countryside catching butterflies and counting them. Which, when you think about it, isn't such a bad deal. Gets you out and about. Better than living here. Which, in turn, gives her an idea. They're sitting by the fire now, eating his homemade stew. She doesn't know what's in it, but it tastes all right. "So," she says, going all nice-friendly-conversation, no-big-agenda on him, "where do you come from? You're not from around here."

He shakes his head. "I'm not from anywhere," he says. "Or maybe I'm from all over. I even lived here once."

"Here?"

"When I was a kid." He glances off toward the plant and it's like he's looking back through time. He seems like the kind of person who can see what he talks about, what he remembers. Not just words or thoughts, but pictures. "My old man worked here a few times," he says.

"Really?" Elspeth doesn't know of anybody working here who didn't stay right here. "What did he do?"

"He worked for Lister's."

"What's that?"

"George Lister and Son," he said. "One of the companies that built the plant. He helped design it, then he came back, when it all closed down, to help decommission it."

"What does that mean, exactly?"

"He helped to shut it down."

"Oh," she says. "He'd be popular, then."

The man gives a rueful smile. "I don't think so," he says.

"So, what's it like?" she says, to get him off this subject. She wants him a bit more cheerful.

"What's what like?"

"Out there. You know. In the real world."

He laughs. "It's *all* real," he says. "But it's different. It varies, place to place." He looks around. "Wherever you go, this is the best of it."

She laughs. "*This?*" she says. "You have *got* to be kidding."

"Well," he says, "not exactly this particular spot. But the open air, the land. Places where you can sit quiet, or just get on with your work, and nobody bothers you. You don't find that very often."

"Tell me about it," she says. She leans forward and rests her chin on her wrist: warm, sympathetic, interested. She can do that stuff in her sleep, if she needs to.

He laughs. "Anyway," he says, like he's avoiding a question she hasn't asked him yet, "I'm almost done here."

"Yeah?"

"Yes," he says.

"So you're leaving?"

He nods. "Soon," he says.

She nods. She's about to give up, at this point, because she can feel him slipping away, but she gives it another try. "Can I come with you?" she asks him.

He looks surprised, but he isn't really. "Why would you want to do that?" he says.

"To get away from here," she says.

"What about your folks?"

"Don't got any folks," she says, which isn't quite true, even though it is really. "Look, all I want is a lift. I won't jump you or anything."

"Is that right?"

"Well," she says, "not unless you want me to."

He smiles. He has a nice smile and she feels a bit wistful, right then. She feels kind of sorry for him, to be honest. He should fuck her, it would probably cheer him up. It would cheer *her* up, that's for sure. Still, there's no point ruling anything out. Farther on down the road, and all that. There's nothing as sexy as heading off down the road at night, not quite sure where you're going. Mile after mile of house lights and country lanes, the fields all around full of dreaming cattle and owls flitting in and out of the headlamps. Just like that French film she saw over at Leonard's house. She wouldn't be surprised if he didn't pull over and give her one before they even got off the peninsula. "Well," he says, after pretending to think it over, "I won't say I'm not tempted. But there's something I still have to take care of before I go." He looks away across the wasteland, toward the old plant. He seems sad, or maybe a little scared, and she wonders what it is he has to do.

"Your loss," she says, trying to shrug it off and come out with her self-esteem intact, but he's starting to worry her now. He's gone all scary and preoccupied on her, and Elspeth can't help thinking that something terrible is about to happen. Because he's different now and, for a moment, she sees it. It's only a glimpse she catches, and she doesn't understand what it is she is witnessing, but she looks into his face and just for that one moment she sees the dark light of the sun, so she has to turn away, out of fear and confusion. It's only a glimpse, though, and when she looks back, out of the corner of her eye, that dark light is hidden and all that's left is sadness. She feels so sad, in fact, that she's on the verge of bursting into tears, like she does sometimes at home for no reason, watching some stupid film on TV or listening to one of her mum's old records.

The man gives her a long look, then he nods. "I'm sure it is," he says. He leans forward and pokes at the fire. "It's getting cold," he says. "It'll be autumn soon."

He looks up and smiles—but Elspeth feels cold now, cold and tired, and she really does start to cry. "Don't say that," she says.

The man shakes his head. "It's all right," he says.

Elspeth wants to believe him, but she can't. She's really crying now; the tears are running down her cheeks and she wishes that, just this one time, everything would work out the way it was supposed to. She looks at the Moth Man, and she thinks, if he could only have been someone else, if he could have just touched her, it would mend everything. Home and school and Jimmy Van Doren and Leonard and the Innertown—it would all melt away and she would be free forever. All he need do is touch her, and that new story can begin. Roads, bedrooms, cities, oceans. Summer. She wishes he could see that. She wishes he would stop being so scary and just put his arms around her and then, after they have fucked for hours in the long grass by the hedge they would drive away in his green van, and the terrible thing wouldn't happen. The terrible thing wouldn't happen and somebody, somewhere, would stay safe—and that's when she thinks of Leonard, without knowing why, without really believing that he's the one who's in danger. She sees Leonard for a moment, in her mind's eye, lifting his head and putting aside his book to welcome someone he has only just noticed and hadn't expected to see, the way he did that first time, in the library, then the cold and the sadness engulf her, till all she can think of is driving away in a green van, traveling west to where it's still summer. Because it's still summer, somewhere, she knows that. It's always summer, somewhere or other, for someone.

LEONARD

I WAS BEING FOLLOWED. OR NOT FOLLOWED SO MUCH AS
watched. Someone was watching me, from among the trees, or in
one of the ruined kilns. Still, it didn't bother me to begin with. I
was scared that Morrison, or somebody, would come for me, but I
didn't think this watcher was from the Innertown. Which wasn't
that logical, maybe, but I figured, if I was next—and for a couple of
days, there, I really was *convinced* that I would be the next kid to be
taken—if I was next, if the bastards wanted me, they could find me
anytime at home, but I didn't think they could touch me out here
on the headland. Which was stupid because I had to have known

that, if they wanted me, they would just come and get me, and there wasn't anything I could do about it. The police were in on it, that was obvious now, and the town hall was probably in on it too. The Homeland bloody Peninsula Company weren't just in on it, they were probably running the whole thing from somewhere in their Outertown offices, some kind of ethnic-cleansing scheme, clearing the streets of potential troublemakers or whatever, or maybe just keeping us all scared, so that when their great Homeland plan finally kicked into motion, they'd have a docile population to man the waste-incineration units or whatever it was they were going to build to replace the plant. Or maybe it was some weird religious thing, like when God let Satan kill Job's sons, or when He sent the angel to kill all the eldest sons of the Egyptians, but spared the Israelite kids. You had to give it to those Israelites, they were hard bastards. They just painted a white mark on the lintel of the door, or whatever, brewed up a mug of Ovaltine, and went off to bed. Some fucking angel was going to be running through the town killing children, and they just lay down and had a good night's sleep, without a second thought. Me, I'd have felt a bit bad about some of those Egyptian kids. I'd have wanted to tip somebody off, maybe that nice brick merchant across the street, or the baker at the end of the road, the one with the cute wife. Or I'd be up all night, in case it rained and the white mark on my door got washed off. It's your eldest kid for God's sake. You wouldn't want any misunderstandings.

I had thought I'd be safe for a day or two, time enough to think what to do about what I knew, which was next to nothing, but I had a start and as a start it was better than torturing that guy Rivers with razor blades. Now, I was being followed. I didn't know who it was and at first they kept their distance, but midmorning

the next day I was in one of the old warehouses, one of the big
echoey ones with ivy and such growing through the holes everywhere in the roof and birds flying in and out all the time, and I
could feel that someone was close. Very close. Only I couldn't see
anybody. All I could see was sun and shadow, and bird shapes flitting here and there, and all I could hear was the singing. I stopped
dead still and looked around, then I called out: "Jimmy?" That was
more wishful thinking than anything else, because Jimmy I could
deal with, but I pretty much knew it wasn't Jimmy out there
among the shadows. This was something else altogether. This was a
person, I thought, someone bigger and quieter than Jimmy or any of
his crew. Someone who was used to being alone and very quiet. A
watcher, like one of those characters in old mystery books. The
Watcher in the Shadows. The Watcher of the Skies. Only, now, I
didn't know if he was there because he was *after* me, or because he
wanted to protect me. To watch over me. Or maybe he was just
there, watching. It didn't matter that it was me, it could have been
anyone. And maybe it wasn't a person at all, maybe it was just a
presence. The spirit of the place. They say every place has its own
spirit, but when they talk about it in books and poems and stuff,
they always mean places like bosky groves, or dark reed beds where
Pan sits playing his pipes to some lost nymph, or maybe some lake
with a lady sleeping just beneath the surface, but why not an old
warehouse, or a cooled furnace? Why not a landfill? Don't they play
that game just so that these things—these spirits—get to belong to
somebody else? I'd always felt something out at the chemical plant,
no matter where I went. You could call it a spirit, or a genius loci—
why not? It was present, and I always thought it was trying to talk
to me. Not in words, though. Not like that. It was more like pointing. It was there, pointing to something I should know about,

something I should have seen beyond the things I was seeing, but it wasn't concerned with what you could say in words. You get a huge moon in an indigo sky, floating over the dusty water by the docks, over the rusty cranes and the old boat eaten away by rust, you get that big moon over the harbor and you can hear owls calling from the woods above, on the West Side—what words are you going to have for that? It's not a description you want, anyway, it's something finer. It's like parsing, or chromatography. Sometimes, the whole world points to something you can't see, some essence, some hidden principle. You can't see it, but you can feel it, though you have no idea how to put it into words. And sometimes, it's just that things are beautiful, only what you mean by beautiful is different from what people usually mean when they say that word. It's not sentimental, or choccy box. It's beautiful, and it's terrible too. It takes your breath away, but you don't know if that comes from awe or terror. Sometimes, I wonder why people think so little of beauty, why they think it's just calendars and pictures of little white churches or mountain streams in adverts and travel brochures. Why do they settle for that? I'm only fifteen, and even I can see there's more to it than that.

I know what ugly is, too. That day, in the broken warehouse, standing there in that dance of sunlight and shadow, nobody there but me and the birds, and this person, whoever or whatever it was, the world looked more than usually beautiful to me, but I knew that was partly because of the contrast with how ugly things were back in the town. Everybody thought the plant was a terrible thing, that they should finally demolish what was left of it and build something new on the headland, but they were getting it the wrong way round: it was the town they should demolish, the Innertown and the Outertown, the terraces and the villas, the poor and the rich, everything. They should pull everything down and start over, maybe in shacks or mud huts, so the people could learn how to live again, instead of just watching TV all the time and letting their kids run wild. They should move the people farther along the coast and teach them to fish, give them little plots of land to look after, little allotments, and some tools and a few bags of seed, and they should leave them for a generation, learning how to live, and how to teach their children. It wouldn't take any more than that. In one generation, they would have new skills, new homes, new stories. Then they could start moving out from there, a few at a time, moving out into the world to teach others, beautiful nomads, moving from place to place, making it good to be alive again.

I was standing there, thinking all this, and I wasn't sure whether it was me thinking it, or whether it was someone else. Thoughts came into my head of their own accord, from nowhere, or maybe from whoever was out there, watching me: thoughts at first, then pictures and sounds, pieces of memory, fragments, but not fragments, because I could see that somewhere, behind it all, everything was connected to everything else, only I couldn't see all the connections, because I wasn't ready. I wasn't used to connections, I was used to the bits and pieces. I was used to the fragments.

Then, after I don't know how long of just standing there, I looked round and saw a shape. It was the shape of a man, a living man who had just stepped out from somewhere. Only there was nowhere to step out from, he was in the middle of the place, right in the midst of all the song and sun and shadow, and yet, still, he looked like he had just stepped out from somewhere because he had. He had just stepped out of that—out of the light, out of the shadow, out of the birds' singing. He was a man: taller than me, but not much; he was standing very still, just gazing at me, no intentions, nothing to be afraid of.

"Who are you?" I asked him. I really wasn't afraid. I was just curious—only it wasn't the usual curiosity, where part of you wanted to know and part of you didn't really give a damn, because what difference does it make anyway, right? This was a pure, sweet, delectable curiosity that was an end in itself, and maybe it didn't have an answer anyhow. It was the wondering that mattered.

It was a long moment before he stepped forward into a pool of sunlight and I saw his face. He looked familiar, but at first I couldn't place him. I'd seen him somewhere, but I didn't get it till he spoke, though even then, I didn't quite hear what he said. It was just a sound, a voice on the air, like something you might hear if you tuned your radio to some new wavelength. For a moment I thought I had wandered into some new place, into some dream of heaven, or the afterlife at least, and I was in the presence of something unworldly, some otherworldly being that, as strange as it might seem, saw me as a friend. Because it seemed to me that this was *my* friend. The one I had been looking for, for as long as I could remember. Then he moved, just a little, and I saw that it was the Moth Man. I recognized him now, though he looked different; or rather, he was the same as before, only bigger—not larger, but bigger in himself, more defined and, at the same time, full of possibilities. He was the Moth Man and nobody else, yet as he stepped out of the shadows, I thought I saw someone else in him, someone I knew, and I was confused for a moment, and I almost turned away, because I thought something was wrong, but then I looked again and I saw that it really was my friend the Moth Man, and he was smiling. He took another step forward and looked into my face, as if he were checking to see if I were awake or sleepwalking. Then he laughed softly and turned away. "Come on," he said, as he walked away. "I'll make you some tea."

———

I kept going back and forward from the place where I was sitting by the fire and some other place that I must have seen sometime in a film or a dream, but neither of those places was an illusion and neither was more real than the other. And I was sure I wasn't hallucinating. One moment I was sitting on a low concrete wall, listening as the Moth Man talked about the machine his father had built deep in the inner reaches of the plant, the next, I was standing in a field of bees, up to my waist in oxeye daisies and goldenrod, the bees swaying in their hundreds back and forth around me, the sun on my face in a place that was impossibly clean, the air scented with grass and pollen. Then I was back by the fire, looking up at him, listening. I had no idea what was in the tea he'd just given me, but it had made me sleep and in that sleep a dream had come, though now, almost awake, I couldn't remember it exactly, I could only see pictures. I knew I had only slept for a short time because it was still daylight there, in the campsite at the edge of the woods, and then, a moment later, in the wide meadow where I stood in the to-and-fro of the bees. That's a surprise: I don't remember falling asleep, I don't even remember feeling strange or drowsy, but all of a sudden I'm waking up and everything is altered—though it feels, not that I'm still in a dream, but that I'm too awake, every detail of every leaf of grass and curl of flame is utterly there in my head, so it's almost unbearable, how real and close it all is.

After a while, I realized we were walking, but I didn't know where we were, or where we were going. It surprises me now, looking back, that I didn't recognize the building we were walking toward, or the room that he led me into, after producing a key and opening a real, working lock on the door, but we must have been in a place that I'd never come across before that day, an enormous, dusty room that looked like a school laboratory at one end—three rows of careworn laboratory tables with sinks and gas taps, a single not quite dead houseplant on a blackened windowsill by the door—then stretched away into a cold, dim space beyond, a long emptiness as far as my eyes could see in the half-light, as much corridor as it was room. As soon as we were inside, the Moth Man closed the door, and everything went dark.

"Wait a moment," he said, before he ventured into the darkness, leaving me alone in the blackness. I know, looking back, that the wait was no more than a few seconds, but at the time it felt long—so long, even, that I forgot he was there, forgot why I had come to this place, and, like a child lost at a carnival, I had begun to feel abandoned, when a faraway gold light came on and the Moth Man came back for me, his face kindly, and perhaps a little concerned, as if he had read the fear in my eyes and wanted me to know there was nothing to worry about, that everything was good. All will be well and all manner of thing shall be well, I thought, as he reached out and touched me gently on the arm: words from a book, I knew, but they had been something else once, they had been words that someone had thought, in a moment like this one. "Come on," he said. He gazed at me for a moment, his face calm, his eyes empty of all emotion, then he turned and started walking slowly, back into the gold light. I followed. All the way, I had the sense of something watching me—not a person, not people, but something small, something concealed in the fabric of the room. Some animal in the wainscot, whatever a wainscot is, some creature hidden in the shadows.

"This is a sacred place." He was standing in front of some kind of machine, maybe a kiln, or a gas chamber—I couldn't make it out, but then I couldn't make anything out, it was hard to see clearly and it was hard to hear what he was saying. I kept missing things, phrases melting on the air before I could pin them down, his hands moving as he spoke, the metal fascia of this machine I'd never seen before, in a room I didn't even know existed, even though I'd been wandering around this old plant all my life. I made that out, though, that phrase he liked so much. He'd said it before, said it more than once when we were outside, in the woods, or trapping moths in the waste ground between the town and the foreshore. I'd laughed the first time he said it, though even then I think I had a glimmer of what he meant. Still, sacred wasn't a common word for people to use when they talked about the plant and I'd laughed.

"Yeah," I'd said. "*Sacred*. It leaps right out at you."

He'd smiled at that, but he'd persisted with the idea. "You know what sacred means?" he'd asked.

I'd thought for a moment, then shook my head—though I knew where he was going. I always knew where he was going, even when he talked about the bizarre life cycles of the Lepidoptera, or the inner workings of fungus colonies; it was like listening to another version of myself talking about the world, filling me in on all the things I hadn't had time to notice yet. "OK," I'd said, "enlighten me."

He'd laughed. I didn't know how he saw me, if he thought I was another version of him, maybe a there-but-for-the-grace-of version from the Innertown, the smart-arsed kid he never got to be growing up. He'd said it often since that first time, how the headland was sacred, but this time it meant something else, something harder, something as dangerous as it was beautiful. This time he's talking about something more specific, some piece of machinery he has made, but I can't really follow because of the tea I've drunk. All I can do is stand there, trying to stay in one place, in my body and in my head, trying not to sway as I watch his lips moving, like someone who's suddenly gone deaf and is trying desperately to lip-read from scratch. Not that it would have mattered, I think. He isn't explaining anything. At one point, I think, he's telling me about how he's found some old drawings and plans on his father's computer system, how he's sat down and worked it out, how they have something to do with the plant. At first, he just thought they were plans for some kind of purification process, maybe something his father designed to help clean up the mess the plant created, but after a while he sees through to something else, some ghost of a notion to begin with, but enough to make him see that what the old man was working on—during his very last days, according to the dates, days when he knew he didn't have very long—what he came close to achieving, is a portal of some kind, a gateway that's already partly built into the plant's inner workings, and has only to be completed. I *think* that's what he is saying, though I might have imagined it, or maybe I put it in afterward, to make some sense of what will happen later, when I walk into that huge light without a second thought and come to where I am now. I don't know. What I do know is that he shows me a machine at the dark end of a long, cold room that looks like a cross between a warehouse and a laboratory, then he tells me about something that's going to happen. It concerns me, but it doesn't sound like anything that will matter. It sounds abstract. In another twenty-four hours or so, this machine will be ready— right now, it's going through some special process, like charging up or something—and we will walk, or maybe I will walk, I'm not sure about the details, somebody will walk through this rusty old door and enter into—something. Another world, another time. Or nowhere, never. I can't really follow him, I'm too far gone in my own mind. There are times when I want to laugh, times when I want to cry, but I don't laugh or cry, I just stand in that long room, listening to him speak and swaying in the half-light, not even sure I'm there at all. Not even sure I'm not dreaming.

———

Later, when the effects of the tea have almost worn off, I find myself sitting by a fire again, in the same clearing we'd camped in before, just ten or so yards from the old farm road. The Moth Man is sitting opposite me, tending a large pot of what smells like soup or stew, the gold light off the fire playing on his hands and face as he sits gazing into the flames. He appears to have forgotten I'm there—maybe I've been sleeping again—but he looks calm. Not happy, but calm. I can't say for sure, and maybe this is something else that occurs to me afterward, but he looks like a man who has made a final decision about something and is just waiting for events to unfold.

His decision has something to do with me, I know—only I don't know what it is he, or I, or both of us have decided. Something to do with the machine in the enormous room. I want to ask him about it, but the questions just don't form right in my head and I start thinking about other things, like seeing Morrison in the woods, or finding the watch, or the theory I had come up with about the lost boys. I even get myself together enough to start telling him about it all. I want to lay out my suspicions, maybe get his views on who is involved with Morrison. I want him to help me make sense of everything. He's not interested in that, though. As far as he's concerned, we've gone beyond the Innertown. He listens patiently for as long as I talk, but he doesn't say anything. At first I think it's because I'm not making any sense—I'm still pretty confused, and not saying things right—but then I see that it doesn't matter what I say, or how clearly I say it, because he has moved on to things that I haven't even begun to consider, much less understand. Which is true, of course.

"None of this is your concern," he says, after I show him the watch.

I shake my head. I feel like I'm saying the words of a script, like one of the minor characters in some whodunit, telling the great detective about my hopelessly mistaken theory. "Somebody killed all those boys—" I say.

He waves his hand. "Don't bother yourself with that stuff," he says.

And that's it. Case closed. I'm tired and confused, and he has other things on his mind. Yet just when I start to think it's hopeless, he stands up and starts setting out two lots of blankets on the ground by the fire. He's thinking something through, but he's not in any hurry. He lays out the blankets, puts some more wood on the fire, then stands up and looks back toward the woods, in the direction of the Innertown. "Tell you what," he says. "We'll go and have a chat with the constable tomorrow. Maybe then you can forget all this and we can move on."

I am surprised by that. I almost laugh, not at what he's saying, but at the way he says it. *Have a chat*. It sounds so ordinary; like we'll just pop by the police house and ask Morrison if he's killed five boys and, if he hasn't, does he know who did. I almost laugh.

He lies down on a groundsheet and pulls some blankets over himself. "Get some rest now," he says. "It's going to be a long day."

I don't expect to sleep again, but I do. It's the sleep of exhaustion this time, not some drug-induced hypnogogic reverie, though there are dreams in my head that must have come from the hours I was under the influence of the Moth Man's strange tea, dreams from the gaps in the day that I can't remember, not with my conscious mind at least—whatever that is. I am exhausted, and I sleep deep, but when I wake it's still early—and very cold, much colder than I would have expected. I lie on the ground under the Moth Man's camphor-scented blankets and I try to remember, if not everything, then the points at which one thing connects with the next, so that I can tell myself the story of what has happened. The story of what has been decided. I know that I have pledged myself to something, but I'm not sure what it is. It has to do with that machine the Moth Man showed me, it has to do with passing through to some other place. At some point during the previous twelve hours, I know I have seen something, and I know that it is sacred to the Moth Man in a different way than anything he's shown me before, and I think it has to do with some kind of deity, or spirit, but I don't know if I have actually seen it, or if he has told me about it, or even if it was something that came up out of a dream and slipped into the story he was telling me in the enormous room—out of a dream, or out of the earth, which is much the same thing by then. Lying there, in the cold dawn, I think that, for the Moth Man, it is a god, a wildness beyond his imagining that took form one bright afternoon when he was out here alone and showed him another way of being in the world. A wild god, but not savage. Not cruel. I don't know what is about to happen, or where the silent machine in the enormous room might take me, but I do know, beyond all doubt, that this is so. Whatever happens, wherever the next twenty-four hours take me, I know that the god of that place is wild but it isn't cruel. Cruelty, I know, is a human quality, and whatever I might find in the enormous room, I know it will not be human.

I sit up. The fire is still burning, though it isn't quite as bright or as warm as it had been when we were talking, before I fell asleep. I look for the Moth Man, but he isn't there. That doesn't worry me, though. I know he won't be far away. He's probably gone to fetch more wood for the fire, or maybe he is gathering leaves to make more of that tea he'd given me. I don't like the idea of that. It *was* amazing and beautiful in a way, but I don't like that I can't remember everything that happened. Though it might have been better if I'd forgotten everything. What really unsettles me, though, is the procession of disconnected images running through my head, and the sense I have of a story all disjointed and out of sequence.

I struggle to my feet and walk away from the fire, away from the campsite, out to the edge of the clearing, and through the trees to where the old farm road runs down to the sea. The headland is always at its best in the early morning, but that day it's more beautiful than ever. When I say beautiful, I don't mean tourist-brochure stuff, because it could never have been that. For one thing, there is nothing much to look at, just a wide field spotted here and there with cold, red poppies and a line of twisted trees turning from black to gray in the first light. Overhead, a few gulls are drifting up from the shore, and what might have been a little owl flutters out across the gray-green grass to the cover of the trees as I cross the road and stand watching, my mind empty—though in a good way, as if absence was what it has promised itself for years. Absence. Nothingness. There's a saying—nothingness haunts being, and I understand what that means, only if you say it in those words it sounds too abstract, too philosophical. Kind of drab, too—which it isn't in the least. John would have said it sounds better in French, but that's not it. It sounds better when you stand at the edge of a field of cold poppies and let the nothingness come, just like that, no huge thing, just that matter-of-fact nothingness. It sounds better when you don't say it in words, when you don't even remark on it, but watch and listen as it takes you away—not some negative thing at all, not some existential condition, but a kind of blossoming, a natural event. Something that, when it finally comes, is no big deal. The self bleeding out. The red of the poppies. The cool of the morning.

———

When I get back, the Moth Man is back by the fire, doing what he always does, as if nothing out of the ordinary has happened. He looks up when I cross over and stand a few feet away, staring at the fire as if it is some kind of miracle, but he doesn't say anything. He just finishes what he is doing, then he feeds me some breakfast and a cup of regular, non-hallucinogenic coffee. I know I've missed something in what he told me about the machine and his father's blueprints and I'm wondering if he knows it too. If he does, I think, he'll surely say something else, he'll surely try to explain—but he doesn't say anything. We sit around for a while, not saying much, just tending the fire and listening to the woods as they go about their business around us. It's not awkward, there's no tension, no sense of delay or expectation. If anything, it's like any other morning: just two friends out camping in the woods. It's friendly, though, with that light, unspoken sense of being comfortable together in the quiet. We sit there a long time, not saying a word; then we put all his stuff in the van and drive down to the Inner-town, like a pair of God's closest angels, to pluck a man's soul out of hell.

DREAMING

In the police house, Alice Morrison is trying not to dream. She is awake now but, as she has discovered, this makes no difference, because the dreams keep coming, even when she stands with her head down, her hands pressed to the wall, her eyes wide open. She has always been afraid of what is happening now, afraid that, one day, the shakes won't pass after a few hours, or even after a day or two, that they will stay with her, always, her permanent, vigilant companions. Now, faces loom up at her out of the floor, or they come leering out from a wall, dead faces, but mocking, mocking and desperate at once, terrible, unknown eyes and mouths, flaring out from wherever she turns. Worse still, though, are the noises in her head—not voices, never voices anymore, just a noise like furniture being moved, wooden table legs dragging across a floor, or saucepan lids falling and clattering on tiles, or maybe the sound of piano wires resonating in the dark, where someone is rocking the frame back and forth, back and forth. Or there are bells in the distance, a sound that should be peaceful, a beautiful sound if the bells were out there in the world, and not inside her head. Then, through all that, through the sudden deceptive moments of quiet, comes the sound of a child, the same child over and over again, sitting or kneeling in a corner somewhere, weeping and whispering to itself, a boy or a girl, she doesn't know, and she can't make out the words the child is saying. All she can hear is this dreadful whisper.

She knows Morrison is somewhere in the house. Somewhere downstairs. He's letting her get on with it, because there have been times when she's told him to leave her alone, and now he is leaving her alone, now he's given up and she has the solitude that she's always wanted. Except that, now, she doesn't want it. She can't take it. She's told herself that this won't last, because this is hell, and she's done nothing to deserve hell. Smith, Jenner, and the others from the Outertown, they deserve this more than she does. Morrison deserves it. She doesn't know what he's done, but she knows he's done something. Nobody who works for Smith is innocent. But then, hell doesn't come to the guilty. It comes to people like the O'Donnells, who haven't done anything wrong. That's the twist about hell, the one they don't tell you about in religious studies, the fact that, in hell, it's not the guilty who suffer, it's the innocent. That's what makes it hell. Some random principle wanders through the world, choosing people for no good reason and plunging them into hell. Grief for a child. Horrifying sickness. Noises and faces coming from nowhere, punctuated by terrible minutes of lucidity, just long enough to take stock of where you are. And you are in hell.

Hell, hell, hell, hell, hell. The sound in her head grows and something tightens all along her arms and legs—like cramps, only much worse—and she feels like her body is about to burst open, tendons and muscles snapping and tearing, the bones cracking. She has known about this forever, she has been at the threshold for so long and now it is finally happening. Morrison is downstairs, fixing tea, or reading a paper, ignoring her. She doesn't want him, but she wants *something*. She wants help. A drug, maybe. It could be that simple. They could come and give her one tiny injection and this hell could end. All she needs is someone to make the call. But she can't do it. She can't ask him. Her whole body wants to scream with the agony, her mind wants to beg for something to free her, and she can't make a sound. She is in hell, and hell is for eternity.

She doesn't know when she first sees the man. She thinks this is one more face, screaming out at her from the doorway, as she turns, searching for an exit. A phantom. God, she knows these are phantoms, she knows these things are hallucinations, or she does some of the time anyway, and it makes no difference. This is the place where mad people live, and she doesn't know how she got here. A few drinks, a few pills? Surely not. She has never believed in that kind of injustice. She has believed in blame and private horrors and shameful acts behind closed doors. She hasn't imagined that the mad deserve their suffering, but she has believed in a route, a road taken, or a history of pain and loneliness, running from the darkest secret of childhood to the asylum, where doctors come and go with needles, and the mad lie down to sleep in oblivion, for precious hours at a time. But where was her route? Nobody abused her as a child. Nobody stole her innocence or made her a witness to unbearable truths. She doesn't know how she got here. She doesn't know how her life got to be unbearable.

But then, nothing is unbearable. When she first sees him, he's one phantom among many, but after a while she becomes aware of a real presence, a warmth that fills the room and she looks out from her hell and sees him there, standing in his own island of light and yet only a few feet away. He has the shape of a man but his face, when she makes it out, is the face of a boy. A gentle, serene boy, gazing at her, calm, forgiving, silent. She knows he will not speak to her, but she needs to break the chain of sound and pain in her head and, when she finally sees him there, she has to ask. He doesn't reply, and she hasn't expected him to reply, but she repeats the question anyway.

"Who are you?" she says. It's a simple enough question.

He doesn't answer, but he comes closer and reaches out his hand—and that, for one terrible moment, is the most painful thing she can possibly imagine. The reaching, the moment before touching. But when he touches her—his hand laid flat across her face, covering her eyes and mouth—she staggers into some new state, some unknown brightness. He lays his hand over her face and her eyes close, and the noises stop. The noises stop and the pain in her arms stops. The pain ebbs away, like water. The noises stop and her head is silent, cool, empty. The gratitude is almost unbearable, but she knows, at the same time, that he has not come here to bless her. She is someone he has found in passing, and his mercy is so huge it costs him nothing to heal her. It's as if she met the Angel of the Lord in some old Bible story, and he has touched her for a moment, and healed her, but she knows that, all the time, his purpose is elsewhere. She falls to the floor then, falling away from his healing hand and into herself, the self she was before, the self she has forgotten in all this noise and pain and fear. So that when she looks up, he is already gone, a shadow passing away, on its way to its divine appointment. But she doesn't care. She is still. Her body is silent. She is capable of sleep.

It may be minutes later, it may be longer, when she hears something from downstairs, from one of the rooms below. Morrison's voice calls out, maybe in fear, maybe in anger, she can't tell, and she can't make out what he says. She is only mildly curious, though, and after a moment the silence returns. The silence of her exhaustion. Outside, somewhere in the trees, a pair of owls is hunting, and closer in, near the window, she hears a gust of wind. Fresh new sounds, sounds that come from beyond her own pain. She hears one thing, then she hears another, but it's fading even as it happens, because she is finding her way to a place where sleep is total, and on the far side of that, a new life. Her name is Alice. Her father loved her, and she had a happy childhood, for the most part. Sleep is her due, and she takes it, with gratitude and relief, and it barely troubles her that, as she slips down and into that dreamless place, the last thing she registers, the last tiny fragment of awareness, is that Morrison is gone and she is in the police house, alone.

MORRISON

When he wakes, Morrison is upright, very upright, in a wooden chair that is too small for him, a heavy, polished old-fashioned chair with a padded back and armrests, the kind of chair that nobody has made for years. He is cold, which doesn't surprise him, because he is also naked, his skin surprisingly white and loose under the unforgiving white light that comes from somewhere above. He is immediately aware of the restraints that someone has fastened around his arms and legs: tight, not rope, maybe leather, or some kind of insulating tape, wound around his arms from the wrist to the elbow, and around his legs from the ankles to the knees, holding him almost incapable of motion, pinned in the chair like an insect pinned to a specimen board. His legs have been bound in such a way that his knees jut slightly outward, his soles raised off the floor, so he cannot gain purchase and push himself up. Whoever did this has very specialized skills—and his mind goes straight to Jenner, who has probably been waiting years for an opportunity to do exactly this, and so eliminate a potential problem. That's the kind of man Jenner is: tidy, ruthless, cool, but, at the same time, someone who takes real care in his work, a man who doesn't like loose ends.

The chair to which Morrison is pinned is set in the middle of what feels like a large, empty space, a wide, echoey space under a single lightbulb, suspended above his head, casting a pool of light that spreads for several feet around him, though it's not enough to fill the room, which feels vast—and Morrison knows, without knowing why, that someone is out there, just a few yards into the dark, invisible, but watching him, waiting for him to be awake, as he now is. Somebody out there wants his fear—a fear that Morrison is suddenly, defiantly, pointlessly determined to conceal, no matter what.

"Hello?" He gives a short, mocking laugh and turns his head as far as he can, first to the right, then leftward; though he knows whoever has him is somewhere directly ahead. "Is anybody there?"

He listens. There is nothing to hear, but he knows someone is watching. He can feel it. He can feel breathing, he can feel a tension, like someone standing very still, keeping himself in check, breathing quietly and slowly, watching, listening. Observing: yes, that's it. This man—and he is sure, now, that it is not Jenner, who would have done things simply, quickly—this patient, self-contained man is one of life's watchers, one of the observers. This is what he works for, not because he enjoys what he does, when it comes to the last act, but for this, this moment of power. A careful planner, obviously, but not possessed of animosity or any other emotion, simply someone who enjoys having power over others. With someone like this, there is no strategy other than delay, a chance to work out what will gratify him, and maybe find some kind of compromise. Try to get him to forget his initial plan, or take things beyond the initial bounds of that plan, or possibly of his instruction set, so he might possibly come to a place he had not anticipated. Maybe, if the initial plan fails, he will do something else, make a mistake, show his hand.

"Who's there?" he calls again. He's strangely confused by his predicament. On the one hand, he is angry at being tied up, angry, too, that he has been restrained with such expertise, but part of him doesn't care anymore, even about that. He is tired. He doesn't know where this is—somewhere out in the plant, no doubt, but he's never seen the interior of this particular building before. He looks up. The room has a high roof, with crossbeams and what looks like a gantry somewhere in the shadows off to his left. He feels cold, slightly damp. "Jenner?" Morrison is almost certain that it isn't Jenner out there, but he can't think of anyone else who would be capable of this. "Jenner, if that's you, just tell me what it is you want."

It isn't Jenner. Jenner doesn't work like this. Whoever is out there is watching a spectacle, maybe playing with him, taunting him with this silence. They are enjoying the mystery, playing. Suddenly, he has the idea that it's kids, that this is some kind of stupid prank. This notion, no matter how far-fetched it seems, is a better explanation for his present situation than Jenner. Jenner would be here now, standing in close where he can do his work, not skulking in the shadows. Jenner is a professional, but this is something a gifted amateur would do—an amateur in the true sense of the word.

Someone who *loves* what he is doing. Not the person who killed Mark Wilkinson and the others; this is a different thing altogether. There is no awe here, no tenderness. This is all hard. Again, the idea comes that there are children out there. But how could a child, even a group of them, do this?

"I'm not sure who you think I am," Morrison calls out to the darkness, not too loud, but clear enough to show that he isn't afraid. "But I'll tell you one thing, you're wrong. I'm nobody special." He laughs again, a soft laugh that is for himself, and nobody else, even if they are watching him. He wants to laugh at the whole thing, the whole situation. This enormous room, these presences in the shadows, him strapped to this chair. It's ridiculous. At the same time, laughing isn't such a bad strategy either. It does him no harm, because it's not a defiant laugh, he doesn't even intend it to be that. It's soft, sad, even a little pathetic, yet it's strangely good-humored. He hears it himself when he laughs again, a note of pathos, of self-pity for a man who has no real work and a phantom for a wife, a man of his age without children or good memories or love. A man who had already arrived at nothingness before whoever is out there caught him off guard and brought him into this new, but not particularly interesting limbo. "Really," he calls again, "I'm *not* who you think." And yes, it does sound pathetic; it *is* pitiful. Sad. Which may work to his advantage because whoever is out there may well have a soft spot for sadness. People like to look at sadness, because it isn't pain, and because it echoes something in themselves.

Nothing is happening, though. Still no response. "Where are we, anyhow?" Morrison asks, sounding to himself more than a little foolish. Which may be exactly what is needed because he thinks he hears something, somewhere off to the left. "It's bloody cold," he says, in the same foolish tone.

He hears another sound then. Nothing much, just a sound, like something rolling across the floor, five or so yards to the left. It's not a sound he recognizes, but he knows it isn't good. Still, he tries not to let it show that he has heard, and he tries to seem unaware that anything bad is going to happen to him. This is the one thing he remembers from school: don't look like a victim, and there's less chance you will become one. Bluff it out. Letting yourself imagine that something bad is going to happen is already a beginning, a first step into the shameful collaboration between the victim and the one with the power, a recognition that pain, deliberately inflicted and profoundly satisfying, is inevitable. He listens. Nothing, then something. Something, then nothing. Whoever is out there is getting closer, or circling perhaps, but he's not visible yet.

Then a voice comes. It is clear, youthful, though not perhaps boyish, and surprisingly gentle. "You are Morrison, the policeman," it says.

Morrison isn't sure if this is a question or a statement of fact, but he answers anyway. "I am," he says. As he says it, he feels a thin, vestigial shiver of pride, not in himself, but in the position. The *office*. He listens. The man in the dark is moving, coming forward, hovering at the edge of the light. He is carrying something—it looks like a bucket—and the lower part of his face is masked. In any other circumstances, Morrison would think the mask was a good sign—but as soon as he sees this tall, rather slender, youthful figure, he realizes that the man is beyond influence: that, however much he may like to observe, he is also someone who acts. He knows what he is going to do, it's just that he has a preordained script for the event, and it pleases him to follow that script. Now, finally, Morrison gives in to defiance. "You know who I am," he says. "So tell me. Who are you?"

The man doesn't speak—and now, from some sign that is so subtle that even he can't tell how he read it, Morrison realizes that someone else is there too, standing farther out in the darkness, watching.

"Who's your friend?" Morrison asks.

The man looks at him now, his eyes blue and surprisingly soft—and Morrison realizes that he is not much more than a boy. "Who's *your* friend?" he asks, not echoing, not mocking, but genuinely asking the question.

Morrison smiles. "I don't have any friends," he says. He's not being sad, or pathetic. He's not playing tactics. He has no friends and this man, this boy, knows as much. In fact, this boy knows everything about him. Or he thinks he does—only, he doesn't, because nobody knows everything about anybody. In fact, Morrison thinks, nobody knows very much at all. "When I was a kid—" he begins, changing tack.

"Not good enough." The man's voice is still quiet, but suddenly hard.

"What do you mean, not good enough?" Morrison is genuinely annoyed. He had just remembered something about himself, something true, and he had wanted to make it real as well, in the telling. "You haven't heard what I was going to say."

The man takes a step closer, then stops. He is in the light now and because he is in the light, Morrison can see that what he is carrying really *is* a bucket. "No childhood stuff," the man says. "It's too easy."

"But that's where it all begins," Morrison protests. He hears the slight crack in his voice and is annoyed with himself. He's let something go now, and he can't get it back. It was the surprise of the bucket, of course, that broke his concentration. Right now, all he wants to know is: What is in that bucket? "Where are you going to find an explanation, if not in the distant past?"

The man nods, and puts down the bucket. "Do you *have* an explanation?" he asks. He seems genuinely curious, not about the question itself, but about the question of whether Morrison—who is beginning to see himself now, through this man, as a type, as a character in a story—has even bothered to look for an explanation. It's something that Morrison finds insulting, as if this man wants to deny him everything, not just a life, or an explanation, but even a soul. Or maybe what he is denying is the soul itself. The very possibility of a soul. Someone like Morrison can't have a soul of his own, because the soul is intrinsically good, intrinsically clean, a piece of property borrowed from God and all His angels, to be returned some day, pearly and clean and undamaged. The idea makes Morrison angry, and he wants to tell this man, this boy, that he's wrong, that the soul is wet and dark, a creature that takes up residence in the human body like a parasite and feeds on it, a creature hungry for experience and power and possessed of an inhuman joy that cares nothing for its host, but lives, as it must live, in perpetual, disfigured longing. "Well?" The man is still gently curious, and waiting now, making space for Morrison to speak.

And now Morrison can see into the bucket, or at least one side of it, which is spotted and streaked with something white, but he doesn't want to seem too curious. "When I was just a kid," he begins, deliberately, with the air of an invited speaker, "my mother took me on holiday. My father couldn't come, he had to work—"

"What did your father do?"

"He worked here, at the chemical plant," Morrison says. He looks the man in the eyes. "I assume that's where we are. At the chemical plant?"

The man ignores the question. "*This* is your explanation?" he asks. Morrison nods. "All right," the man says. "Go on."

Morrison looks at the bucket. The contents are white and wet and he can smell something. A familiar smell, like chalk, but not quite. "We went to visit my aunt," Morrison continues. He feels sad, more or less resigned, not that interested in what he is saying. "She lived by the sea, but it wasn't like this. It was beautiful. Just by her house was a little beach, with this very white sand, and on the beach, a little pier or jetty running out into blue, clear water. I can't tell you how blue it was, or what a gift that pier was to a boy like me. A boy from this place." He looks at the man. He must be a boy from this place too, but who is he?

The man nods. "Go on," he says.

"Well," Morrison says, "I swam there every day, of course. They could hardly get me out of the water, even to eat or sleep. It was summer, really warm, but the water was cool, very cool. And I loved that water. It was my home, my element, a friend to me." He looks at the bucket. He suddenly knows that something terrible, truly terrible, is in store for him, and it has to do with this white, chalky substance splashed and spotted across the side of this bucket. "What's in the bucket?" he asks. The question surprises him. He hadn't intended it.

"Finish the story," the man says. "We have *lots* of time."

In a panic, knowing the story will have no effect on anything, Morrison goes on talking, but now he can hardly bear to talk. It's as if the story itself were a form of torture and not whatever it is that this man, and some accomplice out in the shadows, have planned for him. "I loved that water," he says. "I thought of it as my friend, my companion. Slipping into it, off the end of that dark pier, was like returning to something that had always been there, something that predated everything else in my life. I trusted it utterly." He pauses: he is breathless now, tired again. "Then, on the last day of the holiday, a current came, out of nowhere. It was a real force of nature, a mysterious black current—not a ripple on the surface, but this quick dark force under the water that grabbed me like an animal and started pulling me under and away, away from the pier, out into the sound." He stops, breathes, sees the bucket. Plaster of Paris, he thinks, without knowing why. He remembers the smell, an old smell, a childhood smell. "I almost drowned," he says. "I thought I was going to die. And it really happens, at that last moment. You know, how they say you remember everything, your whole life flashes before you, every detail, all in a flash. Well, that's true, because it happened and I remember it. Only, it wasn't my life. It was somebody else's memories that flashed through my mind." Morrison stops. He is surprised by what he has just said, because it isn't what he had meant to say. Yet, oddly enough, it has a ring of truth to it. "I was remembering somebody else's life," he says. "Somebody I didn't know." In spite of everything, Morrison is almost pleased by this.

The man doesn't say anything for a moment. Instead, he kneels to the bucket and starts pulling out a length of what looks like wet bandage. Morrison can't tell whether he is listening, or if he has been listening all along. Finally, however, the man speaks. "So what happened?" he asks, as he separates one strand of bandage from another.

Morrison watches, fascinated. "I died," he says, almost as an aside.

The man laughs softly. "But you're still here," he says. He carries a length of the wet plaster-covered bandage to the chair and begins winding it around Morrison's right arm. "You know what this is?" he inquires, softly. He sounds like a doctor, with that good bedside manner.

Morrison nods. "Why are you doing this to me?" he asks.

The man doesn't answer, but continues to dress Morrison in the wet bandages.

"I didn't do anything wrong," Morrison says.

"No?"

"No." There is no mistaking, now, what is happening. Morrison knows he is going to die, but he doesn't care about that. He just wants it to be over. "I made mistakes, but I didn't do anything wrong—"

"What about William Ash? What about—"

"I didn't *kill* anybody."

"But you knew what was happening."

Morrison hesitates a moment, then. It isn't deliberate, and it isn't what he knows the man thinks it is—a calculation, a guess at how much the man knows and what he might get away with—but he does hesitate, and he knows right away that this is a terrible mistake to have made. He doesn't know why it happened—he has been through it all a thousand times, and he has resolved it all as well as he can, but he's never heard anyone say it out loud before. He's never been *accused*.

"Well?" The man looks him in the eyes.

"I knew," Morrison says. He feels an almost unbearable sadness descend upon him, a weight, hanging in his bones. "But I couldn't do anything—"

Suddenly, another voice is speaking, a boy's voice, coming out of the dark. "You could have done *something*," this boy's voice says, and Morrison turns to see who it is. The boy is masked, like his companion, but he seems familiar to Morrison, a boy he can almost place, unlike the man who is working still, working steadily, building up a casing of wet bandages around Morrison and the chair.

"I couldn't do anything," Morrison says softly, to the man by the chair. Then, after a pause that really is deliberate, he plays his one last card, speaking even more quietly, even intimately. "I have a wife," he says.

"What was that?" It's the boy talking, angry, mocking. "What did you say?"

"I said, I have a wife," Morrison repeats, still speaking to the man, who has turned back to the bucket.

"What has your wife got to do with it?" the boy shouts. "You were the police. You were supposed to protect people."

The boy is right, of course. Morrison knows that. But he is also wrong, because he thinks Morrison is someone else, he thinks he is worse than he is. Still, he nods. He is about to speak, when the man turns round and starts wrapping Morrison's face with a wet bandage, the cold, clinging plaster chilling his skin, tiny granules of it seeping into his mouth.

"Don't worry," the man says, "I'll leave a space for you to breathe."

Morrison is in a state of panic now, but he cannot move. He cannot do anything. Soon he will be unable even to speak.

"They used to wrap people up like this," the man says, "back in the old days, as a treatment for tuberculosis. Did you know that?" It's like having a conversation with an over-friendly barber: the man even cranes sideways and looks into Morrison's eyes to make sure he is listening. It means something to him, this story. He has planned this carefully, and the story sits at the center of it all, like a spider in its web. "Tuberculosis isn't just a lung thing," the man continues, once he is satisfied that he has Morrison's attention.

"It affects the bones too. They would leave people in these casts for weeks, to prevent deformities. To straighten them, so to speak." He pauses—and Morrison detects a wistfulness in that pause, as if the man is remembering something that had once happened to him. "It would drive them crazy, of course," he says. He steps back to look at his handiwork. "A little more here and we'll soon be done," he says, though Morrison isn't sure if the man is talking to him, or to the boy in the shadows. He can already feel the bandages drying around his arms and legs. He's in a body-size cast now: soon it will all be dry, and he will be like one of those tuberculosis patients of old. Will it drive him crazy? Will it straighten him? Is that what this is about?

The man returns from the bucket. "Yes, it must have been a living hell," he says. "For the patients, I mean." He works quickly now, building up layers, solidifying his creation. Finally he runs out of bandages. He bends to Morrison's face. Only the nose and the eyes are still exposed. "Don't go away," he says.

Morrison wants to look round, to see where the boy is, but already he can't move. All he can see is the man, walking away with the bucket, walking into the darkness, where he stays hidden for some time, before returning with another bucket. The man sets this bucket in the exact same spot as before and begins his work again. *"Enter ye in at the strait gate,"* he says, and continues as he binds Morrison with the bandages, going quickly, building upon the framework he has already created. *"For wide is the gate, and broad is the way, that leadeth to destruction, and many there be which go in thereat: Because strait is the gate, and narrow is the way, which leadeth unto life, and few there be that find it."* He stops speaking and stands back. "There," he says. "You're done." He looks at Morrison. Far away, there is a sound, a small sound, the flutter of a bird, or wind through a broken casement, Morrison cannot tell, but it's not a significant sound, it's not someone coming to the rescue. Still, the man stands a moment, his head tilted to one side. Now, though, it's silent again, a silence that seems to deepen and broaden the longer the man listens, as if he were making this silence happen, simply by giving it his attention. Morrison listens too: for a moment, they are joined together in a fleeting complicity, two men in a room, listening, waiting; then, suddenly, shocked that he hasn't seen it before, he realizes that *this* man, this speaker of Bible verses, is the one who killed Mark and left him suspended in the poison bower. *He* is the one who took the other boys, the one who killed them all and, now that speech has been taken away from him, Morrison desperately needs to ask why he did it. Why the boys and, now, why *this*, when the man knows that Morrison is innocent. Now he can see that, in this man's mind, something has been achieved by this ritual of bandages and Gospel, just as something was achieved in killing those children. He thinks of the verses the man had quoted and, for himself, he adds in the one that seems most significant, for this moment, for this act. He wants to say it aloud, but he can't, because the plaster-of-Paris bandages are already thick around his face, already beginning to dry, and his mouth is set, speechless. All he can do is repeat those verses in his head and look this man in the eye so that, perhaps, by some effort of will, he can communicate his thoughts. *"Judge not, that ye be not judged,"* he begins, putting everything, all the life that remains to him, into the thought. *"For with what judgment ye judge, ye shall be judged: and with what measure ye mete, it shall be measured to you again."* Morrison is not a churchgoing man, in any meaningful sense, but he knows this passage from Matthew, he knows it well. It is written along his bones and along his veins, and in the well of his skull. *"And why beholdest thou the mote that is in thy brother's eye, but considerest not the beam that is in thine own eye? Thou hypocrite, first cast out the beam out of thine own eye; and then shalt thou see clearly to cast out the mote out of thy brother's eye."*

All this time, the man has been watching him. Morrison even thinks he has got through, that the man really is hearing the verses that Morrison is thinking. Finally, however, the man leans in and fixes Morrison's eyes. His look is questioning, like the look the teachers would have when they punished him in school, a look so full of self-righteousness that he would always refuse to dignify it with a response. After a moment, the man says, not loudly, but loud enough so Morrison hears it clearly through the bandages: "I'm giving you time to repent yourself," he says. "Use it well."

With that, he is gone, moving off into the darkness, disappearing for a few seconds, then reappearing in Morrison's line of vision, walking away into the dark again, accompanied now by the boy, who must have been there all along, watching, listening. The two vanish for a long time into the darkness, and Morrison thinks he is alone now, frozen, suspended in time and space, and the panic is almost impossible to bear—like the panic of Thomas à Kempis, when he was buried alive, only worse, since Thomas could at least fight, he could claw at the lid of his coffin, he could scream and moan and pray. Then, when the panic has built to a point at which Morrison feels he might lose consciousness and fold into some kind of mercy, he sees directly ahead of him, where there had only been darkness before, a bright circle of light, fiery, brilliant, utterly inexplicable. For a moment, that is all he sees; then, as his eyes adjust to that sudden brightness, he sees two figures, the man and the boy, walking into this brilliant light, walking into the fire and disappearing into its radiance, as if it had been their natural element all along, sparks returning to the light, flames returning to the fire. It is a terrible moment and, even after all they have done to him, he feels afraid, for them as for himself, because surely they know what they are doing, surely they know that they are walking into the fiery flames of hell, never to return, but to be extinguished, forever.

Then, just as suddenly as it burst upon his eyes, the brightness vanishes and the great room is dark again. The man and the boy are gone, lost in the flames, and Morrison is alone.

HEAVEN

WHY IS HEAVEN SO BRIGHT? WHY DOES THE LIGHT BLIND us? In one story I heard, the first thing the soul wants to do, when it gets to heaven, is to turn and look back toward the life it left behind—but then, if it did, if it could, it would see that everyone it ever knew was still in purgatory. And then heaven wouldn't be heaven anymore. No matter how beautiful heaven is, and even though the soul understands how terrible the old life was, it wants to go back, because of those others. Not because it loved them, or cared so much about them, but because they are calling out from where they are and the soul can't shut out their voices. It belongs with them. It belongs to the earth.

And this is why heaven is bright. This is why it is blinding. So that we can never look back.

The Moth Man hadn't said anything, after he'd shown me the machine he had constructed from his father's notes and drawings. He didn't explain anything, or tell me what was going to happen to me when I passed through the portal. Maybe he had tried to put something into words when he first brought me to the room, but I was still drunk or whatever from the tea and I didn't get what he was saying. Whatever he said or didn't say, though, he didn't explain anything. This isn't that kind of a story. He didn't take hold of my arm and say, "Quick, come with me. I'll get you out of here," like Harrison Ford in some adventure movie. He didn't sit me down and run through the plot, filling in all the gaps, like Hercule Poirot or Sherlock Holmes after the mystery has been solved and the criminals have been taken away. He didn't explain the mystery because he *was* the mystery, only he was the counterbalance to the mystery that had gone before, the first step in a new beginning. Like the crazy photographer says in *Apocalypse Now*: he was yin and yang, thesis, antithesis, synthesis; he was the dialectic in the form of a living, breathing friend. And I still call him my friend because that was what he was. To begin with, I thought I knew him, but then I saw that, even if some of him was old, even if he came, in part, from the world I had known before, he was also new: an unforeseeable new creature, suddenly released from some secret hiding place to walk and breathe and act, as if for the first time. Like Ariel, maybe, at the end of *The Tempest*. He was a friend, but he was another kind of friend, like the friend you imagine you're going to have, but never quite find, all the way through your childhood. A friend who's so close, he might as well be you—and maybe he is, in a way.

You're partly him, he's partly you. He knows what you don't know and you see what he misses.

I don't really know him, though. He isn't who I thought he was, he isn't even who I thought he wasn't. All that time, I didn't even know his real name. I just called him the Moth Man, because that was who he was for me: the Moth Man, the man who belonged to the woods, part of the landscape, flitting from one place to the next, coming to rest for a while then moving on. I never knew where. I never thought to ask him his name, or where he lived, or whether he had any family, other than his father—but then, who cares about names? Who cares about some address somewhere, or the tax disk on a van, or whether he's on the electoral roll? He doesn't belong to the Innertown, I know that much, but it never occurred to me that he might belong anywhere other than the woods. If I don't know anything about him, it is because I never wanted to know. Not about names and addresses and such, anyhow. I'm not saying he wasn't the person I thought I knew when we were out in the woods looking at plants, or sitting at his campfire drinking strange tea, it's just that there is more to him than I had ever seen, but I suppose you could say that about anybody. I remember John telling me about this girl he knew, back when he was a teenager: she worked in the music shop where he used to go, whenever he had money to buy records, and he was maybe in love with her, only she was older, and really pretty, and John didn't reckon he had a chance with her so he didn't say anything, he just went into the shop and bought his record, or maybe he ordered something that they didn't have, so they could get it in for him a week later, and he was very formal, very proper in everything he said and did, so she would never know she had this secret admirer. This kid.

While he was telling this, I remember my mind was racing ahead to some kind of punch line, like maybe in that Romain Gary story where the guy can't work up the courage to talk to the beautiful woman who lives in the apartment above his, even though he passes her on the stairs every day. He can't think of anything to say, so he doesn't say anything and he just gets lonelier and lonelier, till in the end he's sitting in his cold little room and he can hear the woman upstairs having loud sex with someone and he's so desperate, he's so wretched that he hangs himself out of sheer loneliness. And you have to know already—it's part of the plan of the story that you know already because these things are already written, that's what makes it all so dreary and pitiless, you have to know that, when the police come to file a report and haul the body away, the concierge tells them the woman upstairs is dead, she's taken poison and died in agony, writhing about on her bed, moaning and crying. Etc., etc. Only that wasn't John's story at all, it wasn't one of those all-in-the-diffidence-that-faltered stories at all, it was worse, in its way, because it was just one of John's stories, part of real life, where nothing's ever happening, because nothing ever does. In this story, John keeps going into the shop and standing there all tongue-tied and helpless for months and then he goes in one day and the girl is gone. He doesn't want to ask where she is, in case he betrays himself, but the guy behind the counter volunteers the information anyhow, how she has died mysteriously in the night, just two days before, a twenty-year-old woman dead in her bed from some obscure disease that has the same effect on the lungs as drowning. This is what he tells John, and John can see that he wants to tell it, because he knows John's secret, everybody does, because John is just this obvious boy in love that they're all having a laugh about, and now the guy, who's called Dave, wants to see how John will take it. And

John bursts into tears, because he really was in love. In love enough not to have wanted anything, in love enough not to have said a word. And of course when Dave sees this, he feels bad and he wants to give John something to go away with, some scrap of information about the girl—her name was Kate, I think, but I'm not sure if John ever told me, or whether I just thought it, because in the story she sounded like a Kate. Kate Thompson. Or maybe Katie. Anyhow, Dave tells him that, when they were going through the girl's things afterward, they found a hammer, a plane, a fretsaw, all kinds of tools, mostly still in their wrappers, tucked away in the drawers of her cupboard under the sweaters and socks and bras, a complete set of tools for a carpenter or something, only they'd never been used, and it looked like Kate or Katie had been buying them one at a time over months or even years, because some of them had the receipts still in the bags and the dates were all different. That's what the guy, Dave, had told John, to make him feel better—and that was what John remembered years later, when he told me the story. That, and the words the guy had repeated to him, in that poky little record shop that smelled of vinyl and warm dust, all those years ago. "People are strange," Dave had said and, when John hadn't said anything in reply, because he couldn't think of anything to say, he'd said it again. "People are strange, true enough."

As the story approaches its end, I am still thinking of Morrison as a gift. The Moth Man knows our local bobby hasn't killed anyone, but he also knows that in its own, very particular Innertown way, the policeman's offense is too grievous to go unpunished, the most extreme form of an offense the whole town has been mired in for decades: the sin of omission, the sin of averting our gaze and not seeing what was going on right in front of our eyes. The sin of not wanting to know; the sin of knowing everything and not doing anything about it. The sin of knowing things on paper but refusing to know them in our hearts. Everybody knows *that* sin. All you have to do is switch on the TV and watch the news. I'm not saying we should try to help the people in Somalia, or stop the devastation of the rain forests, it's just that we don't feel anything at all other than a mild sense of discomfort or embarrassment when we see the broken trees and the mud slides, or the child amputees in the field hospitals—and it's unforgivable that we go on with our lives when these things are happening somewhere. It's *unforgivable*. When you see that, everything ought to change.

That's why the Moth Man does what he does to Morrison. Because Morrison knows that it is unforgivable even to be innocent when the lost boys are vanishing into the undergrowth all around us. It's unforgivable not to know where they are, even if it's impossible to know. Morrison knows that it is unforgivable for a child to disappear without a trace, and that is both his worst sin and the beginning of his redemption. Because it is a redemption, or the beginning of redemption, that scene the Moth Man so carefully stages in the Glister room. At the time, I can't be expected to understand that. I think of it as a punishment, pure and simple. I don't know how limited Morrison's involvement in the murders has been, but the Moth Man knows. He knows better than anyone, but he makes his terrible gift anyway. Had I known then what I know now, I wouldn't have accepted it—but then, if I had known then what I know now, I would have known that the gift isn't meant for me. It's meant for Morrison. Grotesque as that might sound, it's still true—for how else would a man be released from hell, if not through some terrible but mercifully terminal agony? In his way, the Moth Man is building Morrison a refuge. When he so carefully and thoughtfully binds him in that plaster cell, he is constructing a sacred place where the guilty policeman can be set aside and so, eventually, absolved from the sin of the world. This is how he sees it, I know, but it's only now that I see what a burden it must have been to him.

So he gives me Morrison as a gift, but he doesn't care about it. Right from the beginning, he is thinking about the Glister, and how he will show me the way through. Not to get me *out* of here, but to get me farther in. All the way in. But he is patient too and he can see that something has to be done, that the old life has to be closed down. So we take Morrison, and we bring him to this enormous room, just fifty yards from the Glister. Which is what, exactly? A door? A portal? What is on the other side? I don't know, and to tell the truth I don't even want to think about it. I just know that, when the time comes, I will pass through and then I will be all the way in.

I didn't know if Morrison was the killer at the start but, by the end of it all, when we leave him there in his cast, I know he isn't. Nevertheless, he was implicated, he made some of it possible, so a little bit of justice has been done. Now it's up to the Innertown to carry on that good work. They will have to get themselves an angel, and go up to the Outertown and wipe off the white marks on the lintels. Or they could just stop collaborating with the powers that be and start playing a new game. Make up some new rules, and forget all that *touche pas à la femme blanche* stuff. But that's up to them, it doesn't have anything to do with me anymore. Dad is dead, a collaborator in his own misery all his life, a sleepwalker I was never able to shake awake. Now I am tired, and I'm not at all sure I have the heart for anything else, so my friend arranges the thing with

Morrison, and by doing this he lets me see that, sooner or later, justice will be done. We shake Morrison awake, giving him the tools to judge for himself how far he is from heaven. Then we walk away and leave him there to rot.

They say that, if you want to stay alive, you have to love something. Though maybe love is the wrong word after all. Maybe you have to *be* something. Not some big shot, or somebody's baby, or anything like that. Not smart, or beautiful, or rich. Not famous or dangerous. You just have to *be*. I don't know if that makes any sense, right at this moment, but I have the feeling, as we stand in front of his strange machine, that we are about to find out. I don't see what he does to open the thing: to begin with, it's just a round door in a metal wall, a rusting metal door with letters I can just make out, all flaky and vague amid the rust and dirt,

GLISTER &

For a moment, everything is quiet and still. I stand staring at the letters engraved in the metal, trying to make sense of them, then the Moth Man steps forward and reaches to open the door—and I realize that I am listening to something, up in the roof somewhere, or somewhere above the roof maybe. I can't make it out at first, then I realize that it's a flock of gulls, a big one, maybe hundreds, thousands even, and they are swaying back and forth above the enormous room. Hundreds of thousands of gulls, millions, risen from the landfill and from the gray inlets all along the shore to congregate above us, crying and calling out, and, behind them, somewhere hidden in all that noise, like the nut in a kernel, I can just make out the sound of the tide rushing through wet shingle, a dark, eternal sound that I know will never end, because it isn't just out there in the sky above us, it isn't just in the world, it's in me, it's written in every nerve and bone in my body. Then the Moth Man reaches out and starts to open the door to the portal.

I turn away then, to look back. Not for Morrison's sake, but to see what I am leaving behind. Or maybe to look for one last time at the place where I once belonged. I just want one last look at the only world I have ever known, reduced as it is to this cold room, barely lit by the single faint lamp that runs off the generator the Moth Man built to get the Glister running—but something off to the right catches my eye, something up in the roof beams that I've not seen before, just to the right of the lightbulb. I'm not sure why I see it, because I'm not looking for anything out there at the edge of the light. I should be looking ahead, to the door that the Moth Man is about to open, the door to another world maybe—but something catches my eye and I turn to see what it is. I don't see how it could have moved, and there's no sound, but I feel as if something has happened, that whatever it is that's out there has somehow attracted my attention of its own accord. Even then, it's hard to make it out, just a shadowy mass that seems darker than the shadow that surrounds it, but after a moment I think I can make out the shape of a body, or a carcass maybe, like those sides of meat you see in the butcher's shop, the mass of it heavy and horribly still, some dark liquid dripping onto the concrete below. And I am surprised not to have noticed it before. Something like that. I am surprised—and he notices that, because he reaches out and touches my arm, gently, without the least hint of force. "Don't get distracted," he says. His voice is softer than usual, and for a moment he sounds almost uncertain, as if he is afraid I will fail in some way at the last moment. I turn back to face him.

For a moment, I see the body again, then it's gone and the

Moth Man is there, watching me, not afraid after all, not even concerned, just curious, noticing that something has distracted me but
not allowing his attention to waver, in case I do falter, and I see, at
that moment, that I'm not doing this for my own sake, I'm doing it
for him and—in his eyes at least—for everyone. Everyone in the
Innertown, everyone on the peninsula, maybe everyone everywhere.
I'm surprised.

"It's time," he says. "You're almost there."

"You're not coming," I say. It's not a question: I've seen in his
eyes that he is going to send me into the Glister alone. Which I
should have known, of course, because he has to stay, he has to go on
with his work. He *is* the necessary angel. I have an image of him
going from house to house all along the peninsula, picking off the
Morrisons and the Jenners and the Smiths, one by one. That's what
I see in him, at the last. An angel going from door to door. The
angel of death. The angel of absolution, gathering in the souls of the
wicked—not as a punishment, but because God has forgiven them
at last, and is releasing them from the hell they had fallen into.
Now, the Moth Man shakes his head softly, a half smile on his lips.
"I have to stay here," he says.

Yet, even as he speaks, his face fades again and I look past him,
out to the edge of the circle—and this time I see it clearly: a body,
suspended in the half-light, the ruined frame of a boy hanging in
the air like Icarus falling in some old painting, a boy my age and
more or less my build, a boy with my coloring, as far as I can see in
that light, and pretty much my height as far as I can tell. A mirror
image of me, traveling on some parallel track, like the me/not-me
I'd seen in the woods, *mon semblable—mon frère*. I'd thought he was
dead when I glimpsed him before; now I see that he is badly cut,
but still alive, the dark blood dripping from his face and hands, his

body bound in something bright, swaying slightly in the air, his mouth open, it seems, as if he wants to say something, or had wanted to say something a moment before—and now I know why I want to remember all this as if it had happened in the past, even though I know it continues in the present, because the boy isn't trying to speak, he's screaming, and the boy is me, only it's me in some parallel version of the story, just as I turn and see that the Moth Man is gone. Gone forever, though I could have sworn he was there a moment before. The Moth Man is gone, and then the boy on the wire is gone and I am stepping forward into this vast, impossibly brilliant light. I step forward with the feeling that I'm going to fall, or be swallowed up, and instead I am standing right in the middle of that unbearable light—only I'm not standing *there* anymore, I'm somewhere else and everything is gone. The Moth Man, the Glister, the boy in the beams of the ceiling, Morrison in his plaster cell—everything I know is gone, and all that remains is the calling of the gulls, above and around me the calling of the gulls and the slow, insistent motion of the waters, slow and far away and barely audible, turning on the shore and in my mind.

ACKNOWLEDGMENTS

My thanks to the Society of Authors for their support in the research and writing of this book. Also to the Conseil Général du Nord, and the staff at La Villa Mont-Noir, *merci à tous*.

Printed in the United States
by Baker & Taylor Publisher Services